D1118755

Jun 2023

THE GIRL BY THE BRIDGE

Arnaldur Indridason

THE GIRL BY THE BRIDGE

Translated from the Icelandic by Philip Roughton

MINOTAUR BOOKS
NEW YORK

First published in the United States by Minotaur Books, an imprint of St. Martin's Publishing Group

THE GIRL BY THE BRIDGE. Copyright © 2018 by Arnaldur Indridason. English translation copyright © 2023 by Philip Roughton. All rights reserved. Printed in the United States of America. For information, address St. Martin's Publishing Group, 120 Broadway, New York, NY 10271.

www.minotaurbooks.com

The Library of Congress Cataloging-in-Publication Data is available upon request.

ISBN 978-1-250-89260-7 (hardcover)
ISBN 978-1-250-89262-1 (ebook)

Our books may be purchased in bulk for promotional, educational, or business use. Please contact your local bookseller or the Macmillan Corporate and Premium Sales Department at 1-800-221-7945, extension 5442, or by email at MacmillanSpecialMarkets@macmillan.com.

Originally published in Iceland under the title *Stulkan hjá brúnni* by Vaka-Helgafell

First published in Great Britain by Harvill Secker, an imprint of Vintage, a Penguin Random House company

First U.S. Edition: 2023

10 9 8 7 6 5 4 3 2 1

Do you believe in angels who have somehow lost their way,
and roam the city's streets and squares, lonely and astray?

Bubbi Morthens

THE GIRL BY THE BRIDGE

1

The young man walked west along Skothúsvegur Street, stopped on the bridge over the Pond and, leaning over the railing, saw the doll in the water.

The bridge formed an elegant, low arch where the Pond narrowed and extended southward into Hljómskálagarður Park. The man stood at the crown of the arch, and as it was evening, there was little traffic on the road. A single car slowed down as it passed over the arch and then disappeared from view, its noisy engine breaking the stillness on the bridge. He thought he saw someone cross Sóleyjargata Street, and another person wearing a trench coat and hat walked by him without looking up. The young man leaned on the railing and looked over the Pond towards the Iðnó Culture House, the city centre and, further still, to where Mount Esja rose in the twilight, solid and immovable. Over the mountain, the moon shone like a fairy tale from a distant world, and when he looked down, he saw the doll, half submerged.

He immediately found something poetic about it, inspiring various musings typical to a young writer like him. From his jacket pocket, he pulled a small notepad and fountain pen that he always carried with him and began jotting down a few words about lost innocence, the impermanence of childhood, and the water that was both a source of life and a destructive force. The notepad, which was bound in black leather and inscribed with the date 1961 in gold numerals, was full of the observations of a young man who was slowly but surely treading the path of a writer and took that role seriously. He had already put together a volume of poetry but hadn't had the courage to show it to a publisher. He feared criticism and rejection more than anything else and spent a good deal of time polishing each poem to perfection, constantly making small changes or adding details, as he was doing now with this new poem of his on the transience of life.

He guessed that a girl who had been walking next to the Pond had dropped her doll in the water and hadn't been able to recover it. This thought, too, he jotted down. He tried to put the stillness of the evening into words. The city lights that were reflected on the water's surface. He looked towards the islet in the middle of the Pond, which the Arctic terns occupied every spring. *Now those birds were as silent as the night that laid its veil over the city*, he wrote in his notepad. Then he crossed out the words 'the night'. Wrote 'dusk' in their place. Crossed out 'its veil'. Wrote 'night' again. Tried 'its curtain' in place of 'its veil', but felt that that didn't work either.

He stuck the pen and notepad back in his jacket pocket and was about to continue on his way when it crossed his mind to fish the doll up out of the water and lay it against the bridge's railing in case the poor girl came there in search of her toy. He walked to the end of the bridge, scrambled down to the Pond's bank and tried reaching for the doll, but it was too far beneath the bridge. He went back up to the street and looked around for something that he could use to catch hold of the doll, a stick or tree branch, but saw nothing useful.

He abandoned his plan and walked up Skothúsvegur Street towards Hólavallagarður Cemetery. He found particular inspiration for his poems in cemeteries. He'd gone a short distance when he found the stick he'd been looking for, grabbed it, returned to the bridge and went down to the bank beneath it. He managed to hook the doll with the stick, but discovered that it was stuck. He poked at and hit the doll with the end of the stick, and was about to give up a second time when the doll came loose and floated away from him under the bridge. He watched it for a moment before dashing back up to the street, crossing it and scrambling down the Pond's bank on the other side, where he fished the doll out of the water as it floated by.

The doll was old and a bit tatty, had eyelids that flicked open and shut, and was wearing a flimsy dress. Its mouth was half open and a little whistle came from it when he pressed the doll's stomach. Its hair was frazzled and in some places there were holes in the scalp where it was missing. He pressed the doll's stomach again and water leaked from its eyes, as if the doll were crying.

The young man stood there looking south along the Pond, and now caught a glimpse of something else half submerged in the water. At first he thought he was mistaken, but when he looked closer, he let go of the doll and jumped into the water. It reached up to his armpits and he waded through the mud at the Pond's bottom without noticing how cold the water was, and before he knew it, he'd grabbed the flotsam and managed to pull it towards him. His suspicions were confirmed.

He waded back to the bank, absolutely stunned to realise that he'd found the body of a girl who had fallen into the Pond and drowned.

2

Eygló felt awkward and uncomfortable at the birthday party, without really knowing why. There were lots of children and adults there in the large, two-storey detached house. All of the girls in her class had come, along with three of the boys, although boys weren't usually invited to girls' birthday parties. The birthday girl's fun and energetic aunts had organised all sorts of entertaining activities and games for the kids, including hide-and-seek, board games and tag in the garden, which was enormous. The kids downed fizzy drinks and popcorn and sugary birthday cakes decorated with sweets, and they even got to watch a movie, because the birthday girl's parents had a projector and copies of American animated films.

All of it should have been enough for Eygló to have fun like the others, but something was holding her back. Maybe it was the environment. She'd never been in such a fancy house before and had a hard time tearing her eyes away from all the wonders within it. Large paintings hung on the walls and there was a gleaming black grand piano in one corner of the drawing room. All of the furniture seemed brand new. The white sofa looked unused, as if it were still on display in the furniture store. The carpet on the drawing-room floor was white as well, and so thick and incredibly soft that her feet sank into it. The home also had a television set with beautifully curved glass and buttons that seemed to be from an alien world. Eygló had never seen such a device before, and when she ran her hand over the glass, the birthday girl's father came to the door and said in a kindly tone that she mustn't touch the screen. Eygló was alone in the room, spared from the birthday party.

Her mind wandered back to her own home: the small, dark flat with the leaky tap in the kitchen and the basement window that was so high in the wall she couldn't see out of it without climbing onto a chair. There was no soft carpet on the floor, just worn lino-leum. Her mother worked all day in a fish factory, and there was usually nothing besides fish for dinner. She didn't know exactly what her father did. She did know that he was drunk sometimes, and her mother scolded him for it. She didn't like seeing it because her father was a kind-hearted man and her parents were generally affectionate to one another. And he was always good to his daughter and helped her with her homework and read her stories before disappearing for maybe a few days, without her mother knowing where he was.

The birthday girl, who was turning twelve today, was no special friend of hers. Eygló was at the party only because all the girls in their class had been invited. Actually, she shouldn't even have been in the same class as these kids, seeing as how their families were all better off and poor kids like her were usually put in worse

6

classes. Her teacher had quickly recognised the girl's aptitude for learning and saw to it that she was put in the best class, where conditions for education were better and the teacher's energy went more into teaching than maintaining discipline. The kids were quite accepting of her. Only two boys had pinched their noses and asked why her clothes smelled so bad. 'It's probably the smell of mildew from my basement,' she'd said.

Maybe she felt like she didn't belong there, surrounded by all that wealth. She had decided to skip the games for a bit and instead walked through the house, from the bedrooms to the sitting and drawing rooms, the kitchen and laundry room, admiring everything she saw. Her mother had told her to have fun and get to know the kids, and Eygló knew she said that because she was worried that her daughter was too much of a loner, feeling happier when she was by herself. Said that she inherited it from her father. But it wasn't as if Eygló didn't have many friends. She was sharper than most others her age and knew how to talk to the kids in her new class, and made sure they gave her her due. The other kids recognised that she had something about her and sought her company, rather than the opposite.

Eygló had been wandering around the house for a while when she found herself again in the beautiful room with the soft carpet and the white furniture, and saw a girl she hadn't noticed before at the party. She was around the same age as Eygló and even more poorly dressed, compared to the other kids.

'Hello,' said Eygló, catching a glimpse of her own reflection in the rounded television screen.

The girl seemed depressed, as if something had happened to her. She was wearing a well-worn dress, knee-high socks and summer shoes with buckles.

'Is everything OK?' asked Eygló.

The girl didn't answer her.

'What's your name?' asked Eygló.

'I've lost her,' whispered the girl as she walked towards Eygló and past her without stopping, then onward out of the room. Eygló watched the girl disappear out of the drawing-room door, then looked down at the carpet and saw something she never forgot, because it was all so new and exotic to her. When the girl walked past, her reflection didn't appear in the television screen and she had left behind no footprints in the thick carpet, as if she were completely weightless.

3

The couple's anxiety was plain to see as they recounted their difficulties. The man's mobile phone rang twice, but he didn't answer either time, just checked the numbers and went on detailing the troubles they'd been having. Konrád understood their concerns but wasn't sure if he could do anything to help. He was loosely familiar with them, but had never met them before. His wife, Erna, had known the woman for years, without Konrád ever involving himself in their acquaintanceship. The man had called him out of the blue and asked if there was any chance they could meet. The couple's granddaughter had sometimes been problematic, and they wanted to know if Konrád could give them any advice on dealing with her. They knew that Konrád had worked for years as a police detective, and even though he was retired, the two of them were convinced that he was an expert in the types of things their grandchild was entangled in, but which were like a closed book to them. Konrád was reluctant to meet them, but gave in to the man's urgent plea. He remembered Erna speaking well of the woman, saying that she was always genial, and vaguely recalled that the couple had lost their daughter in a car accident and raised her child.

Wanting to be completely honest, they admitted to Konrád that they were talking to him rather than the police because they hoped to keep this matter away from the media. The wife had been prominent in politics, although some time had passed since then, and they feared that the tabloid press would have a field day with this story if their connection with the girl got out. Often, it was as if the police could barely keep anything confidential. But Konrád mustn't misunderstand them. If, in his opinion, they should turn to the police for help, they would do so without hesitation.

'The truth is,' said the man, 'that we haven't heard from her for a few days now. Either her phone is dead or she doesn't have it with her; she's not answering it, in any case. Of course, it's happened before that she hasn't picked up for a while, but never this long, and besides –'

'We recently learned from her that she'd been acting as some sort of mule or whatever it's called,' said the woman, looking at her husband. 'She wasn't caught in customs or anything like that and said that she'd only made one trip for some people she didn't want to name, but that could just be a lie. We don't trust anything she says any more. Nothing. Except . . . this is something new . . . this about her being a mule.'

The woman's expression revealed her frustration, but also her genuine concern for the girl. Maybe she blamed herself for the girl's situation. Maybe she'd had no time for her when her political career was at its peak. Maybe the grandchild could never replace the daughter she'd lost.

'Do you think she's left the country?' asked Konrád.

'She might have her passport with her,' said the woman. 'We can't find it in her room. That's one of the things we wanted to ask you to look into for us. If you wouldn't mind. We're getting no answers from the airlines.'

'I think it's best that you talk to the police,' said Konrád. 'I –'

'We don't even know who we should talk to there. She doesn't know what she's doing any more and has started smuggling in drugs and we really don't want her to be arrested and thrown in jail,' said the woman. 'We know she's using drugs. First it was alcohol. Now it's other stuff. We simply can't manage her. She's so hard to deal with. She's so terribly difficult.'

'Does she travel a lot?'

'No, not particularly. At most, a weekend trip with her boyfriend.'

'We thought you might be able to talk to him,' the man said. 'He's never been here and we haven't met him, but it occurred to us that it might be her boyfriend who's using her.'

'Have they been together a long time?'

'We first heard about him a few months ago,' said the woman.

'But does she still live with you?' asked Konrád.

'Supposedly,' the woman said, taking out a photo of the girl and handing it to him. 'We can pay you for your trouble. It's just so awful to think of her out there somewhere with those junkies and be unable to do anything to help her. Of course, it's up to her what she does, she's twenty and we have little say over her, but . . .'

'Even if I managed to find her, she would just disappear again,' said Konrád, looking at the photo.

'I know, but we want to try . . . we want to know if she's OK. Whether anything can be done for her.'

Konrád understood their concerns very well. While working on the force, he'd met parents who were in the same situation. Parents who had tried to do their best but witnessed their child sink deeper and deeper into the world of drinking and drugs without being able to stop it. It could be such an ordeal for the families. Many gave up following repeated unsuccessful attempts to help their kids. Sometimes, however, they managed to lead the wayward child out of that terrible rut and steer him or her towards a better life.

'Did she admit to you that she'd been smuggling in drugs?' Konrád asked, slipping the photo into his jacket pocket.

'She didn't need to,' said the man.

'That's why we're so worried,' said the woman. 'She may have got herself tangled in something she can't handle.'

She looked desperately at Konrád.

'I found her in the loo. Three days ago. She'd just returned from Denmark and must have been in a rush because she forgot to lock the door. I didn't even know she was in there when I opened the door, and found her dropping those things into the toilet bowl. Little condoms that she . . . that she'd hidden in her vagina . . . it was shocking to see it.'

'We haven't seen her since,' said the man.

4

Every time Konráð drove along Sæbraut Road, he couldn't help but glance towards Skúlagata Street, where the slaughterhouse of the South Iceland Abattoir had once stood, with its black iron gate barring its courtyard. It was an involuntary reaction, almost a quirk that he had a hard time shaking off. Now there were high-rise flats along both sides of the street, which Konráð found ugly. In his mind, the new high-rises destroyed the well-established, beautiful area called the Shadow District, which was a part of old Reykjavík. Konráð had been brought up there, long before the city planners threw up the high-rises, and he resented how his old neighbourhood was treated. He couldn't understand why human stupidity had chosen that place and made it the ugliest spot in the city.

A planning failure, however, wasn't the reason why he looked to where the slaughterhouse had been. It was there at the gate that his father had died in 1963, fifty-three years ago, fatally stabbed by an unknown assailant. Ever since Konrád retired, that incident had come back to haunt him ever more insistently. One evening not long ago, he'd gone and stood for a while in the place where his father was found lying in the street with two lethal stab wounds. He hadn't done that in many years. The police report on the stabbing remarked on how much blood had flowed out onto the pavement.

Konrád parked his car behind police headquarters on Hverfisgata Street and went in to see a man he knew who was in the Drugs Squad. He told him about the concerns of the couple who had got in touch with him, without mentioning the condoms in the toilet bowl. The couple had said that the girl had called her boyfriend Lassi, but was tight-lipped when they pressed her for more information. 'Just a friend of mine,' she had said, putting a quick end to the conversation. They didn't know how to contact him. Didn't know what he did. Didn't really know his name.

'The boy she's with could be named Lars or Lárus or something like that; Lassi is just a nickname, probably,' said Konrád. 'I was wondering if there might be anything on him in your files. The girl's name is Daníela. Called Danní.'

'Why are you interested in these people?' asked the policeman, who was middle-aged, unusually slender, and had a scraggly beard and hair down to his shoulders. He liked heavy-metal music and had once played in a band.

'Acquaintances,' said Konrád. 'The girl has run away. Is into drugs and alcohol, according to them. They asked me to look into it.'

'So, what, are you some sort of private eye now?'

'Yes, exactly,' said Konrád. He'd been expecting such a comment. 'Would you mind checking on this for me?'

The policeman's chair creaked as he turned to his computer and started typing in Daníela's name, saying at the same time that he really shouldn't be doing this, and in fact wasn't permitted to. Konrád said that he was aware of that, and thanked him for the favour. Nothing came up on the screen. If the Drugs Squad or Directorate of Customs had had any dealings with her, that information would have been recorded in the database. On the other hand, three Lassis did come up: one, named Lárus, was the same age as the girl. He'd been given suspended sentences for theft and done time for drug smuggling.

'If she's with him, she's in trouble,' said the metalhead. 'He's a complete moron.'

'We'll see,' said Konrád, jotting down the names. 'The couple are worried about their granddaughter. That's all I know.'

'Will you tell me if you uncover anything meaty?' said the rocker, just for formality's sake. Konrád knew that he was overwhelmed with assignments and wasn't being serious.

'Of course,' Konrád answered, with just as much conviction.

He didn't intend to spend much time on the girl, who probably wasn't lost, but only avoiding her grandparents. She was quite far gone if what they said about the incident in the loo was true, and Konrád doubted that she would get right back onto the straight and narrow even if she did come home now. It was mainly in memory of Erna that he even let it cross his mind to make inquiries about her; these people were her friends. If he didn't find her on his first attempt, he would speak to the grandparents and repeat his advice to them to talk to the police, even if it meant staining the family's honour. He knew that no matter how things went, he would have to report the drugs.

While pondering these things as he walked back to his car,

Konrád came across an old friend from work. Her name was Marta and she came up to him and asked what he was doing there. She was the most rough-and-ready woman that Konrád had ever met, big, tall and mouthy, and she lived alone after unsuccessful relationships with women who left her for one reason or another. She had started in CID under Konrád's guidance and they soon became good friends. He knew no better police detective than her.

'Hello, Marta,' said Konrád. 'You're as cheery as ever.'

'Shouldn't you be playing golf or some such shit? Has Leó been pestering you?'

'No. What's up with him?'

'He's such a pain in the arse. He's had a few things to say about you. About your days together on the force. Insinuating things. You know how he is. Started drinking again and thinks that no one can see it. Poor bugger.'

'Didn't he just get out of rehab?'

'Well, that was last year. It did nothing for him. What do you do all day? Aren't you bored out of your mind?'

'I may end up that way, I suppose,' said Konrád.

'Yeah, but I still envy you,' Marta said, waving him goodbye. 'Damn, I'm going to have it nice when I quit this crap job.'

Konrád smiled to himself. She'd often made similar remarks, but he knew she didn't mean a word of it. He'd sometimes pointed out to Marta that she'd never be able to hold on to a woman because she was already married to the police.

He drove off with the addresses of the three Lassis from the database and started with the one he thought most likely to be accommodating the girl. His name was Lárus Hinriksson, a typical habitual offender since adolescence, with various types of convictions for drugs and petty crime behind him and constantly in trouble. His address was in Breiðholt, which was on Konráð's way home. It was a late-autumn evening, at dusk. The cold north wind signalled the approaching winter.

He found the right block of flats, parked the car and stepped out of it. Rooms in the basement were rented out, and Lassi lived in one of them, according to the information found by the metal-head at police headquarters. A row of garages stood in front of the building. The entrance was locked and Konráð rang one of the doorbells, but no one answered. He rang another one, to no response again, but when he rang the third one, someone buzzed the door open without saying anything. Konráð entered the stair-well and started descending the steps to the basement. A man appeared on the landing of one of the floors above and asked who had been ringing the bell. Konráð kept quiet and waited for the man to return to his flat.

In the basement was a dark hallway with locked storage spaces for the residents, along with two rooms. Konráð knocked on the door of one of the rooms and listened, but no one answered. He tested the doorknob. The room was locked. He repeated this at the other room, and when he turned the doorknob, the door opened. Walking into a messy, foul-smelling den, he saw that he was too late.

A grimy folding bed stood against the wall and the floor was littered with leftover food and other rubbish, among which lay a girl of around twenty years old, wearing jeans and a T-shirt that revealed her bare arms. A needle and syringe hung from the elbow joint of one arm. Konráð knelt down next to the girl and felt for a heartbeat, but there was none. As far as he could tell, her death wasn't recent. She was lying on her side with her eyes closed, as if she were asleep.

As he got to his feet, he swore under his breath and took the photo from his pocket, to check whether this was the same girl the couple were worried about. His mobile phone broke the silence. The name Eygló appeared on the screen and he immediately recognised the caller's voice, despite not having heard it for some time.

'I need to see you,' said Eygló.

'Any special reason?'

'We need to talk.'

'Yes, but I'm a bit bu—'

'Preferably tonight, Konrád. Can you come to my place?'

'All right,' he said. 'It might be a little late.'

'Doesn't matter, just come.'

Konrád said goodbye and called Marta's mobile. She answered after a few rings.

'Yes, what?' she said bossily.

'You should get up here to Breiðholt, quick as you can,' he said, 'and bring a team from Forensics with you.'

5

About half an hour later, the place was crawling with policemen. The Forensics team closed off the entrance to the block of flats and the stairs to the basement, the basement hallway and the room where the girl lay. No one was allowed down there apart from a doctor, who pronounced the girl dead. Marta waited patiently with other members of CID for the Forensics technicians to finish their work. An ambulance had arrived to transport the body to the morgue of the National Hospital. All the evidence pointed to the death having been an accidental overdose. Forensics wanted to rule out all other possibilities.

Konrád told Marta about the meeting he'd had earlier that day with the girl's grandparents and their worries about her drug and alcohol use and clear involvement in drug smuggling. They'd been reluctant to take their concerns to the police for personal reasons, probably hoping that they could talk some sense into her themselves. She had responded by disappearing. Konrád had got Lassi's address from the Drugs Squad and decided to pay him a visit on his way home, with this result.

'Friends?' said Marta as they stood there in the stairwell, watching the Forensics team work. The block's residents were slowly starting to return home from work and were soon allowed to go up to their flats, carrying bulging bags of groceries and towing their kids, who, no less than their parents, stared open-mouthed at all the goings-on. Detectives walked up the stairs, knocked on people's doors, and asked about the tenants in the basement. The room's owner lived on the first floor and appeared to be away.

'The woman was a friend of Erna's,' said Konrád. 'I don't know them as well as she did. Hardly at all, actually.'

'Would you rather talk to them?' said Marta. 'Tell them about this?'

'No,' said Konrád pensively. 'I think it's right that you do; it's procedure.'

'It won't be fun telling them the news.'

'It won't be the first time they've had to hear such a thing.'

'Oh?'

'They lost their daughter in a car accident many years ago,' said Konrád. 'The girl's mum. Break the news gently.'

'Jesus and Joseph,' he heard Marta sigh.

He gave a police officer a detailed report of his involvement in the case and the tenuous thread of events that led to his opening the door to the basement room. He didn't recognise the officer, who was extremely pedantic in his questioning, leading to it taking a fair amount of time, with Konrád waiting impatiently to be able to get out of there. He wanted to disconnect himself from the case as quickly as he could and leave it to the police, and he regretted having entangled himself in those people's lives and the girl's death. He had great sympathy for the couple but wasn't the right man to alleviate their suffering.

Finally, he said goodbye to Marta and was driving away from the block when he remembered his phone call with Eygló. She had sounded rather down, which was unlike her. They hadn't known each other for very long, having only met a few times to discuss Konrád's father after Konrád became more curious about his fate. His and Eygló's fathers had met during the war years and held séances that were thought rather dubious before their scam eventually came to light.

Engilbert, Eygló's father, took it quite to heart and cut all connections with Konrád's father. The years passed. A few months after Konrád's father was murdered, Engilbert fell into the sea and his body was found washed up on the shore at Sundahöfn harbour. It was uncertain whether his death was accidental or if he had committed suicide. Konrád had contacted Eygló recently. He didn't have much to go on, only some old newspaper clippings of his father's, but had the hunch that he and Engilbert had taken up their old wartime occupation during the war years of duping people out of their money through sham séances. Eygló considered the notion preposterous.

Eygló had never invited Konrád to meet her at her place; they'd only spoken on the phone or met in cafes, usually at his request. Eygló was reluctant to meet him and preferred not to talk about her father, besides having an obvious dislike for Konrád's father, whom she blamed for Engilbert's melancholy and cruel fate. Yet she was a little more at ease now than she'd been at their first meeting and he noticed a change in her attitude towards him, as if she found it good to be able finally to talk to someone about her father.

Konrád pulled up to a small terraced house in the Fossvogur neighbourhood. He saw a faint light in its living-room window, and the silhouette of a person in it: probably Eygló, waiting for him. He walked up a few steps to the door, which opened as he approached, and Eygló invited him in. He was met by a faint smell of incense, and from the living room came a soft sound of music, so low that it could barely be heard. Konrád had never seen Eygló dressed in anything but black and it was the same now: a black skirt and black blouse, with a silver cross hanging at her neck. She was in her sixties, black-haired and petite, looking ten years younger than she really was. She had delicate features, with searching eyes that didn't miss a thing. He thought she probably coloured her hair, and had tried to imagine how she would look without her doing so. Erna had never coloured her hair, but just allowed nature to do its own thing.

'Excuse my impatience, but I felt I needed to see you immediately,' Eygló said, showing him into the living room. 'Where have you been?' she asked, trying to be discreet as she sniffed the air. 'Have you just come from the recycling centre?'

He suspected that what she smelled was the odour from Lassi's basement room, which had hung on his clothing. He knew that at one point, she, like her father, had worked as a medium, and he wondered if a good sense of smell was useful in that job. All the senses were, probably, he thought, in one way or another.

Konrád saw no reason to keep his whereabouts secret and told Eygló about the couple, the girl and the girl's fate, adding that she had called just as he was standing over her body.

'I'm sorry,' she said, taken aback. 'I called at the worst time.'

'No, it was fine,' Konrád reassured her.

'So she overdosed, the poor girl?'

'So it seems. The police will be giving it a closer look. What was it you wanted to discuss?'

Eygló clutched the silver cross hanging from her neck. She did so reflexively, as if it calmed her when she needed it.

'There are two things, actually,' she said, so softly that Konrád had to lean forward to catch her words. 'The first is something I heard last night, and couldn't believe. The other is about a girl I remember from when I was twelve years old and . . .'

She looked at Konrád.

'I haven't held a séance in many years.'

6

One by one, the guests left the terraced house in Fossvogur until only Eygló and the old woman were left. Eygló felt tired and empty, as she always used to do after helping people catch a glimpse of the afterlife. Having no more energy after saying goodbye to the participants, she sat back down in her chair at the round table where the séance had taken place. The old woman was still sitting there, dignified, slender and almost completely blind and deaf, with two long plaits hanging down her back, wearing sunglasses to protect her eyes and hearing aids in both ears. She looked more like an old Indian chief waiting to be picked up and taken back to her reservation. Her son, who was going to give her a lift back to the nursing home, had been delayed.

Eygló had known the old woman for ages, but hadn't seen her for many years. It had been a very long time, too, since she had held a séance at her home, but it all came back to her quite quickly. The participants were comprised of those who had consulted her over the years, some of them again and again, asking if she could put them in touch with the deceased. They were old clients of Eygló's from when she held séances regularly, even at homes where someone was plagued by a serious illness, and she would try her best to alleviate their suffering. From the time before she stopped holding them, for the most part, and then finally quit altogether. She had exercised her gift of clairvoyance very little for years now.

Eygló had called each client and invited them to a séance at her home. A total of six people gathered there in Fossvogur, four women and two men. None declined her invitation. They sat down at the table and everything was as before, except that they had all aged considerably. Nothing that could be called remarkable happened. One participant had become a widower since Eygló's previous days of séances, and sought answers about his wife. He got none. The mother of a woman in the group came forth. Eygló said that she sensed her presence in the living room, and that it was linked with a serious illness. The woman confirmed this. 'Is it your husband?' Eygló asked, without knowing why. The woman nodded again. 'The illness is quite advanced,' said Eygló. 'He's in palliative care,' said the woman. 'Do you know if anything can be done for him?' The presence faded. 'She wants you to trust the doctors,' said Eygló.

After around half an hour of these sorts of questions and answers, Eygló apologised to her guests; she hadn't done this for a long time and had quickly grown tired. They were understanding, and talked among themselves for a little while before getting ready to go. Everyone except for the old woman, who waited for her son.

Her name was Málfríður, and she had been an active member of the Icelandic Psychical Research Society in the sixties and seventies. She was married to a well-known medical medium and acted as his assistant, in charge of organising séances and consultations of those who were eager to benefit from her husband's gift and believed that he could contact the deceased. She herself had no doubts about the existence of the afterlife and often spoke of the ethereal world, where human souls gathered after parting from their bodies. A steady stream of people came to see her husband, seeking answers about or from the great beyond, and the old woman had witnessed incidents that were impossible to explain to anyone who didn't believe in the supernatural. Eygló remembered the long conversations she'd had with Málfríður when she was younger and just discovering her gift, which she didn't understand, but wanted to learn more about and harness if she was able. She had turned to the Psychical Research Society for guidance, and Málfríður helped her not to fear those faculties of hers, but rather live with them as an inseparable part of herself and accept the fact that she was a little different from others.

'Isn't he coming, the boy?' the old woman asked, referring to her son, who himself was rather old.

'He probably thought it would last longer,' replied Eygló apologetically. 'Maybe I could have gone longer.'

'Don't worry about it,' said Málfríður. 'You did well. You always did. You have a soothing presence. Same as your father.'

The old woman leaned forward.

'Why did you organise this séance?'

'What do you mean?'

'Why did you bring us together?' said Málfríður. 'Why have you become interested in séances again?'

'I wanted to see how it would go after all these years,' said Eygló hesitantly. She had expected such a question, but hadn't made up her mind about how she would answer it.

'Only that?'

Eygló nodded but Málfríður wasn't about to let her off the hook so easily.

'What are you looking for?' she asked.

'Nothing special,' said Eygló.

'Did you think that you could summon it with our help? The energy that formed here tonight?'

'I don't know what you mean,' said Eygló.

'You really remind me of Berti sometimes,' said the old woman. She never called Eygló's father anything else. 'It wasn't nice to see him squandering his gifts. He was always hiding something from us. If he hadn't drunk so much, he could have used his talents for good.'

'I think he was never completely at ease with his gift.'

'No, of course not. Any more than you? It's a pity how things went with him. Your dad was a good man. You must never forget that. Weak-willed, of course, and extremely sensitive. Liked to drink. Which is maybe not the best mix. Did this have anything to do with Berti? This séance?'

'No,' said Eygló.

'Have you ever sensed his presence after he left us?'

'No.'

'He stopped all his involvement with the society,' said Málfríður, repositioning herself. 'We didn't know what he was doing or if he was acting as a medium in any capacity before he died. It was of course tragic how he treated himself, and how he broke off old friendships. My husband tried to talk sense into him but gave up, saying that he couldn't possibly have been OK considering his state.'

'Mum said the same thing, that he was very unhappy in his final months.'

'Yes, the dear, of course it's been difficult for her. And for the two of you. Extremely difficult, I can imagine.'

The old woman looked at Eygló through her sunglasses.

'Later, we learned that Berti had taken up again with bad company,' she said. 'It was as if he sought out those losers, probably because they provided him with alcohol. Someone said they'd seen him with the man who had done him so much harm.'

'Who? What man?'

The old woman took off her sunglasses. Her eyes were nearly white and sensitive to light and brightness, and no longer perceived anything but hazy movements.

'The one who used him to hoodwink people during the war and was then stabbed near the South Iceland Abattoir.'

After Eygló repeated what the old woman had said, Konrád looked up.

'Did she mean my father?' he asked, scarcely able to conceal his surprise.

Eygló nodded. 'I don't see who else she could have meant,' she said.

'Does she, this woman, think that our fathers were up to their old tricks?'

Again, Eygló nodded.

'We thought . . . you thought that that would have been preposterous.'

'Yes.'

'The two of them together?'

'Yes.'

'What were they doing?'

'God knows. Málfríður had just heard it somewhere, and knew nothing more.'

Konrád looked towards the round table in the living room and imagined Eygló's guests sitting around it, holding hands. In one corner of the room was an old piano that Eygló said was a Danish heirloom.

'Why did you hold that meeting now?' he asked. 'That séance. What was it that you didn't want to tell the old woman? Is it a sensitive issue?'

'Actually, I told her before she left.'

'Told her what?'

'You don't believe in such things,' said Eygló, who knew Konrád's views on the afterlife and the supernatural. 'It's pointless talking to you about it.'

'About what?'

Eygló hesitated.

'She appeared to me again,' she then said.

'Who?

'A little girl I saw when I was twelve years old, and she was just as lonely and helpless as she was then. I can feel that she misses a doll that belonged to her. She thinks that I can help her find it.'

7

Accompanied by a uniformed officer, Marta went in person to Danní's grandparents' home to inform them of the girl's death. Konrád had told her where in the westside they lived. She'd requested the assistance of the parish priest, who was waiting for her in his car when Marta and the officer arrived in his squad car. The officer was young and inexperienced, and had never had such an assignment before. Marta wasn't familiar with the priest, but told him the main details about the young girl and the needle stuck in her arm.

'Those poor people,' said the priest.

'Yes, it's terrible,' said Marta. 'Just terrible.'

It was rather late in the evening, and as they walked up to the house, they noticed that a large flat-screen TV in one of the rooms was on and showing a wildlife programme. While ringing the doorbell, Marta thought that once before, these same people had been paid a visit that ruined their lives. Had it been in the evening, like now? Or in the middle of the night?

The woman came to the door and looked questioningly at the trio, and Marta paused a moment before explaining the reason for their visit. She tried to choose her words carefully.

'God, no, don't say that!' moaned the woman. Her face paled and she burst into tears.

The priest stepped forward and helped her back into the house. Her husband was standing there, still as stone.

'Is this true?' he said softly, looking at Marta.

'Unfortunately, it is, yes,' she said. 'You have my sympathies. I'm sorry to have to bring you this awful news.'

The man went over to his wife and took her in his arms, led her into the living room and tried to comfort her with soothing words, but was clearly having a hard time swallowing this himself. The priest followed and sat down with them. Marta kept a suitable distance. The police officer remained standing in the hall.

After the priest had spoken to the couple for a little while, Marta decided that it was time to disturb them. She said that she had to get some information from them, and that either they or someone they trusted would have to identify the body formally, at the first opportunity.

'Identify?' said the man. 'Isn't it certain . . . ? How do you know that it's her?'

'The man you asked to look for her, Konrád, had this photo with him,' said Marta, taking out the photo of the girl. 'I expect it came from you?'

'Was it Konrád who found her?' asked the man.

'Yes.'

'Where is he? He isn't with you?'

'He's not a police officer,' said Marta. 'I'm sure he'll get in touch with you as soon as he can.'

'What happened?' asked the woman. 'What happened to her?'

'At first glance, it appears she was careless with drugs,' Marta said. 'Chances are she died of an overdose, but we don't know if it was accidental, or if it was a premeditated suicide.'

'Suicide? My God . . .'

'Did you ever hear her say anything about suicide, or did she show any signs of depression? Anxiety?'

The couple shook their heads as if the idea was entirely foreign to them.

'Do you know if she'd been doing a lot of drugs or drinking a lot lately?'

'We know so little,' said the man.

'Of course. Sorry. Most indications are that it was an accident,' said Marta. 'Unfortunately, this happens far too often. I understand that she was in a relationship with a man called Lassi or something like that. Can you confirm that? I'm sorry about these questions, but it's important that we get as much information as we can, as quickly as possible.'

'We don't know his name; she just called him Lassi once when we asked about the relationship,' the man said.

'A man named Lárus Hinriksson rents the room where she was found,' said Marta. 'Could that be him?'

'Isn't that likely?' said the man. 'Was he with her when this happened?'

'We haven't been able to find him,' said Marta. 'But it shouldn't be so difficult. Do you know where he spends his time?'

'Us? No, we've never seen him.'

'When you spoke to Konrád about your granddaughter, you mentioned drug smuggling. That she'd been a mule.'

'She admitted to having brought drugs into the country,' said the woman. 'She couldn't deny it. I saw them.'

She looked at her husband.

'God, how awful this is. Poor Danní. How could it have come to this? She was so . . . she was such a good and beautiful child, and reminded us so much of her mother. How could it have come to this? How could this have happened? She was just a child, and was lured into this . . . this . . .'

The woman hid her face in her hands.

'Do you have any reason to believe that she worked for someone here in town?' Marta asked. 'That she didn't smuggle the drugs in for her personal use?'

'She swore and insisted that she'd only done it that one time,' said the man, 'but of course we know nothing about it. I think she was lying to us. She said she did it for some men but didn't want to tell us who they were. She didn't want to tell us anything.'

'Do you think she meant this Lassi? Or people connected to him?'

'We don't know,' said the man. 'We know nothing about these things. It's completely incomprehensible to us that such a thing could have happened. Incomprehensible.'

'Is there a reason why you didn't contact the police?' asked Marta. 'When you saw what was going on? How deep she'd sunk? When you saw the drugs?'

The couple looked at each other. The priest's expression suggested that Marta could have left this question for another time.

'Danní begged us not to do that,' said the man. 'We said we were going to. We told her that we had to talk to you. That she couldn't behave like that and smuggle in drugs in front of our noses.'

'She flipped out,' said the woman. 'Said that she had to deliver the drugs, otherwise she would be made to pay for it. She promised that it was just that one time, and that she would never do it again.'

'Who would make her pay for it?'

'She didn't want to say,' said the man, sighing. 'And I don't even know if she was telling us the truth. Whether the stuff was just hers. I . . . we always wanted the best for her. We didn't want to anger her. That was always our first thought. To make her happy.'

'And this is the result,' whispered the woman.

The priest signalled to Marta that he thought that was enough.

'Yes, I guess that's enough for now,' said Marta. 'What about her father? How can we find him?'

'Her father?' the man exclaimed. 'Good luck with that.'

'Oh?'

'I guess he's somewhere in Brazil. He's lived there for years and never cared about Danní. Never had anything to do with his daughter. Acted as if she didn't exist.'

8

Konrád had just come in the door when his mobile phone rang. He'd sat a good while with Eygló before going home, discussing with her what the old lady at the séance had said about their fathers. It was the first real evidence they had that the two men had been in contact with each other after working together during the war years, and it came as a great surprise to them. Especially Eygló. She'd always said that Engilbert had turned his back on Konrád's father and wanted nothing more to do with him.

On the phone was Marta, who was back at the station after her visit to the elderly couple, and she filled him in on what had taken place there.

'It doesn't sound like fun,' said Konrád.

'They said they expected to hear from you before too long,' said Marta. 'Were you thinking of looking in on them?'

'Yes, I suppose so,' said Konrád. 'Of course, I don't know those people at all, and don't know why they got me involved in this. Do you think it was an accident?'

'Looks like it,' said Marta. 'The girl just screwed up. It's as if she'd only just begun shooting up, which may explain why it went the way it did. She only has a few needle tracks on her arms; not many at all.'

'What was in the syringe?'

'MDMA, they think – a toxicology study remains to be done – there's been a lot of that stuff in circulation. It's been in the news quite a bit recently.'

'I don't pay much attention to the news,' said Konráð.

'Could be from the stuff that the girl smuggled into the country. She has no police record, and we don't know her connection to the drugs world apart from the kid who rents the room where she was found – maybe. Lárus Hinriksson. She seems to have been a complete newbie to it all, the stupid girl.'

They said goodbye shortly afterwards, and Konráð had a bite to eat and poured himself a glass of red wine. He put some old Icelandic pop music on the record player. He still played his LPs as if he'd never heard of any of the technological advances that had revolutionised music publishing. He knew every scratch on the record and liked the little hiss before the start of the first track, which was like a prelude to the music. He sat down at his dining table, looked at the newspaper and magazine clippings scattered over it, and thought about his father and Engilbert. These clippings had been his father's, and Konráð had found them after his death. There were articles about clairvoyance, stories about fraudulent mediums and how their scams were discovered, an interview with the chairman of the Psychical Research Society, and pieces on the ethereal world where human souls gathered after the deaths of their bodies. The clippings were an indication that his father had become interested in the afterlife again before he was stabbed. What had sparked that interest, Konrád didn't know. His father had never talked about it. He had, however, told his son all about his and Engilbert's activities during the war years, when they held séances and profited off people who looked to them for answers. His father made fun of believers and saw nothing wrong with making money from other people's troubles.

He'd once mentioned that Engilbert considered himself to be possessed of real psychic abilities and had held séances before their paths converged. On the other hand, he'd been insecure and hesitant and hadn't had many clients before Konrád's father suggested they work together. Konrád didn't know how they first met, or why Engilbert agreed to join his father in the scam. He did know, however, that nothing was sacred to them. Not even the most bitter sorrows. Even parents who had lost their children could seek solace from that 'trusty' medium.

Konrád rummaged through the clippings and thought about his father's stories. If he and Engilbert had started scheming again after a twenty-year hiatus, it likely had to do with séances. They hardly had anything else in common. It was difficult to imagine what else it could be, if anything.

Another question was bothering Konrád; one that he hadn't asked Eygló. It had only occurred to him suddenly and unexpectedly, when Eygló told him that the old woman had said that Engilbert and his father had been seen together shortly before they both died. He didn't know if Eygló had been thinking the same. If she had been, she didn't mention it, in any case.

His mobile rang again. He looked at the clock. It was midnight. Not recognising the number, he hesitated for a moment before answering. He immediately knew who it was from the voice on the other end: a man he'd worked with and been friends with for many years, although their friendship had long since gone cold.

'Are you already in bed, you lout?' he heard Leó say, and knew that he was drunk.

'Marta told me you were drinking again,' said Konrád. 'So all that therapy yielded no results.'

'Shut up –'

'Apart from the cost to those of us who stand on our own two feet.'

'Shut up!!'

'Shut up yourself,' said Konrád, before switching off his phone.

9

No one knew better than Konrád that old police reports didn't tell the whole story. The main points were recorded, whatever details were considered most relevant from witnesses' testimonies, a description of the facts of the case, locations and times and personal information about the people who were spoken to and whom the case touched. Details that seemed irrelevant, informal conversations, unsubstantiated rumours, calls from people who thought they had vital information, especially ones who'd obviously been drinking, were for the most part left out, unless there was some special reason to follow up on them. Many things that witnesses themselves considered negligible were never mentioned, unless the questions put by the police brought them to light. Some people lied for reasons that they alone knew. Others relied too heavily on their memory, which was quite often unreliable, not least among his father's acquaintances.

The files on his father's murder weren't very substantial. The autopsy revealed that he had died from two stab wounds. One went through his heart, causing him to lose a huge amount of blood in a short time. This coincided with the description of the murder scene. The bloodstain was in front of the iron-barred gate to the South Iceland Abattoir facility, and judging by the description, it was as if the man had been led to the slaughter there.

The police reports stated that, according to their neighbours, Konrád and his father had quarrelled the same day that his father was found murdered. During questioning, Konrád had flatly denied that there had been any argument. He was convinced that it had absolutely nothing to do with the case. He had certainly got into a fight with his father, which ended with Konrád storming out and meeting some friends in town. Two of them had moon-lighted with him in construction work, and the third was a loser heading fast towards drinking himself to death, which he ended up doing a few years later. The three of them could confirm that he'd been with them the evening his father was murdered. The investigation having come to a standstill, the police had resorted to the process of elimination, wanting to remove all doubt that Konrád had killed his father. Parricides were extremely rare.

Only one of the three policemen most directly involved in that murder investigation was still alive. He'd quit the force a few years after the incident and gone to work for the Directorate of Customs, but had retired many years ago and now lived on the Reykjanes peninsula, south of Reykjavík. Konrád hadn't been out to Reykjanes for a long time and decided to go for a drive, wondering, along the way, whether he should pay the man a visit. They knew each other only through that particular investigation. The man was no longer on the force when Konrád began working there. He'd always treated Konrád with respect and had shown himself to be understanding towards that young man who had grown up in difficult circumstances, considering him to be something of a misfit who struggled with anger that he didn't really understand and couldn't always keep in check.

Near Keflavík, Konráð turned off the road to the south and headed for the former military base, recalling the summer when he'd worked there for an Icelandic contractor hired by the US military. At the time, the military had an extensive presence on Miðnesheiði Heath. That was the summer after he graduated from the Technical College, and he got the job through a friend of his. He was put on a crew in charge of the maintenance of the base's roads and streets. He enjoyed the work, the food in the mess was good, he slept in the contractor's bunkhouse five nights a week and went to Reykjavík at the weekend. Some of those working on the base smuggled cigarettes and beer through the main gate; he himself did the same and was well stocked by the end of the summer. The base was like a smaller-scale model of life overseas. It was there that he went to a fast-food place for the first time, and had a hamburger and chips.

He still hadn't made up his mind, and before reaching the gate he turned left and headed towards Hafnir. Then he noticed a road he'd never driven before, a coast road by the international airport. He drove along it at a relaxed pace, admiring the view of the shore and the sea before reaching Stafnes, where there was a small cluster of buildings. He drove on in the gentle autumn light past the church at Hvalsnes, where, centuries ago, the hymnist Hallgrímur Pétursson was minister, and carved his grief onto stone following the loss of his daughter. Finally, Konráð decided that he wouldn't return home without stopping first to see the ex-cop.

The man was working in a tool shed next to his house and

immediately recognised Konrád as he drove up and parked his car. Despite his advanced years, the man was healthy, had a sharp memory and was attentive. He had run into Konrád several times in the past, when he dropped by police headquarters to say hello to his former colleagues. His name was Pálmi, and he invited his visitor in for coffee.

'To tell the truth, I've been expecting you for quite some time,' he said, showing Konrád to the kitchen. 'I'm just surprised that it's taken you so long to get started.'

'I wouldn't say I've got started on anything,' said Konrád, sitting down at an old kitchen table with a faded plastic tablecloth. 'There's hardly anything left to uncover, is there? You guys did all you could.'

'Apparently not,' said Pálmi. 'We never came to a conclusion as to what happened. It's uncomfortable, not being able to close such a case. Even just a few days ago, I was speculating about it, so you see that such a thing can really haunt you. Which, of course, you already know. Doubtless better than me.'

Pálmi poured Konrád a cup of pitch-black coffee.

'Weren't you in charge of the investigation of the man they hid up on Langjökull glacier?' he said.

Konrád said that he was.

'You must have been relieved when he was finally found. Wasn't it, what, around thirty years later?'

'It was definitely a relief when he was found,' said Konrád. 'Nothing in the investigation pointed to the glacier. Nothing at all.'

He tried not to sound too apologetic. He had no reason to be ashamed. The case had been the most difficult one in his career.

'Isn't that why you're here now? Because of unfinished business?'

'No . . . I don't know,' said Konrád. 'I was going through the old reports, trying to see if you'd ever questioned a man named Engilbert. I found nothing about that, but thought maybe you hadn't put it down on paper. He purported to be a medium or seer or whatever it's called. Do you remember him at all?'

'Yes, I remember him, but not in connection with this case. Didn't his body wash up at Sundahöfn harbour? It wasn't until he was found dead that someone recalled that he and your dad knew each other during the war. Were engaged in some sort of fraudulent activity. Is that right?'

Konrád confirmed this, and added that he'd recently spoken to Engilbert's daughter and learned that he'd been found dead just a few months after his own father was killed.

'They were scamming people who believed in the afterlife.'

'The afterlife?' said Pálmi sceptically. 'I don't think that was ever a part of our investigation.'

'I know my dad had become interested in the subject again before his death, and Engilbert's daughter learned that the two men had been in contact again.'

'Well, I can assure you we had no information on that at the time.'

'No one looked into it?'

'Nothing would have led us to establish a link between Engilbert and your father outside of their collaboration during the war,' Pálmi pointed out. 'Either Engilbert fell into the sea by accident, or he'd decided to end his own life. But I doubt it had anything to do with your father, if that's what you're thinking.'

'I don't know what to think. I find it interesting – something that might be called a new twist in the case if it turns out that they had indeed got up to their old tricks again.'

'Engilbert's wife thought that he occasionally spent time down at the harbour. On the boats. That he'd met up with sailors who gave him alcohol. She thought he'd fallen between one of the boats and the dock, without anyone seeing it. At least no witnesses came forward. Two or three fishermen we questioned knew who he was, but they didn't know what happened.'

'And Engilbert's name never came up in connection with my father's death?'

'As I said, after your father's death, we tried to interview everyone who knew him or was acquainted with him in some way,' said Pálmi. 'But no, Englibert's name never came up in the investigation.'

'Engilbert's daughter told me he took the news of my father's murder quite to heart,' Konrád continued. 'He reacted very badly when he found out.'

'Well, I of course know nothing about that. How long have you been in touch with her?'

'I've met her a few times.'

'So you've started digging around a bit in the case?' said Pálmi, smiling, as if having just won a bet that, sooner or later, Konrád would resume the investigation.

'Were there any other unusual occurrences at that time?' Konrád asked. 'Anything that you needed to look into? Fraudulent psychics? Acts of violence? Unexplained deaths in Reykjavík?'

'Unexplained? No, nothing comparable to your father's murder,' Pálmi replied thoughtfully. 'Fortunately, murders are rare here in Iceland, and were even rarer in those days. No, nothing comes to mind.'

'Peculiar accidents . . . ?'

'No, or . . . no. What exactly do you mean by unexplained?'

'I don't know. Just, anything.'

'Like a fire, or . . . ? There was a fire at one point in those years, I recall, and it took the life of an old man. It started with the stove. Is that the kind of thing you're thinking of? And there were always a few suicides, unfortunately, and . . . a girl found dead in the Pond.'

'A girl?'

'Yes, twelve years old.'

'Did she fall through the ice?'

'No, it happened at the end of the summer. She probably dropped her doll in the water, and then tried to fish it out.'

'Her doll?'

'Yes. The girl was found close to Skothúsvegur Bridge. It was definitely an unexplained death. There were no witnesses to what happened. But it has nothing to do with the things you're looking into. Nothing at all.'

10

Konrád would have liked to have a chat with Marta before driving back to Reykjavík, but since she wasn't picking up her phone, he assumed she was in a meeting. He felt guilty about not having contacted Danní's grandparents and hoped that Marta could update him on the progress of the investigation. He was planning on going to see them, but preferred not to do so empty-handed. In fact, he didn't really want to go, and would do so only out of a sense of duty. He was bad at such things. Bad at making conversation. Bad at showing compassion to strangers, or offering them support. He didn't know how to go about it. He thought for a moment about stopping to buy them some flowers, but decided not to. He would go and see them one more time to show his respect, but that would be it, as far as he was concerned.

His son, Húgó, called him to see if he would mind babysitting the twins while he and his wife went to the theatre one night next week. Konrád said that it would be no problem. He really liked the two boys and was always up for babysitting them. Húgó, who was a doctor, asked how he was doing. Konrád replied that he had nothing to complain about, and after a brief conversation, they said goodbye.

Just as he pulled up outside Danní's grandparents' house, Marta called and asked if he'd been trying to reach her. He replied that he just wanted to know how the investigation of the girl's death was going, and she told him that there actually was no investigation, for the moment. The body had to be autopsied first. Lárus Hinriksson hadn't been found yet. Inquiries had turned up nothing. No one seemed to have seen him recently. Those who knew him, his family and friends, had no news of him. When they called the mobile number registered in his name, all they got was a message saying that the number was currently unavailable.

'Don't you find that a bit odd?' Konrád asked. 'That you couldn't contact him?'

'Not really,' Marta replied, clearly with her mouth full. 'So far, we haven't been looking for him very actively. He's sure to turn up.'

'Do you know anything more about the drugs the girl had on her?'

'No – she could just have smuggled them in for herself. For her own use. It might be as simple as that. But we're still looking at the other possibility, that she was working for someone else.'

'Can you tell me anything about her relationship with Lárus?' Konrád asked. 'I'm about to go and see her grandparents, and would love to have something to tell them.'

'I'll see they're kept in the loop,' Marta replied, sighing wearily. 'Though they certainly have no qualms about calling the police station now.'

Konrád shut off his car's engine and went up to the house. The husband came to the door and invited him in. He looked as if he'd aged by several years. His wife was sitting in the living room. They had brought out the family photo albums, and the table was covered with photos of their daughter and granddaughter. Most had been taken on special occasions, Christmas, birthdays, others abroad, at the Tivoli amusement park in Copenhagen or in front of the Eiffel Tower. Konrád looked them over. In some of them, their daughter was holding her little Danní in her arms, and both were smiling, beaming.

In shock and distraught, the couple asked Konrád how he'd discovered Danní's body and to describe what he'd seen. Looking at the photos cluttering the table, Konrád consciously tried to avoid adding to their pain. He told them that as far as he could see, she hadn't suffered at all. It was more as if she'd fallen asleep and not woken up again. Her expression had been peaceful.

'I'm guessing that Marta, the officer in charge of the case, told you that this Lárus is an old acquaintance of the police. He's quite difficult,' Konrád clarified, considering that a real understatement.

'He didn't do this to her?'

'The police think she wasn't careful with the dosage,' said Konrád. 'At least that's their initial assessment.'

'I don't understand,' said the woman. 'She was always so afraid of needles, always refused injections.'

'I guess it's not the same when it comes to injecting that damned poison,' her husband interjected.

The couple continued to ask Konrád questions, which he tried to answer before eventually referring them back to Marta, telling them not to hesitate to call the police station for further information or to pressure the police into moving the investigation along. This brought the conversation to an end. Before leaving, Konrád hesitated; glancing again over all those captured memories of the two girls who had filled their lives, he searched for the appropriate words to say goodbye. He had just brought them to his lips when, suddenly, the doorbell rang, and the husband went to see who it was. Konrád caught a few muffled greetings and then the visitors appeared, a couple a bit younger than Danní's grandparents. The husband introduced the new arrivals: his brother and a female friend of his. Konrád said hello and took the opportunity to leave, stating he had business to attend to.

'Thank you for all your help,' said the husband. 'It was Konrád here who found Danní,' he explained to his brother.

'Oh, you're the policeman?' said the brother.

'He was married to Erna – you probably remember her. She was a doctor, like you. At the National Hospital in Fossvogur, right?' The husband glanced at Konrád, who nodded.

'I just remember she was a doctor,' said the brother. 'But our paths never crossed. She passed away a few years ago, didn't she?'

'Yes, from cancer,' confirmed Konrád, who didn't want to go into it in any detail.

'It's all just a big game of chance, nothing else,' said the woman accompanying the doctor, with a contrite air that seemed to say that the ways of the Lord were inscrutable. 'No one knows when their number's going to come up.'

As soon as he got home, Konrád phoned Eygló. When she didn't answer, he finished what was left of his glass of red wine from the night before, thinking about his visit to Pálmi, the old policeman. As he took his last sip, his mobile rang, and he saw that it was Eygló.

'Did you call me?' she asked as soon as he answered.

'Yes,' said Konrád. 'It's about that girl you told me about last night.'

'What about her?'

'Do you know anything about her, who she is or who she was, or . . . is she dead, since you . . . since she appears to you?'

'You don't understand these things at all. Are you actually calling me to make fun of me?'

'No,' Konrád replied, regretting his clumsy question. 'Absolutely not. I have my doubts, yes, but I –'

'What do you want?'

'You told me yesterday that you saw a young girl who was unhappy and was searching for her doll.'

'Yes.'

'Do you know about the accident at the Pond?'

'The accident at the Pond?'

'A young girl drowned there,' Konrád said, trying to remember what Pálmi had told him. 'It was in 1961. She was twelve years old. It was thought that she dropped her doll in the water, and when she tried to fish it out, she drowned. There were no witnesses. A man passing by . . . Are you there . . . ? Eygló . . . ?'

Hearing only a slight disturbance on the other end, Konrád thought she'd dropped her phone on the floor.

11

Lárus Hinriksson seemed to have disappeared off the face of the earth. His family had long since cut ties with him, and knew nothing of his whereabouts for months. His parents were divorced and had no contact with each other. Lárus had two brothers who were doing much better in life. One of them, who was co-owner of a garage, told the police that he'd last heard from his brother more than a year ago, and that he'd been having money problems, as usual. He'd refused to lend him any, which Lárus had said he needed and promised to pay back as soon as possible. The brother said that he'd long since stopped listening to his whinging; Lárus was 'a hopeless case' and owed him loads of money, which he had probably never intended to pay back. The other brother told pretty much the same story. Lárus was always pestering him for loans and trying to scrounge money off him. They'd met last at that brother's house a year and a half ago, but he had thrown Lárus out and told him never to come back. Both brothers thought that all the money he said he needed so badly went directly on drugs.

They didn't know Danní and had never heard of her. Nor had Lárus's mother; she didn't know that her son was in a relationship with a girl, and was devastated to learn that the girl had been found dead in his room. She didn't know where he lived, and repeatedly asked the detective who had been sent to question her about the girl, her relationship with her son, and how she had died. The mother worked as a cashier at a Nettó supermarket, and when the detective asked her if Lárus had tried to extort money from her as he'd done with his brothers, she replied that she had no extra money to give him. Her wages were pitifully low, and the rent she paid for the broom cupboard that was supposed to be a flat was absolutely killing her. She moonlighted doing cleaning work to pad her income, and was proud of it. The detective had nodded sympathetically – never admitting that due to the pittance paid him, he also moonlighted as a mason during his holidays, not declaring a single króna of what he earned.

'Are you looking for Lassi because of what happened to the girl?' she asked the detective as they stood talking behind the supermarket.

'Yes, we have a few questions for him,' replied the detective.

'Does it have to do with him? Her death?' asked the woman worriedly.

'We need to talk to him about it.'

'Lassi would never hurt anyone,' said the mother. 'He may do drugs and all that, but he would never hurt a fly.'

'No, of course not,' said the detective, jotting down in the small notepad he used on such occasions that he wouldn't hurt a fly.

The father, Hinrik, appeared to be the last member of the

family to have seen Lárus. Hinrik was a bus driver; he had moved to Akureyri a few years earlier and took tourists to Lake Mývatn. He'd met his son there in the north a few months earlier. Lárus had said he'd come to attend a concert with some friends, his father told the female detective sent to his home by the Akureyri Police. He knew nothing about his son's relationships and didn't know the girl found dead of an overdose in his son's room in the south.

'Do you know the others who were with him?' asked the detective. 'When he was here?'

'No, I don't know Lassi's friends,' said the father. 'I only knew his playmates when he was little. Then he got into all kinds of crap. I tried to help him, but had to throw in the towel. The poor kid went to the dogs in just a few years, without anything being able to stop it. We tried all kinds of therapy, got him to talk to loads of counsellors and social workers, but none of it helped. His addiction was stronger. He stole money from us and used our credit cards if he could. His brothers wanted to help him, but they soon realised that all the money they gave only went towards deepening his addiction. He started breaking into businesses and people's homes and finally got caught with ecstasy tablets in Seyðisfjörður as he was getting off the Norræna ferry. He was sentenced to a year and a half in prison, which he served at Litla-Hraun.'

'And that didn't set him straight?'

'I went to see him there two or three times,' the father replied, 'and I got the feeling that he wanted to move on. He said he was thinking about going back to school and that sort of thing. But as soon as he got out, the first thing he did was get drunk and high, and I realised then that it was hopeless.'

The detective jotted this information down.

'You don't really think he would have hurt that poor girl?' Hinrik asked, no less worried than Lassi's mother.

'We just need to speak to him,' said the detective. 'That's all I can tell you.'

When CID finally managed to contact the owner of the room where the girl was found, it turned out that she had been planning to kick Lassi out, not only because he hadn't been paying his rent, but also because of the general nuisance he made of himself and complaints from the residents upstairs.

The owner was a woman of around sixty who had wanted to give the boy a helping hand, as she told the police. She had occasionally worked as a volunteer for the Red Cross and met a number of young people who had strayed from the right path. When she placed an ad to rent the room, Lárus was one of those who came to have a look at it, and he had honestly admitted that he'd just served time in Litla-Hraun for a petty crime. The woman took pity on him. As a pious Christian woman, she believed that it wasn't her place to judge others, but that, on the contrary, she had a duty to try to help them return to the right path. To that end, she kept the rent at a low rate, or at least a very reasonable one, as she put it. He never paid a single króna of it.

He always said that he was on his way to doing so, and acted surprised when she told him that she still hadn't received any transfers. 'But I went to the bank to pay it yesterday,' he said, flabbergasted at the misunderstanding and blaming the bank for it. He assured her that he would fix it at the first opportunity. Worse was that hanging around him were all sorts of people who stayed up late into the night and visited him at all hours, often buzzing any flat to get into the building. It didn't matter if it was three in the morning. Understandably, it was a great nuisance to the building's residents and the woman bore the brunt of their anger. She vowed that she would get the boy out of the basement as soon as possible.

Lassi had sworn to make amends, but the situation quickly deteriorated again and a month later, such a violent fight took place in front of the building between some of Lassi's friends that even the police finally intervened, despite having long since stopped following up on the residents' complaints.

'I'm not surprised a girl was found dead there,' a woman living on the ground floor told the police officer sent to question the building's occupants.

'Too bad it wasn't the kid,' her husband added.

'Do you think he was the one who killed her?' asked the woman.

The residents hadn't really noticed Danní, and couldn't say if she visited Lárus regularly. Nor did they know any of the others seen in Lassi's company, either coming up from the basement or going down there. All those people chain-smoked, and everyone in the floors above could smell it. And it wasn't just good-quality American tobacco. Those in the know said it was cannabis, too. Joints. Marijuana. And even worse.

'Just a bunch of junkies,' said a man living on the second floor.

Signs of this were visible in the little room. Found among all the rubbish, empty bottles and beer cans was a panoply of drug paraphernalia: pipes, straws and lighters. There were also syringes and needles, empty boxes of Ritalin and Contalgin. Some with special Icelandic labelling. Others imported illegally.

'The poor girl,' said a man on the third floor.

'Serves her right,' said his wife.

12

As so often, Konrád had trouble sleeping. He got up in the middle of the night, switched on his computer and browsed the internet for a while. He went through the Icelandic news sites, reading about a government minister caught up in some scandal, an association providing assistance to Albanian refugees and wage negotiations that had stalled.

Much of the news at the start of September 1961 would not have stood out as particularly unusual in today's papers: death sentences for rebels in Algeria, herring sales agreements made with the Russians, a man who narrowly escaped drowning in the Akureyri harbour. In the cinemas, the American blockbuster *For Whom the Bell Tolls* was being reshown in commemoration of the untimely death of the great American writer Ernest Hemingway, as one advertisement stated.

The largest daily published a small insert with the black border normally used for death notices mentioning the accident that had taken place at the Pond. It gave few details. A young man crossing the Reykjavík Pond Bridge had discovered a drowned twelve-year-old girl. The circumstances of this terrible accident were unknown. The police thought that the girl was alone when she fell in the water. She couldn't swim.

Three days later, the same daily quoted a police inspector as saying that a preliminary investigation had revealed nothing to suggest that the girl's death was a homicide. The article didn't give the names of the girl, her parents or next of kin, it being common practice not to do so under such tragic circumstances. Nor was the name of the young man who found the girl stated in the papers.

Konrád continued to surf the internet. Prominent these days was news of websites set up by women who had been the victims of sexual assault or abuse, having been raped at some point in their lives or abused as children. Every day, new stories were added to those sites. Some victims had no qualms about publishing their stories under their own names, and their testimonies were honest and straightforward, giving details of gross sexual violence and the suffering it caused. Sometimes, the names of the perpetrators were given and the shame 'handed back to them', as it was called. Konrád was especially surprised by just how many women had terrible stories to tell of their relationships with men. Of course, he had witnessed such violence during his career as a policeman, but hadn't realised that it was so widespread and pervasive.

He switched off the computer, lay back down in bed and thought about Eygló. They had arranged to meet the next day, but he dreaded the meeting, knowing that he would have to ask her questions that haunted him, and which he expected she would take badly.

*

Eygló sat waiting for him in the cafe, deep in thought. The clinking of tableware carried from the kitchen. The noise from a large espresso machine spewing hot steam occasionally drowned out the noisy chatter of the customers. This was a popular, crowded place in the city centre, and as Eygló watched Konrád park his car outside and pay the parking meter, she thought that she probably should have suggested someplace a little quieter. Moments later, he sat down opposite her and ordered a coffee.

At first, when Konrád had asked to meet her to talk about his father's friendship with Engilbert, she hadn't taken the idea well. She had no answers for him. Furthermore, she was reluctant to discuss her family affairs, and particularly her father, with strangers, given the tragic circumstances in which he had departed this world. She had never spoken of it to anyone, barely even her mother. The two of them had avoided the subject, for the most part. So it took her by surprise when Konrád called and began asking her all those questions. She hadn't been prepared for it, and wasn't particularly cooperative. When they met later, she hadn't been as stressed, and came to understand that he was only in search of answers to questions that had been bothering him for years, not unlike herself.

She didn't know exactly how old he was; probably just a few years older than her. The more she got to know him, the more she liked him. He had a good presence, she felt; he was calm, composed and interesting. Unlike, for example, the man she'd met two years earlier when a friend of hers tried to hook her up with one of her work colleagues. He started annoying her almost the minute they met. He was twice divorced, with a tan the colour of chicory, and couldn't stop talking about his trips abroad, his golf games and his house in Florida, a property he'd managed to wrest from the claws of wife number two.

She and Konrád had agreed to meet when they spoke on the phone the night before, after he mentioned the girl who drowned in the Pond. Eygló had been so shocked by the news that she'd dropped her phone. She knew immediately that it was the girl she had seen when she was twelve years old.

Konrád had promised Eygló that he would look into the matter and try to find out who the girl was.

'I didn't find much,' said Konrád when he told her about his search in the police records. It seemed that everyone was convinced that it was a terrible accident. 'It looks as if the girl's body hadn't been examined. I don't know if there was even an autopsy done on her. Maybe they thought it was unnecessary. I found the coroner's report. He concluded that the girl died accidentally, by drowning. And then it's as if no one bothered to look into it any further. The case was closed.'

'What was her name?'

'Nanna.'

'Nanna,' Eygló repeated slowly, letting the name sink in. 'And who was she?'

'A very ordinary Reykjavík girl, I think. Born here in the city. Attended Eastside Elementary School. Her mother was single and lived in the old military barracks neighbourhood up on Skólavörðuholt Hill. Probably one of the last residents there, before all those old Nissen huts were razed. I looked her up. She died years ago. At the time, she was working in the kitchen of the National Hospital. She seems not to have given the name of the girl's father to the civil registry office, but lived with a man and his son, who was a few years older than the girl. The man was a labourer and never had any run-ins with the law, from what I can gather. He died about ten years ago. From what I could see on the civil registry website, his son is still alive, as is the young man who discovered the girl's body. He's a retired teacher. I wrote down his name. I found another man in the registry with the same name, but the age fits with the teacher. He was nineteen when he happened upon the body. His testimony is very precise. Very clear.'

Eygló listened to Konrád in silence.

'And nothing is known about the girl's father?' she then asked.

'He may have been from the Suðurnes peninsula. The girl's mother was from Keflavík, and I believe she was pregnant when she moved to Reykjavík. She may have been fleeing the gossip. In any case, the girl is registered as having been born in Reykjavík.'

'A case like that would be much more thoroughly investigated today, wouldn't it?'

'I suppose so,' Konrád replied. 'There are specific procedures. What's on your mind? Why are you interested in this girl?'

'I was twelve years old, at a birthday party,' said Eygló. 'It was two years after that accident. The party was held at a house on Bjarkargata Street, close to the Pond, and I remember feeling quite uncomfortable there. I've seen apparitions of the deceased. It happens without warning, and sometimes I don't even realise what's going on. The girl was there. I'm sure it was her I saw. It was one of the very first times I experienced such a thing, and to this day, I find it hard to explain the unease and sadness I felt when it happened. I didn't know about the accident. I spent the summer of 1961 with my mother and relatives in the village of Kirkjubæjarklaustur and only returned to Reykjavík in the autumn, at the start of the school year.'

'And did the girl appear to you again recently?'

Eygló nodded. 'Yes, not far from Bjarkargata Street. It was in Hljómskálagarður Park. I was taking a shortcut to the Nordic

House and came across a little girl standing next to a bench there in the park, looking at me imploringly. I took my eyes off her for a moment when I stepped aside to let a man approaching me pass by, and when I looked again, she was gone. But I remembered her very well. Remembered having seen her before, and knew that she'd passed from this life a long time ago.'

13

The espresso machine hissed loudly again and the cafe patrons' chatter grew louder. Again, Eygló regretted not having chosen a quieter place.

'And what's the story of the girl's doll?' Konrád said. 'You said you thought she was looking for a doll.'

'That was just the feeling I had. I really don't know where it came from, but I just felt as if she was looking for her doll.'

'The man who found the girl's body and pulled it out of the Pond said he saw the doll first, and when he went to fish it out, that's when he noticed her.'

'The girl must have lost it.'

'Yes, the police believed she dropped it in the water and tried to get it out. Of course, we have no way of being sure it really happened that way, but they considered it a plausible explanation for the way things went.'

'She could also have lost hold of it when she was fighting for her life in the water,' Eygló said.

'Do you think there's a particular reason she appears to you?' asked Konrád. 'Is she connected to you in some way?'

'No, not that I know of. But we may have some connection I don't know about. Do you want to talk to any of those people?'

'What people?'

'The ones named in the police reports.'

'No, not at all,' answered Konrád. 'Why should I do that?'

'For me.'

'No, I . . . it was a terrible accident. I don't know what I could say to them.'

Eygló sat there silently for several moments, watching the passers-by through the window.

'Of course, you don't believe me,' she said.

'Believe what?'

'There's a darkness surrounding this girl, an unclean aura. She's discontent . . . you don't believe a word I say, do you?'

'It's not a question of what I believe, Eygló. I think you believe in what you see and experience and sense, which is fine. Even if I don't understand it. I hope you don't find it disrespectful of me to say this. I know you take these things seriously, and I can feel how personally you take them, but –'

'But you want nothing to do with it?'

'Not under these premises, no. I'm just saying it as it is. Not under these premises.'

'So you wouldn't want to find out where it is?' asked Eygló, after a short silence.

'What?'

'Her doll.'

'Her do—? No. Because I think it's impossible. It's been gone for so long, of course. Do you really think it's still out there somewhere?

'No, not me,' Eygló replied, apparently unwilling to give way to Konrád's doubts. 'But she seems to think so. The girl.'

Konrád said nothing. He didn't know what to say.

'You have no interest in it whatsoever?' said Eygló.

'No.'

The espresso machine hissed out another plume of steam.

'Well, I guess I need to get going,' said Eygló, preparing to stand up, as if she saw no reason to sit there any longer.

Konrád looked at her and wondered if she took after her father. In his youth, Engilbert had dreamt of becoming an actor and performed in a few plays at the theatre by the Pond. Apparently, he'd had an innate gift for dramatisation, which could lift the séances to another level. At his best, according to Konrád's father, his gestures and facial expressions were worthy of the finest actors. The smallest piece of information that he had dug up about a gullible client could become a theatre production in his hands, with the client confirming everything laid before him and Engilbert seeing more clearly than ever into the ethereal realm. Some came back again and again, which made things easier for Konrád's father. He would sometimes even send a friend of his to a séance, with instructions to play the part of a grieving but grateful relative of someone in the beyond, a charade that inevitably left little doubt in the minds of those gathered of the extraordinary connection of the clairvoyant with that world.

People had cash to burn during the war years; in fact, Konrád's father said that he'd never seen so much cash in his life. Eventually, however, he grew careless and suspicions were aroused. Then one day, during a session, the two accomplices were unmasked, destroying Engilbert's reputation. To Konrád's father, it was all the same; he just shrugged and turned to something else.

'There's actually one other thing I wanted to talk to you about,' Konrád said, gripping Eygló's hand. He sensed her growing frustration and knew it was his fault, to a certain degree. Because of how he doubted everything she told him. His remarks had touched a nerve and he knew it wouldn't get any better the longer their conversation went on. He needed to broach a painful subject, and hadn't yet decided how he should go about it. He just knew that he didn't have the patience to wait with it much longer.

'Which is?'

'Our fathers,' said Konrád. 'About what the old woman told you.'

'That they'd been seen together?'

'Do you have any idea what they were up to? I know we've gone through it already, but this is new information.'

'You probably shouldn't read too much into it. Málfríður said they were seen together, but she didn't remember where she heard it or who told her, or why it was mentioned at all. They may simply have crossed paths by chance. Were seen together, without it having the slightest significance.'

'No, of course not,' Konrád admitted. 'It may be better not to read anything into it, but I still have this one question that I really need to ask you. You told me once that Engilbert reacted very badly when he learned of my father's death.'

'Yes, that's right. My mother told me he seemed very stressed and became so afraid of the dark that he couldn't bear being alone after nightfall. I think I told you before that he was a very sensitive man.'

'Could there have been another explanation for his reaction, one that your mother hadn't known?'

Eygló looked inquisitively at Konrád.

'What do you mean?' she asked.

'You also told me that Engilbert hadn't spoken well of my father. Said that he was a despicable character and a lousy rotter who led him to do things he regretted. I assumed that he was talking about their collaboration during the war years.'

'Yes.'

'What if he meant their more recent collaboration?'

'I don't understand what you mean.'

'When my father died, he left behind newspaper articles on mediums. The articles weren't very old. He'd apparently regained an interest in the subject, long after working with Engilbert during the war. Engilbert is the only clairvoyant or medium my father knew or ever worked with, as far as I know. Now we find out that they were seen together not long before my father was stabbed. Taken all together, the articles, Engilbert's reaction, the way he spoke about my father, accusing him of having led him to do things he regretted . . .'

'What are you saying?'

'Do you think that Engilbert was capable of such a thing?'

'I can't believe this,' said Eygló. 'Do you think my dad did it?'

'Please don't take this the wrong way, Eygló – I'm just looking for answers. A lot of time has passed and I don't have much to go on –'

'Do you think my father picked up a knife and stabbed your father? That he killed him?!'

'I'm simply saying that the police never explored that possibility. But now we know that they may have worked together again –'

'What you're saying is that my father was a murderer!'

Eygló was furious, and could no longer stand the sight of Konrád. She jumped up, knocking over her chair. A few of the cafe's patrons turned to look at them.

'I told you about my father because I trusted you!' she hissed, before rushing to the door. 'I trusted you!'

14

Konrád stood up and put the chair back in its place. He went to the counter and paid for their coffees, then left. He cursed himself for being so clumsy, regretted what he said and wondered what he could do to put things right with Eygló. As he was getting into his car, his mobile rang. Konrád hesitated, but finally answered after several rings. It was Danní's grandmother. She asked if she was disturbing him and he politely replied that she wasn't, telling himself at the same time that he needed to be more tactful than he was at the cafe. He was about to ask her if everything was all right, but realised that the question was absurd. Nothing was all right for the elderly couple. The grandmother came straight to the point.

'Do you know if the police have found the boy?'

'The boy?'

'That Lassi.'

'No, not that I've heard. But it won't take them long to get their hands on him. I know that they're doing their best and are asking around.'

'I'm afraid they have bigger fish to fry,' said the woman. 'They say that it wasn't a homicide, that Danní died of an accidental overdose. Do you think they'll leave it at that?'

'I can't say,' Konrád replied delicately, trying by all means to avoid ending up in another argument. He preferred to try to suggest in a few well-chosen words that the woman speak to the police herself.

'We would really like to speak to the young man,' the woman said. 'About Danní. 'As soon as possible.'

'Do you think he had something to do with her smuggling?'

'Yes, that too.'

'You should take it up with the police,' Konrád advised, looking for a way to end the conversation. 'It's just a matter of time before they find him.'

'Would you mind coming to see us?' the woman asked. 'We're counting on you a bit in this matter. Erna always spoke so highly of you.'

'Erna?'

'You can't imagine how proud she was of you.'

Konrád didn't know what to say. The woman had managed to throw him off balance.

'We found a little something we'd like to show you,' she continued. 'It's a sensitive matter, and we thought you might be able to give us some advice.'

'What did you find?'

'May I just show it to you when you come?'

Konrád bit his tongue; the refusal that sprang to mind was downright rude. He hadn't yet composed himself after Eyglo's angry departure. Feeling that his hesitation was becoming awkward, he promised he would stop by the grandmother's house later that day, as soon as he had the chance.

While consulting the old police reports concerning the girl who had drowned, Konrád had noted down certain details, for example the names of her mother, the mother's partner and his son, as well as the name and last address of the man who had discovered the body in the Pond. He hadn't imagined making any particular use of that information, but now he'd unleashed Eygló's fury by making light of what she claimed to have seen at the birthday party and in Hljómskálagarður Park, and worst of all, had accused her father of the most horrendous crime. Going over their conversation in his mind, he saw that he had only himself to blame, due to his insensitivity and bluntness. He should never have approached the matter as he did.

With these things in mind, he drove to a terraced house in east-side Reykjavík and rang the doorbell, hoping the owner would be home. The name next to the bell was Leifur Diðriksson, and ever since setting eyes on it in the police reports, it seemed familiar, although Konrád couldn't think why.

He was about to ring the doorbell again when the door opened, revealing a bearded man with messy grey hair, wearing a checked work shirt and worn-out felt slippers. He eyed Konrád, his gaze cold and tired, as if the spark of life within him had dwindled over the years. His expression changed to one of surprise when Konrád began explaining what had brought him.

'. . . and I'd like to ask you about what happened at the Pond, if you wouldn't mind,' Konrád concluded after introducing himself and verifying that the man in front of him was indeed the same Leifur he was looking for. It had taken him a bit of time to explain the reason for his visit there in the doorway, and he saw that the man was quite startled, as if he hadn't heard mention of the girl in the Pond in years. Konrád also saw that he'd managed to pique the man's curiosity.

'Why do you want to do that?' asked Leifur. 'You're with the police, you said?'

'No, I'm not with the police. I was for a long time, but I'm retired now. I'm actually here on my own account.'

'Why are you asking about this case now? Has something new turned up?'

'No, not at all. I just came upon it in some old police records and saw your name, and it occurred to me to pay you a visit because you're the one who found the girl in the Pond.'

'It was pure coincidence,' said Leifur. 'I was passing over the bridge and . . . I don't really understand this. What . . . ?'

'To be completely honest, a friend of mine is interested in this case,' Konrád confessed, hoping that he wouldn't have to reveal Eygló's name or tell him about the séances and the appearance of the girl, whom she thought was still wandering around in the vicinity of the Pond. But Leifur wasn't about to let him off so easily.

'Why?'

'She's a bit special.'

'In what way?'

'She's a medium,' Konrád said, 'and she thinks she saw the girl in Hljómskálagarður Park.'

'She did?'

'Personally, I don't believe in ghosts,' said Konrád, 'but this story interests me, which is why I thought of contacting you. I hope I'm not disturbing you.'

Leifur Diðriksson looked at him for a moment without saying

anything, before inviting him in and asking him who this medium was. Konrád replied that she hadn't been active on the psychic scene for a number of years and wasn't a household name in those circles now. She was just a friend of his, who had managed to pique his interest in the case in some peculiar way. Leifur had turned one of his bedrooms into a study, and he invited Konrád into it. The room was covered with books wherever one looked. Magazines and newspapers lay strewn about alongside handwritten letters and papers, and a large computer system unit stood humming next to a monitor. Shelves were overflowing with books and Konrád ran his eyes over the spines: books of poetry, biographies, Icelandic novels, works on ethnology and Icelandic folklore.

'Sorry about the mess,' Leifur said, taking a seat behind the desk. 'I'd vowed to clean this all up when I stopped teaching. You can see how that's gone.'

'How long were you a teacher?'

'All my life, really,' Leifur replied, and Konrád thought he detected a twinge of regret in the man's voice. 'High school. Mainly Icelandic and literature. There's been a serious decline in students' aptitude. Kids today can barely read and write. They know hardly any literature, and even less poetry. In the past, we wrote about spring and the arrival of the golden plover, or about the atomic bomb and Vietnam. Things that mattered. Now they just rap about shagging.'

When he said this, Konrád remembered why the man's name was familiar to him. Leifur himself was a poet, although he hadn't published anything for decades. Konrád vaguely recalled a collection of poems by him published in the 1960s, which had drawn attention to that promising young writer. Another had followed in its wake a little later, but then it was as if his pen had dried up. Konrád remembered reading an interview with Leifur many years ago, in which he said he found writing difficult, and that poets needed to be a little more critical of their own works.

Konrád returned to the incident at the Pond. Leifur told him that all he'd done was find the girl's lifeless body and drag it up to the bank. After making certain that it was too late to help her, he'd run to a house on the nearest street and told the people there about his discovery, and then they'd called the police. They had taken care of him, cold and drenched as he was after wading into the Pond. Then, wrapped in a blanket, he and they had stood watch over the body until the police arrived. He had given them a statement, telling them how he'd first seen a doll floating in the water, and then, a few moments later, the girl. The body was driven away in an ambulance, and soon afterwards, only a couple of police officers were left. The small group of people that had gathered there at the bank of the Pond soon trickled away, and before he knew it, the remaining police officers had driven him home and it was all over.

'It all happened very quickly,' said Leifur. 'Suddenly it was finished – just as quickly as it had started, really.'

'It can't have been easy for such a young man as you were to deal with.'

'I . . . I have to admit it took me a while to get over it. Yes, it was an unpleasant experience, as you can imagine. To see that girl's body. So young. It was completely awful of course. Today I would have been offered counselling. For a long time, I was in a state of shock, without really realising it. I had trouble sleeping and was conjuring up all sorts of crazy things in my head. Whether it would have changed anything if I hadn't sat so long at Cafe Mokka.

Whether I would have got there sooner and been able to save her. Naturally, those sorts of thoughts follow in the wake of such incidents. I don't know. I never spoke to anyone about it.'

'Yes, it would probably be dealt with differently today,' said Konrád.

'Without a doubt. I was writing poetry in those years, and it took me a long time and a lot of effort to find inspiration again.'

'There were no signs of struggle or violence on the body?' Konrád said, avoiding the subject of poetry.

'No, not that I saw. It was at the end of summer, as I'm sure you know, and she was lightly dressed, in a dress and knee-high socks.'

'Did you notice anything unusual as you crossed the bridge? Any traffic? Passers-by?'

'No. There was nothing going on there. A car or two on Skothúsvegur Street. I saw someone on Sóleyjargata Street, and remember that another man walked past me without looking right or left. That's all.'

'Did you tell the police about those people?' asked Konrád. He couldn't recall having seen anything about passers-by in the reports.

'Yes, I think so ... or ... I can't remember. I just can't remember.'

'Was he on Skothúsvegur Street? The man who passed you?'

'Yes, he was walking eastward. I didn't get a good look at him. I was lost in thought.'

'How old do you think he was?'

'I have no idea. I barely saw his face. He was wearing a trench coat and hat.'

'A middle-aged man?'

'Yes, could have been. I was so young. For me, any man like that was middle-aged or elderly. Wearing a trench coat and hat.'

'Naturally. And the one on Sóleyjargata Street?'

'I didn't see him clearly either. Just a vague glimpse. I wasn't there to observe passers-by.'

'No, of course not.'

'Then she wanted to see me,' said Leifur.

'Who?'

'The girl's mother. Wasn't her name . . . Nanna? The girl? The police asked me if I would be willing to go and meet her mother. Actually, it was more of an order. I didn't know what to say.'

'And what did you do?'

'I went,' replied Leifur. 'Up to Skólavörðuholt Hill and met the poor woman.'

15

Leifur had given the police his address and phone number in case they needed more information. At the time of the incident, he was still living with his parents. His two brothers had left home, his mother was a housewife, and his father, a wholesaler, made a good living. Their home was near the city centre, and he used to walk to Reykjavík Junior College, as his brothers had done before him. His father came home every day for lunch, which would be ready and waiting for him. After dinner, he would sometimes play bridge with friends whom he invited over. At such times, his mother would go to her sewing club or her 'Fitness for the Mrs' group, after providing the men with refreshments. The couple were very active in the Oddfellows society. They could hardly believe that their youngest son, the naivest of the three boys, a bookworm with his head in the clouds, should have ended up involved in something so shocking as coming across the body of a twelve-year-old girl in the Pond.

The police had called him the next day with their request. The girl's mother wanted to meet him to thank him for his part, and of course to hear from the horse's mouth, as it were, the whole story of how he'd found the body. She lived in the old barracks neighbourhood on Skólavörðuholt Hill, and the police had given Leifur the number of their Nissen hut, while adding that hardly anyone lived up there any more. Most of the former residents had by then moved on to better housing. No, the police wouldn't escort him there; they had other things to do.

Leifur wasn't sure he wanted to go. He'd never set foot in one of those huts and didn't know those people. What he'd experienced the night before continued to haunt him, the eeriness, the muddy water, the girl's cold body. He just wanted to forget all about it, but knew that it would take time.

His mother had urged him to visit the poor woman, and offered to go with him or to order his father to do so, but he replied that he could do it himself. It shouldn't take too long. He set off for the hill and reached the neighbourhood around twenty minutes later. He'd often walked past those former barracks scattered around Reykjavík and seen how the poor people lived, putting varying degrees of attention into maintaining their abodes. Many of the huts there on the hill were in bad shape, and there were outhouses interspersed between them. Wooden shacks had been thrown together next to some of the huts, and there were also special sheds where people came to fetch water for their daily needs, as the neighbourhood had no running water. Smoke wafted from the chimneys, and the smell of rubbish and mildew filled Leifur's nostrils. Two rats scurried past his feet and disappeared beneath a rusty barrel. Those neighbourhoods were disappearing. Leifur knew that the times were changing and, soon, all this squalor would be a thing of the past. All that was left was a dying cluster of buildings that was home to the last slum dwellers in Reykjavík.

Some of the Nissen huts were numbered. The number 9 had been painted in white on one of them so long ago that it was practically invisible. The door was ajar. Leifur knocked but got no response, and he stood awkwardly for several moments on the doorstep before pushing the door open and entering.

A curtain had been hung up at the back of the hut, likely to create a separate sleeping space, it looked to Leifur. From behind it appeared a woman of around thirty, who was startled to see him. She was wearing a dress, a wool jumper and a dirty apron. The woman had been crying. Leifur introduced himself and said that the police had asked him to come here to see her.

'Was it you who found Nanna?' the woman asked, wiping her eyes with the sleeve of her jumper.

He nodded.

'Thank you for coming,' she said. 'I wasn't sure you would agree to it. I wanted to thank you for finding my daughter.'

'Unfortunately, there was little I could do for her,' he said. 'I'm sorry that I didn't pass by there sooner. I might have seen what happened.'

'You didn't see it?'

'No, unfortunately, I . . .'

'The police told me that she hadn't been in the water for very long when you discovered her, which is why it occurred to me that you might have seen something. Seen what happened to her.'

'No, unfortunately. I . . . you have my condolences. I don't know what happened to her. I jumped into the water as soon as I saw her, but unfortunately, it was . . . unfortunately, it was too late. I'm so sorry.'

'I don't know what she was doing there,' said the woman, wiping her nose with the corner of her apron. She was slender and bony, her eyes protruding slightly from her thin face. 'I don't understand why she went to the Pond. I don't understand what she was doing there alone and . . . I spoke to her friends here in the neighbourhood, and they said they'd been playing with her yesterday afternoon up here on the hill, but that she'd disappeared without saying anything. She must have wandered downtown for some reason. To my knowledge, she'd never played down there at the Pond. I have no idea what she was doing there.'

The woman sat down on a rickety old chair. She was alone there in the hut, forlorn and grieving, making him wonder where her husband was and if she had anyone who could come and stay with her for a while. He saw that she attempted to keep the hut welcoming and tidy, with curtains on the windows and rugs on the cold floor. There were dark streaks of mildew on the ceiling, from which hung two lights. 'I have nothing to offer you, my friend.'

'I don't need anything. Thank you.'

'I started wondering where she was when she hadn't come home by dark,' said the woman. 'But that was nothing new. The kids here on the hill play until late in the evening and usually there's no reason to worry about them. Especially in the summer. They're good kids. Still, I found it a bit unusual and went looking for her, but of course didn't find her. Then I heard people talking about something having happened down at the Pond, but no one knew exactly what. It didn't even cross my mind that it was Nanna. I was on the point of contacting the police, but somehow, they'd learned that I was looking for my daughter and came and asked me if she had gone missing. By then, my little Nanna had already been taken to the National Hospital's morgue.'

The woman burst into tears, and Leifur didn't know what to do. He stood there at the door, stepping from one foot to the other, desperately wishing that he was back at home.

'She was so small for her age,' said the woman. 'And was always so skinny, my poor girl. She was born prematurely. Had the appetite of a bird. But I never really had the means to feed her properly until I started working at the National Hospital and could bring a few things home with me to eat.'

Leifur didn't know what to say to this. The doll that he'd seen beneath the bridge was lying on the table in front of the woman, and she picked it up and smoothed its dress and ran her hand over its tangled hair.

'The police told me that the Pond isn't very deep in that place. But it was deep enough for my girl. She was so small for her age, and special. It was odd how much attention she gave this raggedy old doll of hers, at her age. I don't think I could have ever got her to part with it . . .'

Leifur sat there silently for a moment or two, then reached for his pipe in among all the clutter on his desk and began filling it.

'It was one of the most difficult experiences of my life,' he said. 'That awful environment and the poor woman's pain. She simply couldn't understand what had happened to her daughter. It was incomprehensible. She didn't understand how her daughter could have died that way.'

'Did you ever speak to her again?' Konrád asked.

'No, I didn't. I never saw her again afterwards. Maybe she passed away?'

Konrád nodded. 'She left Reykjavík after the tragedy,' he said.

'Moved back to Keflavík, where she was from. It looks as if she lived alone, afterwards. She died years ago.'

'What does that medium, your friend, say?' Leifur asked in a tone that clearly implied he had no regard for that type of person. 'Is the girl pestering her?'

'No,' Konrád said. 'According to her, the girl is unhappy. She has an unclean aura, something like that. As I said, it's all quite alien to me. I don't get it.'

'She's unhappy?' Leifur repeated, making no attempt at hiding his scorn. 'They're all the same, those mediums. All they ever do is state the obvious.'

'I don't know about that,' Konrád said. 'My friend is a very upright woman.'

'Upright? Sure. I don't doubt it for a second.'

'Do you recall anything else from your meeting with the woman, there on the hill?'

'No, I think I told you pretty much everything. Except . . . as far as I recall, the woman hinted that the girl lacked a certain maturity.'

'Oh?'

'Yes, I remember it now.'

'Maybe because she was a bit old to be clinging to her doll like that?'

'Exactly.'

Konrád hesitated, silent and ambivalent. He'd never attended a séance and didn't believe in ghosts, and viewed ghost stories as little more than interesting fantasies belonging to folklore and the old peasant society. Those stories no longer had a place in a world lit by electricity. He had to disregard everything his experience as a policeman had taught him, where only the cold, hard facts of life counted. He had to put aside the doubts of a man who believed only what he could touch with his own fingers. He hardly knew how to word his question. Let alone get it out of his mouth. 'I don't suppose you know what became of the girl's doll?' he finally asked.

16

On the floor of an abandoned shed on the Vatnsleysuströnd coast, so close to the ocean that the surf could be heard, a young man lay motionless. He was on his side, bound tightly with duct tape to an old chair. His head was bloody, his face was cut, three of his fingers were broken and he had various other injuries from being assaulted and tortured. Lighter fluid had been sprayed on his crotch, and the smell of it mingled with that of the sea. His screams had been drowned out by the cries of the seabirds that hovered around the shed and the surge of the powerful waves that crashed over the basalt shore and splashed over the rocks.

He could only open one eye; the other was too swollen. His entire body was in terrible pain. He couldn't see much, lying like that on the floor, bound to the chair and with one eye closed. He didn't know where he was. They had put a bag over his head somewhere in Hafnarfjörður, a plastic bag they said they were going to suffocate him with. They made a game of holding the ends of the bag shut until he couldn't breathe and then letting go. Held it shut. Let it go.

He could hear the birds and the surf, and knew that he must be near the sea. Lying there on the wooden floor, he could see a stack of firewood against one wall and a little table, upon which stood a Thermos. On the floor next to him was an old claw hammer. There was a broken window on one of the shed's walls, and a gas mower next to the stack of firewood, with a gas-powered grass trimmer leaning against it. There were also two shovels and the pickaxe that they had repeatedly threatened to drive through his skull.

They had left him lying there in his blood. One of them had taken a flying leap and kicked him so hard in the chest that he fell backwards, hit his head on the floor and was nearly knocked out cold. Before leaving him there alone, he had heard them argue about what they were going to do next. He'd heard the slamming of doors and a car being started, as well as the sound of the engine fading into the distance, until it died out and not another sound was heard apart from the crying of the birds.

Listening to it, he fell asleep. In spite of everything.

When he woke up, the daylight that had previously shone through the shed's window was gone, and he was lost in complete darkness. His whole body ached and he could barely move a muscle, bound as he was to the chair. Every time he tried to move, a searing pain tore through his chest, and he thought that the kick he'd received must have broken some of his ribs. His broken fingers burned with pain. After a while he began shouting for help, and then simply screaming as much as the pain in his face and chest allowed him, in the hope that someone would hear him. After screaming himself hoarse, he finally gave up, and then started sobbing and cursing his terrible fate.

He couldn't understand why Danní hadn't given him the stuff. Those guys had called him and threatened him, ordered him to come and hand over the goods, or else he and Danní would pay dearly. He knew they weren't empty threats; those guys terrified him, but he tried to man up and said he would fix it, no problem. By the next day, they had lost patience.

They had scoured the town for him and eventually found him sitting over a beer at a sports bar where he regularly went to watch English football matches. They sat down next to him and asked him about Danní, and he told them the same thing as the day before, that she had got the dope past customs, no problem, and was going to turn it over to them. She would deliver the stuff as planned, and in doing so, would settle her and Lassi's debt. That was the deal. They would be free. Just that one trip. Danní had no intention of being their mule for the rest of her life.

'So, what then, is she going to sell it herself?' one of them had said.

'To who?' asked the other. 'Who's she going to sell it to?'

'I'll kill the fucking cunt.'

'She's not going to sell anything to anyone,' he had said. 'She's going to give it to you. Every last bit of it.'

Convinced that he was lying to them, they asked him over and over again about the delivery, but each time, he could only answer the same thing: everything had gone well, and Danní was going to deliver them the stuff. They retorted angrily that they couldn't believe a word of what he and Danní said; that he knew perfectly well where the drugs were and was going to use them himself, but things would get very difficult for them if they didn't deliver the fucking goods at once!

They had squabbled like that in the sports bar until the two guys had had enough and ordered him to follow them. He had refused to go, but knew that it was useless.

'Do you think we're going to let you weasel your way out of this?' one of them said. 'It's worth twenty fucking million krónur on the street!'

'You're coming with us,' said the other one, who appeared even more stoned than his partner. He had gone to the toilet and come back from it hyped up, and sniffing over and over.

'I can't,' he said, 'I need to –'

'Shut up, Lassi! Shut up, you fucking idiot!'

A third man was waiting for them in the car, smoking. They pushed Lassi into the back seat and got in on either side of him.

'What are you doing?' he asked.

'Let's go,' was their only response.

He didn't know how long they had driven before arriving at the shed. Since they had passed through Hafnarfjörður, this place might be somewhere on the Reykjanes peninsula. The plastic bag was over his head when the car stopped. They had dragged him out of the vehicle and dumped him on the ground, then kicked him. A door had opened and they'd plonked him onto a chair. Enraged and higher than kites, they had ordered him to hold out his hand. He did so hesitantly, and they grabbed it and laid it on a cold table. They ordered him to spread his fingers, and he didn't dare disobey. When the hammer hit his middle finger, he heard the bones shatter and screamed in pain.

Now he was lying on the floor, having screamed himself hoarse. He heard the birds and the surge of the sea. Not that that mattered. All that mattered was getting out of there alive.

He must have gone back to sleep. A light that suddenly illuminated the shed woke him with a start, and he heard a car drive up.

Terror overwhelmed him again. He heard voices outside, the door opened, and the same two guys who had come looking for him at the sports bar came in and shut the door behind them. Lassi remained completely still, pretending to be unconscious.

One of the men switched on a torch and laid it on the table, its light half illuminating the shed's interior.

'Is he dead?' he asked.

'The fucking moron!' replied the other.

'How are we going to wake this arsehole up?'

Several moments passed as the men looked around for something they could use. Unable to bear it any longer, Lassi opened his eye just a crack and saw one of them grab the grass trimmer and shake it to check for fuel.

Lassi shut his eye again, knowing that his suffering was far from over as he heard them trying to start the device.

17

After Konrád left, Leifur Diðriksson sat back down in his study, emptied his pipe into an ashtray, reached for his tobacco and began re-stuffing the pipe with his index finger. He moved slowly, almost on autopilot, from years of practice. Then he lit his pipe and took a puff. None of these actions required any concentration. And in any case, his mind was far away. He gazed back over the years until he was standing again on the bridge, looking at the city lights reflected in the Pond and letting himself dream of becoming a poet.

That dream had turned out to be a mirage. He never became the poet he wanted to be; never made a mark on the world of literature. Maybe he had aimed too high. He'd had the drive and passion to compose poems and the willingness to learn from those who had paved the way for modernism in Icelandic poetry, the type of writing that appealed to him most. He had sought the company of those dedicated to composing verses and writing about poetry and fiction, and had kept abreast of trends in the literary world. He had published imperfect poems in the school newspaper and felt a surprising pride seeing his name printed there. He had attended evenings of readings at school and accumulated enough poems for his first collection. It took him two years to work up the courage to submit it to a publisher. He had just started university at the time. The book was rejected. Same story with another publisher. Promising. Talk to us again in a few years. He'd ended up publishing the collection at his own cost, having it printed and bound at a printer's on Nóatún Road. Then he'd distributed it in bookstores and had even considered selling it on the streets like a newsboy, but didn't feel like going to the trouble in the end.

A few years later, his second manuscript was accepted for publication. The biggest daily newspaper published a review highlighting the maturity of his writing and describing him as a promising young poet. At the time, he was teaching at the same junior college whose halls he had walked and where he had written his youthful poems. Many years later, the publication of another of his books aroused some interest. He gave two interviews to the press, one of which was extensive and given a prominent place in the organ of the party, because he'd always been a socialist and the party had wanted to put their poet on show. Then his inspiration dried up. He had a drawer full of poems but saw no point in trying to publish them. Besides, family life and work didn't leave much room for literature. He was never able to fulfil his dreams. His wife and three children had all left him.

He hadn't thought of his visit to Skólavörðuholt Hill for years. The memory of it had grown cold and distant, and the ex-policeman had got only a glimpse of it. But the man's questions had stirred up the old experience inside him: he could see Nanna's mother, alone and distraught, under the patches of mildew on the ceiling. She told him that her daughter loved to draw and had a gift for it. She didn't know where that gift came from. She brought her paper from the hospital, but sometimes the girl had to make do with waxed paper from the dairy. Her daughter would sit there with a pencil and three or four crayons, drawing pictures like the ones the woman had insisted on showing Leifur. She got up, went and opened a ramshackle chest of drawers that was missing one leg and handed him drawings and paintings by her daughter that she kept in it. Every inch of those sheets of paper was used, filled with faces, animals and flowers, as well as two or three images of her doll. Some were in colour, others in black pencil – which had a darker air. Leifur particularly remembered one of them, which was of the National Hospital, gloomy and sinister, surrounded by black night and the windows scribbled over.

She could have become an artist, the woman declared as she sat back down and covered her face with her hands. Leifur wanted to console her, but he didn't know her and didn't know how. So he just stood there awkwardly in the middle of the room until he said he needed to get to class. The young woman hadn't heard him, and he went to her and laid his hand on her shoulder. She snapped out of her reminiscing, held his hand in hers and thanked him for coming to see her. He needn't have gone to the trouble.

'It was no trouble at all,' he replied.

'We'll soon be leaving the hill.'

'Oh?'

'We've been told to move on,' the woman said listlessly. 'They're going to raze what's left of these hovels. I don't know what to do.'

Leifur took another puff from his pipe and his mind wandered back to the bridge that night. He thought about how his discovery of the girl in the Pond had shaped his life and destiny, and even influenced his career as a poet. Then he remembered the notes he'd taken that day. He still had the notepads containing the remarks he'd scribbled down, planning to use them later, which in fact he had done. They were buried beneath a pile of books and papers in a cabinet in his study, but he found them quite quickly and leafed through them while smoking his pipe, until he opened the one he'd had with him on the bridge. He saw how he'd groped for the right expression, having crossed out words like 'veil' and 'dusk' and tried to find others to replace them. He stroked the ink with his fingertips, remembering the young man who had stood there on the bridge. As he meditated on those bygone, optimistic days, he set eyes on his line about the moon:

and the moon limps

Limps? he thought, trying to remember why he'd chosen that strange wording.

It wasn't until he was standing in front of the bathroom mirror the next day, wondering once again whether he should shave off his ashen beard, that the explanation dawned on him.

18

Konrád was once again at the old couple's home. Every time he visited them, it was half-heartedly, and he was determined that this visit would be the last, no matter what. He barely knew them, and was just a spectator to their anguish. Of course he felt sorry for them, and of course what they were going through was unbearable – and that was pretty much the only reason for agreeing to come. He couldn't understand why they were constantly contacting him and not the police, nor could he figure out what role they wanted him to play in their grieving process.

The woman opened the door and told him that her husband wasn't at home; he'd popped over to his brother's but would be back any minute. She thanked him for coming, but he clarified that he didn't have much time, and reiterated that she should contact the police if she had any more information about her granddaughter.

'Yes, I know,' the woman replied. 'But I feel more comfortable talking with you because we know each other, and because Erna was such a good friend of mine. I realise you're retired and all that, but it's a relief to be able to talk to someone familiar with these things. You can't imagine how difficult this has been . . . for me and my husband. Both witnessing Danní go gradually down that path, to the dogs, as it were, and then having it end so awfully. God . . . I know we could have done better. I'm sure of it. We should have looked after her better.'

'Anyone would have regrets in such circumstances,' Konrád said, trying to reassure her. 'But there are so many different factors that play into such behaviour, addictions of that sort. Things that have nothing to do with a person's upbringing. Absolutely nothing.'

'Yes, but still . . .'

'You told me you found something.'

'Her mobile phone,' the woman replied. 'It was in the back pocket of a pair of her jeans lying in a pile of clothes under her bed. She never let us into her room. We weren't allowed to touch a single thing in it. Her phone was dead, but it wasn't locked. We charged it and . . . there are photos on it of Danní, some of which show her naked. We also found numerous messages to her, probably from that boy, asking her where she is and saying that they've got to hand over the stuff. What does he mean? The drugs?'

'Who was supposed to get the stuff?'

'He doesn't say.'

'Contact the police immediately and show them all of it,' Konrád said. 'There's no time to waste. Give them that phone. They'll know what to do with it.'

'But the photos?' the woman said bewilderedly. 'I don't want anyone else seeing them. At first, I thought about throwing the damned phone in the bin. Won't the photos just end up on the internet if I hand it over? Won't they go straight to the media? I couldn't bear it!'

'They may already be on the internet,' Konrád warned, realising immediately that what he'd said would hardly console the woman. 'But I think you can trust the police with it.'

The woman went to the kitchen, opened a drawer, and came back holding the phone. She handed it to Konrád.

'I don't know what the girl was thinking,' she said. 'I don't know what to do with this. I know that the phone is important and could help us find out what Danní was doing before she died, but I don't want anyone seeing those photos.'

Although far from being a specialist in smartphones, Konrád managed to find this one's image gallery – and the first photo he saw was one of Danní, naked. He scrolled through other similar ones. Some were taken by her, in a mirror. Others not, and Konrád wondered if Lassi had taken any of them. Yet they didn't seem to him to have been taken in the boy's basement room.

'Many of these photos were taken here,' said the woman. 'In Danní's room. And here in the living room.'

Konrád checked the call log and messages on Danní's phone, and saw that the same number came up repeatedly: Lassi's. The text messages became more and more desperate as their number grew, talking about 'the stuff' and how 'they' were waiting for it. The words 'dope' or 'drugs' were never used. The final message was a simple exclamation: WHERE ARE YOU!!! Konrád checked the message's date. It had been sent the day before Danní had been found dead.

'Do you think she smuggled in the drugs for her own use?' asked the woman, who had read all the messages. 'Or does the stuff belong to certain others, who are waiting for it to be delivered to them, as she said?'

'It looks to be your second suggestion,' said Konrád.

'It's the lesser of two evils, don't you think? It would mean she wasn't lying to us.'

'Why do you think she didn't hand over what she smuggled in? Do you have any idea?'

'Wasn't she going to do that?'

Konrád looked intently at her.

'Do you know where it is?'

'She told us that they would make her pay dearly if she didn't deliver it. Do you think that they could have done that to her? Injected her with it? That Lassi? He seemed pretty upset about not being able to reach her. Why didn't she answer him?'

'You need to talk to the police,' Konrád repeated. 'I don't have any answers to your questions.'

'No, of course not.'

She thought things over for a few moments.

'Do you think her death wasn't accidental?' she asked hesitantly, as if unsure that she wanted to hear the answer. 'Do you think that someone . . . ?'

'I don't know.'

'To think that we actually have to ask such questions.' The woman sighed, and Konrád could see that this was taking a toll on her. He didn't know how he could comfort her. The first time he'd met her, she'd expressed to him her fears that the press would discover that her granddaughter was involved in drug smuggling and that she, as a public figure, would be raked over the coals. Now all her anxieties were about Danní, and how she could have died under those circumstances.

'It's just as possible that she'd run up some large debts and made that trip to pay them off,' Konrád suggested. 'Maybe then she hesitated and used some of the drugs that she smuggled to shoot up, with this awful result. Unless she stole it all. From Lassi. And doing such a thing is never a good idea. Do you know what she did with the dope?'

The woman was silent.

'Did you find it?'

She nodded.

'At the same time as you found her mobile phone?'

Again, the woman nodded.

'It's still in those awful condoms. My husband and I told the police that we didn't know where the dope was, as we hadn't imagined that she'd kept it. In our house.'

'Can you show me?' Konrád asked, pulling out his phone to call Marta. 'Have you touched anything at all?'

'No . . . well, no, I just found her suitcase and opened it. You see . . . it's . . . Danní rushed out the door and we didn't see her again after that . . . so she left everything here.'

'All of it?'

'There's much more than what's in the condoms. Much, much more.'

19

Marta called Konrád shortly after midnight. She was still at Danní's grandparents' place, where the police had discovered numerous baggies containing a liquid-drug concoction. They were in a sports bag belonging to the deceased, which wasn't particularly well hidden on the top shelf of the wardrobe in the girl's bedroom. Danní hadn't just smuggled drugs by hiding them in her body. The bag also contained packets of cocaine and ecstasy – MDMA – as well as steroid tablets. She must have hidden it all in her suitcase when she returned to Iceland. The drugs' street value ran up into the millions, if not tens of millions, Marta said, exhaling into the handset.

'But you, why are you constantly hanging around here?' she asked. Konrád could hear that she was smoking, and he envisioned her standing outside the couple's house with one of those slender menthol cigarettes of hers. She was tired and cranky. It was past midnight; she'd had enough and wanted to go home.

'I don't know, Marta. They won't leave me alone,' said Konrád. 'It's quite a big haul the girl smuggled in.'

'Yes, it's a lot. The suitcase had been modified to allow her to hide the drugs in it. She was lucky not to get caught. She took a big risk.'

'Her grandparents say she was a mule. She admitted it to them.'

'Those poor people are completely baffled, of course. As for us, we don't know whether the girl was a mule or brought the stuff in for herself or for Lassi. We need to find the boy asap. The Drugs Squad has feelers out, but it's going slowly. He's probably in hiding. We've got eyes on the building where he lived, but he hasn't shown himself there.'

'Do you think the girl's death wasn't accidental?' Konrád asked.

'So far, that's how it looks,' said Marta. 'The smuggling certainly raises questions. Forensics is going to go through her phone to see if they can get anything from it.'

'Lassi's messages to her seem pretty desperate. Isn't it clear that she was supposed to deliver the drugs, but didn't?'

'Possibly.'

'Why didn't she?'

'The guys from the Drugs Squad are here with me, and we've been thinking about using her phone to lure out whoever's drugs these are. If they weren't hers, of course. We'll send a message from her number to this Lassi, suggesting a time and meeting place, and see if we can trap him that way.'

They discussed these matters for a few minutes, until Marta put out her cigarette and said that she was going home. Konrád reminded her that if they were going to set a trap for the alleged ringleaders who were supposed to receive the drugs, they would have to act quickly. Marta asked in return why he didn't just let the police do their job, and then told him to go to bed.

Konrád knew he wouldn't be able to sleep. He sat at the dining table covered with his father's newspaper clippings and thought over his visit to the teacher who was once a poet and discovered the girl's body in the Pond. Konrád's question to him concerning the doll's fate had taken him by surprise, and after a moment's hesitation, he said that he just assumed it was long gone, having probably ended up at the rubbish dump. Konrád had replied that he wasn't so sure about that. An object that played an important role in an event like that had every chance of ending its life somewhere other than on a rubbish heap, and he wondered if he should try to follow the trail of the girl's mother in Keflavík. He hadn't spoken to Eygló since she'd left the cafe in a huff over his questions about her father. Konrád wanted to talk to her and explain what he had meant, but thought it best to wait until most of her anger had passed before contacting her again.

Looking through the clippings again, he tried to remember if his father had spoken about mediums or clairvoyants or worked with them in the months before his death. Nothing new came to mind, but Konrád knew that his memory of those days was hardly reliable – most of it was vague and hazy, lost in the mist. Back then, he had drunk excessively and felt a lot of anger towards his father, and his mother as well, who had abandoned him at a young age in Reykjavík when she moved with his sister Beta to the East Fjords. Konrád had wanted little to do with him and stayed away from home for days at a time, crashing at his friends' places or with girls he met, or even in the stairwells of blocks of flats. The blocks on Háaleiti Street and Stóragerði Road had recently been built and it was no problem sleeping in the stairwell of either of them, and he hadn't minded ending his nights there if he happened to be in those areas in the eastern part of town. You don't when you're nineteen.

One of the last things that Konrád did for his father was go with him to collect a debt from a certain restaurant owner. At the time, Konrád had mainly stopped doing jobs for his father that were meant to be kept under the table. His father would buy large amounts of liquor from the crews of cargo ships or workers on the military base in Keflavík and resell it, either to individuals or restaurants in both Reykjavík and the countryside. Svanbjörn was one of them. The liquor was in litre bottles, gallon containers, or 25-litre plastic casks, its alcohol content sometimes up to 90 per cent. Konrád helped his father water it down and transfer it to ordinary bottles for distribution. This was done mainly in their basement flat, which sometimes resembled a large-scale distillery, from where they delivered the bottles to clients. Konrád's father didn't have a car, but a friend of his, who had a very noisy little English van, helped them with the deliveries and pocketed part of the profits.

Occasionally, Konrád's father would have to go and collect debts, even resorting to violence to get what he was owed. If he was asked for more time to pay up, he would raise the interest rate. This wasn't the first time that Svanbjörn had been slow to pay his debt, and Konrád's father lost patience. He went to see the deadbeat, taking Konrád with him to teach him how not to let arseholes walk all over him, as he worded it.

They met Svanbjörn behind one of the restaurants he owned, an establishment that only opened in the evening. Svanbjörn was the same age as Konrád's father, and didn't look tough at all. He moved slowly and had a pallid complexion, with dark rings under his eyes; in fact he looked ill. He had worked for a long time as a cook on various ships, and appeared to have kept the swaying gait of sailors. He'd been putting out the rubbish and was quite startled by this unexpected visit. He said he had no money at the moment.

Konrád's father didn't believe him, and in no time at all, he was giving him a tongue-lashing.

'Shut your mouth and pay me what I tell you to pay!' he shouted when Svanbjörn complained about the interest that had caused his debt to swell.

'I just don't have the money here with me,' replied the restaurateur. 'You'll have to come back later . . . and then I can pay you.'

'Oh, really! You want to send us an invitation, for when it suits you? Do you take me for a fool? You'll pay me now or I'll burn this piece-of-shit place of yours down!'

'It's . . . it's just that business isn't going very well these days,' Svanbjörn pleaded in a thin, hesitant voice. He seemed to know from experience the monstrous anger that could flare up in Konrád's father, and to fear him. 'I'll have to . . . I'll have it in three or four days, I promise you, and –'

He wasn't able to finish his sentence. Konrád's father punched him square in the face.

'I'm not going to stand here listening to your bullshit!' he yelled.

Svanbjörn stared at his two visitors in turn. Blood dripped from his mouth, and he spat it on the ground.

'I don't have any money on me,' he said. 'There's no need to get crazy about it.'

'No need? You really think so? Do you also think there's no need to pay for what you order? You owe me for three deliveries! Do you think that's fine? Do you really think that's fine?'

When Svanbjörn didn't answer, Konrád's father threw himself at him, punching and kicking him and hurling him to the ground. He looked as if he was going to beat the hell out of the man, until Konrád grabbed him and told him to stop. Konrád had to use all his strength to restrain his father, and then he slammed him against the wall of the building and held him there to try and calm him down. In the meantime, Svanbjörn struggled to his feet.

'You fucking bastard,' he muttered. 'You're a goddamn fucking bastard, you motherfucker.'

'Yeah, pay me, you lowlife scum!' Konráds father shouted, trying to free himself from his son's grip so he could unleash on the man again.

'Can you pay a part of it now?' Konrád asked the restaurateur.

'I don't want a part of it,' his father shouted. 'I want all of my money right now, or I'll kill him! Let go of me, boy! Let go of me! What do you think you're doing? Let go of me, you moron!'

Konrád released his grip on his father, who had calmed down slightly, but still glared hatefully at Svanbjörn.

'I'll be back tomorrow, and you'd better have the money then, you fucker. Is that understood?'

Svanbjörn muttered something that Konrád didn't catch, and they left him there behind his restaurant. The next day, Konrád's father and some friends of his paid Svanbjörn a visit. Konrád didn't know what transpired between them. In the evening, his father returned home, triumphantly waving a wad of notes that he said Svanbjörn had given him, covering nearly all his debt. His father was in high spirits that evening. His knuckles had cuts all over them.

That evening, one of Svanbjörn's restaurants burned to the ground. The news media reported that it was a case of arson, but the perpetrator or perpetrators were unknown.

Konrád's father swore to high heaven that it wasn't him.

Two weeks later, he was fatally stabbed.

Svanbjörn had an alibi. He was in Ólafsvík with his family at the time of the murder.

20

Lassi watched with growing horror as the two thugs tried to start the gas-powered grass trimmer. The engine stalled several times, and he was hoping that they were going to give up when the trimmer suddenly started with an unbearable noise. They seemed not to know how to handle the machine, and he watched them struggle with it. They held it at arm's length and hit the stack of timber with it, causing wood shavings to fly out around the room, some landing on the floor about half a metre from Lassi. Hearing the whirr of the trimmer, he could no longer pretend to be unconscious. He started screaming for help, which only amused his two captors. Having got better control of the machine, they started waving it menacingly at him, at his feet, crotch and face, laughing like crazy as they did. Lassi kept screaming, shutting his eyes and expecting his face to be ripped to shreds any moment, but then the motor began hiccupping and stalled. The thugs looked at each other, tried unsuccessfully to restart the trimmer, and then tossed it aside, to Lassi's indescribable relief – which, however, was short-lived. They righted the chair Lassi was tied to, and everything went black for a second as he found himself upright after having lain there on his side for so long.

'Let me call her,' he begged. 'Let me call Danní back. She got all of it. I'll tell her to come here or . . . wherever you guys want and she'll hand it over to you . . . please, let me call her . . .'

All he knew about his two kidnappers was that one of them had sold them dope a number of times. He assumed that they were in cahoots with whoever it was he and Danní owed money to. The one trip that Danní would take overseas was supposed to be enough to clear their debt. They realised how enormous the risk was when they learned the quantity of drugs that she would have to get through customs. If she was caught, she would probably have to do at least seven years in prison.

Their debt was about one and a half million krónur, and had accumulated in the space of a year or so. The more they used drugs and the greater their need for them grew, the less they could afford them. They had never met the person behind the smuggling oper-ation, only his henchmen, who had threatened them with the worst reprisals if they didn't pay what they owed. It was Danní and Lassi themselves who had suggested the solution. These guys had given Danní cash and instructions, told her how she should dress, gave her information on who she was supposed to meet in Den-mark and how the deal was to go down. They had provided her with a suitcase specially designed for smuggling the drugs into the country and told her to transfer them to an ordinary sports bag once she got back, and then wait for two days. Then she was sup-posed to bring the bag to one of the swimming pools in Reykjavík, put it in a locker in the ladies' changing room and leave the key to the locker in a previously designated place. All the instructions were simple and precise.

Lassi had borrowed a friend's car and driven to the airport in Keflavík. Waiting for Danní near the exit of the arrivals' area in the Leifsstöð terminal, he oscillated between hope and terror. One by one, passengers emerged from the customs area, mainly tourists, who were flocking to the country in numbers higher than ever. Time passed and he was beginning to fear the worst, and even thinking of getting out of there, should the whole plan have gone to hell. The doors opened again and a group of tourists passed through, followed by Danní, towing her suitcase. She was dressed smartly, like a businesswoman, in order to throw the customs officers off the scent. Lassi didn't move. Giving him a signal not to approach her, she walked through the exit doors and out into the car park. It was then that he ventured to join her, and together they got into the car. Danní seemed to be on the verge of a nervous breakdown. She was shaking like a leaf, laughing and crying in turn, and said that she would never do such a thing again. Never in her life had she felt so bad. The customs officers hadn't even looked at her. She'd forced herself to go to the duty-free shop and browse the creams and perfumes, doing all she could to appear like an ordinary traveller and trying her best not to let her nervousness show. Then she'd waited for her suitcase to arrive on the baggage carousel, grabbed it and towed it like a corpse past the customs area, without encountering a single staff member.

Before they reached the turn-off to Grindavík, she asked Lassi to pull over and stop the car, and then she opened her door and puked.

They decided it was best to keep out of contact until she had delivered the goods. For some reason, she hadn't followed through on the plan.

'Where is she, Lassi?' one of the thugs shouted, kicking him in the shin.

'Is she off fucking someone else, Lassi? Is that it?' asked his sidekick.

The two men giggled stupidly, both of them drunk and high. Lassi had smelled the alcohol on them, and they'd gulped down some unrecognisable pills.

'Let me try to call her again,' said Lassi, his entire face aching with every word. 'I'm sure she'll answer.'

'Did you take his phone?' one of the thugs asked the other, who started patting his pockets.

'No. You don't have it?'

They both looked for the phone, finally finding it in one of their shirt pockets. They switched it on.

'Oh, look, she sent him a message,' said the one holding the phone. 'Just now. We didn't hear it over the trimmer.'

The guy read the message and handed the phone to his partner, who did the same.

'What bullshit is this?' he said. 'She's going to hand over the bag to this fucktard?'

'What did she say?' groaned Lassi.

'She wants you to pick up the bag. That wasn't the deal. Why can't she do as she's told? That fucking cunt!'

'Where?' Lassi asked. 'Where am I supposed to pick it up?'

'In a boathouse at Nauthólsvík? What the . . . ?'

Lassi was impassive. He had never heard Danní say anything about Nauthólsvík, and had no idea if she even knew where it was, let alone if there were any boathouses there. He was relieved that she had finally given him a sign of life, despite wondering anxiously what she was doing.

'Has she brought the bag there?' he asked.

'What the hell is she up to, the dirty bitch?' said one of the thugs.

'She's afraid of you,' replied Lassi, seeing his opportunity to get out of this place. 'She wants me to take care of it. I can –'

'Yeah, you're not going fucking anywhere!' yelled the other, driving his elbow as hard as he could into Lassi's face, knocking his front teeth loose and breaking his nose. Blood poured from his nose and mouth as the chair overturned. His head hit the edge of the table, leaving a deep, bloody gash. His neck and the back of his head hit the floor hard, and he stopped moving.

'Damn!' shouted the first thug. 'Is he dead?'

'No . . . do you think so?' asked the other, kicking the inert body.

'You killed him!'

'Me?'

'Yes, you, you fucking idiot!'

21

Konrád heard a knock on his door and looked in surprise at his watch. Wondering if he'd misheard, he didn't move, but then there were several more knocks, more resolute this time. He got up to go open the door, assuming it was his sister coming to see him at this late hour, as she did regularly. He'd been about to call Eygló, despite the lateness of the hour, and his eyes widened when he opened the door and saw her standing there in front of him.

'Were you in bed already?'

'Actually, I was thinking of you,' he replied, inviting her in. Konrád was relieved to see her. He didn't want to be at war with her and had thought up various ways to thaw their icy relationship. He knew now that it hadn't been necessary.

Eygló had never been to his home. She hesitated for a few moments in the hall before following him to the living room. She knew he was a widower, but it appeared that he kept his place in order. Not that she was there to investigate him. The house was dark, apart from a soft, warm light from the light fixture above the dining table. Seeing the newspaper clippings covering the table, she recalled Konrád telling her about his father's collection. Displayed prominently in the living room was a black-and-white wedding photo, showing a young couple on the steps of a church. Háteigur Church, it appeared to her. The photo was on an old smoking table that she assumed was a family heirloom, or had been bought from an antique store. Next to the table was a leather armchair of the sort that she recalled being fashionable in the homes of younger couples around 1970. She caught a whiff of tobacco smoke, mingled with another, more pleasant smell, of candles having been recently snuffed out. A pop song that she recognised from days gone by was playing.

Konrád offered her a glass of red wine called the Dead Arm. She glanced at his left arm, which was withered, but not so much that he couldn't use it when needed. It had less strength and mobility than the right, and Eygló had noticed when they met that he often kept his left hand in his pocket. He doubtless did that to hide his infirmity from those he was unfamiliar with, she thought.

'That's your wife, Erna, isn't it?' she asked, pointing at the wedding photo.

'Yes, that's Erna. The day we got married, as you can see.'

They sat down at the dining table and sipped their wine. It didn't take long for Eygló to get to the heart of the matter. She had calmed down soon after rushing out of the cafe, and with the fog of anger cleared away, she realised that Konrád had tried his best to spare her, having only been looking for answers to events that had haunted him for decades and just happened to be connected to her.

'Do you really believe that Engilbert killed your father?' Eygló asked, looking over the clippings.

'I don't know. I could have worded it better though,' said Konrád. 'I didn't mean to make you angry.'

'You suggested very clearly that my father was a murderer. I don't know how else it could have been worded. It's hard to swallow such an accusation silently.'

'Of course. I understand perfectly.'

'But what do I know? My mum said that my dad really loathed yours. According to her, it had something to do with their collaboration during the war. But maybe it was because of something that happened later.'

'Apparently, Engilbert enjoyed the attention and the money when he and my father were at their best, even if later he blamed him for how things went, and for having destroyed his reputation. Anyway, that's what my father told me. I'm not saying this to disparage Engilbert or to try to justify anything my father did. Don't take it like that. I'm just trying to look at it objectively. I personally had a very difficult relationship with my father at the time. Obviously, it's much more difficult to address these questions when we're so closely tied to them.'

Eygló nodded.

'I went to see Málfríður again,' she said, 'and had quite a long chat with her, trying to get her to remember who told her that about our fathers, that they'd been seen together at that time. She'd completely forgotten. Still, she was certain that that's what she was told, and given what they'd been up to during the war, she immediately thought it must have been some sort of scam. She didn't particularly remember your father, having known of him only through their wartime swindle, but when I started talking about the murder at the slaughterhouse, she said she remembered it perfectly. She was very surprised that I would ask her about my father in that context. But I think I managed to talk my way out of it rea-sonably well. That said, little escapes her notice.'

Eygló took a sip of wine.

'For example, she remembers the girl who fell into the Pond.'

'Oh?' said Konrád, suspecting that the reason for Eygló's return visit to Málfríður hadn't just been to ask her about their fathers, but about the girl as well. 'You were able to ask her about that?'

'Málfríður told me she'd met the girl's mother, who had turned to the Psychical Research Society for advice. She had asked if it could recommend a clairvoyant, as she knew nothing about such things.'

'In connection with her daughter?'

'Yes. It was a few months after the accident. Málfríður said that she'd been extremely downcast, the poor woman, and that she'd pointed her to a man named Ferdinand, a famous medium who lived in the Skerjafjörður neighbourhood of Reykjavík. If her hus-band had been in Iceland at the time, she would have entrusted the woman to him – but unfortunately, he was abroad. She never saw the woman again, but one day she asked Ferdinand about her, whether she'd come to see him, but he couldn't recall if she had.'

'So she'd been looking for answers?' Konrád asked.

'Málfríður told me that the woman hadn't known what she was looking for. She'd apparently asked a lot of questions, wanting to know if such things could be believed and what sort of people were likely to appear at the séances, and was highly suspicious of it all. Málfríður slightly regretted having sent her to Ferdinand, because he charged quite a lot for consultations and was very insistent about payments. Maybe it scared the woman away from him. She didn't seem to have much money.'

'Maybe she went to see someone else?'

'Málfríður didn't know. She only met the woman that one time.'

'And did you tell her about your experience involving the girl?'

'Yes, the evening I held the séance. She asked me why I was interested in her and I told her what I saw when I was twelve, and also about the apparition in Hljómskálagarður Park. It was as if twenty years dropped off her. Málfríður likes nothing more than hearing such stories. Over the years, her belief in the afterlife has grown ever stronger, and she says she can't wait to cross over and have everything she knows to be true proven.'

Konrád smiled and told Eygló about his visit to the teacher who'd been at the Pond when he discovered the girl's body, and about the man's visit to the child's mother and the deplorable conditions in the Nissen-hut neighbourhood in which she lived. Konrád refrained, however, from mentioning his question about the doll and its current whereabouts.

'Did he meet the girl's stepfather or his son?' asked Eygló.

'He didn't mention having done so.'

'Do you know anything about them?'

'No, nothing more than what I've already told you. The man lived with the girl's mother for a few years, along with his son. He and the woman weren't married, which was unusual for the time. I thought about paying the son a visit, but I'm not sure how far I should take this. It's undoubtedly painful for these people to have to dig up the past.'

'Yes, I suppose it is,' agreed Eygló. 'Do you really believe it's possible?' she resumed after a short silence. 'That Engilbert attacked your father?'

'I don't know,' said Konrád. 'The fact that we're sitting here asking these sorts of questions seems to me crazy enough in itself.'

Eygló looked around the room.

'Did you snuff out some candles just before I arrived?' she asked distractedly. 'Sorry – it's none of my business.'

'No,' said Konrád. 'There are no candles in this house. Not since Erna died.'

Eygló looked at him enquiringly.

'She didn't start a day without lighting a candle,' Konrád explained.

Eygló smiled, but said nothing as she continued to look at the clippings. Suddenly, a photograph caught her attention.

'That's the old lady!' she said, pointing at the photograph accompanying a magazine article on the Icelandic Psychical Research Society. 'That's her, there, next to her husband.'

'Who?'

'Málfríður,' Eygló said, handing him the clipping. Konrád scrutinised the photo. Its caption announced the new board of directors for the Psychical Research Society in 1959, and in the photo, four men and two women stared solemnly at the camera. The woman whom Eygló pointed to was plump, wearing a white blouse beneath a jacket, with her dark hair tied in a bun. Her expression was resolute. The caption didn't give any names, but Eygló said that she remembered two of the men from the time when she was active in the society, and one of them was Málfríður's husband.

'Málfríður mentioned how depressed and distraught the girl's mother was,' Eygló went on, continuing to stare at the photo. 'Her distress is of course completely understandable and unsurprising, but there was more to it than that. Málfríður thought the woman had some doubts simmering inside her. She spoke to the woman for a long time, and she got the impression that she was looking for answers to her daughter's fate, as if what happened hadn't been an accident but something else. As if someone was responsible for the girl drowning in the Pond.'

'The old woman said that?'

Eygló nodded.

'How did she get such an idea? Did she have reason to suspect someone? I mean, the girl's mother.'

'She didn't say it directly. It was the feeling Málfríður had after speaking with her. That she doubted that it was an accident.'

'That's probably not an unusual reaction,' Konrád said. 'She'd naturally consider all possibilities.'

Konrád asked again what Málfríður had said, specifically, but Eygló had nothing to add. Again, she caught a strong smell of extinguished candles, and felt that it enveloped them and everything else in the living room, but knew that it was useless to mention it to Konrád.

22

The Drugs Squad implemented the operation quickly, and without much preparation. Three surveillance teams were positioned in the area around Nauthólsvík. The sports bag was placed in a boathouse near the beach, where people from Reykjavík came to bathe. The bag was clearly visible from the path that ran along the small bay, so that anyone on the lookout for it couldn't miss it. One of the vehicles was parked next to the Nauthól restaurant. In it, two men equipped with binoculars and radios kept an eye on the car park overlooking the path. The second vehicle was parked in the car park of the University of Reykjavík, and the officers in it kept an eye on the boathouse. The third car was stationed at Loftleiðir Hotel, to observe traffic on Nauthólsvegur Road, which provided access to the swimming area.

A member of the Drugs Squad had suggested Nauthólsvík because the nearly non-existent traffic to and from it at that time of day could easily be monitored. The police watched a car drive down the road and turn into the university car park, circle round there and then head back towards the city centre. Another car drove all the way down to the beach and pull up on one side of the Nauthólsvík car park, putting the officers on alert. No one stepped out of the vehicle, and soon the car's windows began to fog up. A quarter of an hour later, the car backed out of its parking spot and drove slowly away.

The drugs that Danní had smuggled into Iceland were no longer in the sports bag. They had been replaced with synthetic lures, and listening and tracking devices had been installed in the bag. The objective was to apprehend those in charge of the smuggling operation, rather than the underlings who carried out their dirty work. Lately, the police had received a lot of criticism for arresting only the mules and dealers at the bottom of the ladder, rather than nabbing those who funded the deals, were the main perpetrators in the smuggling operations, and hoarded the profit when things went as planned.

The text message sent to Lassi's phone remained unanswered. It was unclear whether it had been read, and whether the operation would work. Some had suggested waiting and preparing it better, but others thought it better to strike while the iron was hot.

The radio crackled. The car parked at Loftleiðir Hotel reported that a black Land Rover was driving down Nauthólsvegur Road towards the beach. Seeing the approaching beam of the headlights, the officers on guard at the University of Reykjavík did their best to be discreet. Soon, the black SUV passed in front of them and they informed their colleagues that they had seen two men inside it.

The SUV turned right towards the beach and parked in the car park overlooking the path. The driver turned off the vehicle's head-lights, but left the engine running. Several minutes passed without anything happening, but then the passenger door opened, a man got out and stood there looking around for some time. Without shutting the car door behind him, he suddenly dashed to the boat-house, grabbed the bag and headed back to the SUV. The headlights came on as soon as he got in and slammed the door. The vehicle backed out of the car park and drove quickly away, reaching Nau-thólsvegur Road in a matter of moments. The officers posted at the university followed the vehicle without turning on their headlights. They had already transmitted the licence plate to headquarters. Their colleagues at Loftleiðir Hotel announced on the radio that the black SUV had passed them and was heading eastward along Air-port Road, rapidly increasing speed. The vehicle's registered owner was a certain Randver Ísaksson.

'That fucking scumbag,' an officer remarked on the radio.

The decision was made to call in the Viking Squad – the Fire-arms Support Unit.

In the meantime, two of the surveillance vehicles were following the SUV at a reasonable distance, trying not to look conspicuous, which was difficult given the near-total absence of traffic. The SUV stopped at the light on Bústaðavegur Road, waited for it to turn green, then turned right and accelerated sharply. The light at the intersection with Litlahlíð Street was red, but the driver braked late and drifted into the intersection, where he stopped for a few seconds before continuing on Bústaðavegur, ignoring the light. He crossed the bridge spanning Kringlumýrarbraut Road, in the direc-tion of the National Hospital in Fossvogur. The SUV swerved from lane to lane, the driver alternately braking and accelerating. The police suspected him of being drunk or high. They discussed stop-ping him in order to keep him from harming himself, his passenger, or any other drivers or pedestrians, but decided to wait. They still kept a distance, without losing sight of the SUV's tail lights.

The dispatcher reported over the radio that Randver Ísaksson was on probation and should be approached with caution, as he had previously been arrested for carrying an illegal weapon and threatening the police with a firearm. As it turned out, the weapon had been only a toy gun.

The SUV came to the end of Bústaðavegur Road and turned south, onto the Reykjanesbraut Highway, where it picked up speed. The pursuing officers were concerned that its occupants had noticed they were being followed and were going to try to lose them. The SUV continued to accelerate until it ran into trouble on the off-ramp up to Breiðholt. It was as if the driver suddenly lost control of the vehicle; it lurched onto the central reservation and then back onto the road as the driver tried to right its course, crossed the lane and hit a traffic light, which broke in two. The SUV came to a stop, perched precariously on the base of the light pole.

The first police officers to arrive had called an ambulance before parking their vehicle close to the SUV. As they got out of the car, the SUV's driver's door opened and a man staggered out. As soon as he saw the officers, he ran full speed up Breiðholtsbraut Road, eastward, and then turned left towards the church, sports bag in hand. The officers ran after him, just as the second surveillance vehicle drove up and parked behind the SUV. The passenger had been thrown out of the car by the force of the impact and lay there motionless on the asphalt. Blood welled from his head and the officers didn't want to touch him, preferring to wait for an ambulance. They found no one else in the vehicle, but noticed that the boot was full of all sorts of stuff, including a pile of clothes.

'What is this?' one of the officers asked, pressing his face against the back window to get a better look.

The SUV's driver had reached the church. He was still carrying the bag. The officers continued to chase him, without knowing if he was dangerous. They were in radio contact with the Viking Squad, which was driving at breakneck speed on Reykjanesbraut Highway in their direction. If things panned out, the fugitive would run smack into them. They didn't think that he was armed.

The two officers back at the SUV, unable to see clearly into the boot, began fiddling with opening the rear hatch. It was unlocked, but had become jammed in the collision with the traffic light, besides the fact that the vehicle was more or less suspended in the air, stuck on what was left of the pole. They grabbed the hatch's handle and jiggled it a few times until the boot opened. From it fell an unconscious man, so disfigured by the accident that the two officers grimaced before giving him first aid.

'Is he dead?' asked one of the officers.

'Looks like it to me,' replied his colleague, looking towards two ambulances that raced, sirens wailing and lights flashing, up the deserted Reykjanesbraut Highway.

The SUV's driver ran alongside the Mjódd shopping centre, the police officers at his heels. However, they kept their distance and did nothing to try to obstruct him. Ahead, they saw the Viking Squad's two vehicles pull up at the shopping centre and members of the squad jump out, dressed like terrorists, with black bala-clavas over their faces. They immediately set off after the fugitive, who, becoming desperate when the reinforcements arrived, threw down the sports bag to lighten his load. It was useless. Barely a minute later, a Viking Squad member tackled him to the ground.

Out of breath, the SUV's driver tried in vain to resist being handcuffed.

23

Konráð didn't know much about the restaurant owner Svanbjörn beyond the fact that he had had a run-in with his father, and that the police had questioned him in connection with the latter's murder. The records stated that he was with his wife and two sons in Ólafsvík at the time of the crime. Witnesses had seen him in that town that day; he'd gone to the bakery in the morning and to the supermarket around noon. Then he'd spent the evening with his family at his sister-in-law's, who was then in Reykjavík but had lent them her house. In those years, it could take five hours to drive from Ólafsvík to Reykjavík. The records noted that Svanbjörn had a car, and had driven it to Ólafsvík on his holiday.

CID had called Svanbjörn in twice for questioning. A preliminary investigation revealed that he and Konráð's father had been engaged in shady business deals, prompting a closer investigation into the two men's association. During the first round of questioning, Svanbjörn spoke of their strained business relationship, and of how the father and son had assaulted him. He didn't paint a good picture of Konrád, even though Konrád had done nothing other than stop his father from pummelling him.

By revealing their transactions, Svanbjörn was in fact acknowledging that he had purchased contraband alcohol for his restaurants, but to try to make himself look better, he asserted that it had only been in very small quantities, which Konrád knew was a lie, and had only done business with Konrád's father, which was another lie.

In the following interrogation, Svanbjörn was asked a number of questions about the fire at his restaurant, as if the police had got new information about it that gave them cause to call him in a second time.

Questioner: 'Were you there when the fire broke out?'

Svanbjörn: 'No, I wasn't. There was no one there. Luckily. Otherwise, things might have been much worse.'

Questioner: 'I have here the report on the investigation into the fire, which states that in all likelihood, it was an act of arson. The evidence points to the fire having started in two places at once. Do you know of anyone who might have set fire to your restaurant?'

Svanbjörn: 'I answered these questions the other day. No one comes to mind.'

Questioner: 'Are you sure?'

Svanbjörn: 'Yes.'

Questioner: 'During your first interrogation, you stated that you had a dispute with the deceased over unpaid debts, and that he assaulted you. And that his son was with him. Do you have any reason to believe that they had something to do with the fire?'

Svanbjörn: 'No.'

Questioner: 'Why not?'

Svanbjörn: 'Because they wouldn't have got anything out of it. I'd already paid my debt to the man. Our dispute was over. I have no idea who set fire to the place.'

Questioner: 'According to our information, you two came to blows again the evening of the fire.'

Svanbjörn: 'I don't recall that.'

Questioner: 'Did you see each other that evening?'

Svanbjörn: 'Yes, we did.'

Questioner: 'What happened?'

Svanbjörn: 'I paid off my debt to him. And in doing so, ended our business relationship.'

Questioner: 'And nothing else happened?'

Svanbjörn: 'No.'

Questioner: 'What if I told you that we have proof that you went to see a doctor that evening at the Reykjavík Health Clinic?'

Svanbjörn: 'That was for something entirely unconnected. I fell on my face outside my house. My wife can attest to that.'

Questioner: 'According to the doctor on duty, your injuries appeared to be more typical of an assault.'

Svanbjörn: 'I can't comment on his diagnosis. All I can tell you is what happened to me.'

Questioner: 'Isn't it true that your restaurant went up in flames while you were being treated?'

Svanbjörn: 'Yes, that's true.'

Questioner: 'But you deny any connection between that event and your injuries?'

Svanbjörn: 'Absolutely.'

Hearing a noise in the hallway, Konráд looked up from the records. One thing he had learned from them about Svanbjörn is that the man had trouble telling the truth, and did all he could to make it look as if he'd had no reason to harm his father. Konrád had told the police everything he knew about Svanbjörn and his father's business dealings, and also about the evening when Svanbjörn's restaurant burned down and his father returned home in a triumphant mood, with bloody knuckles.

The door opened, revealing Marta.

'I heard you were here,' she said.

'Yes, I . . .'

'What are you up to, constantly poking your nose into our files?' she asked. 'Did Olga let you in?'

'I was just finishing up,' Konrád said, closing the folder containing Svanbjörn's testimony. 'I just wanted to refresh my memory on a few details. Looks like you've got your hands full.'

That same morning, he had read on the internet that an operation conducted by the Viking Squad had led to the arrest of two men. A news site had revealed their identity and details about Randver Ísaksson, who had a long criminal record.

'Yes, never a moment's rest,' said Marta.

'Have you been able to question those fellows?'

'Not yet. We were hoping that this operation would net us a few others. The ringleaders, not just the small fry,' Marta replied, disappointed. 'Anyway, they have connections to Danní and her boyfriend.'

'Oh?'

'We'd like to know who sent her after the drugs.'

'Isn't it this Randver?'

'He could have a part in it,' said Marta.

'And the one who was with him?'

'Hardly. He's a kid who showed up on our radar recently, just a rookie. What I wanted to tell you, which wasn't in the papers, is that we've found Lassi. They had him in the boot of the SUV, and had really worked him over.'

'And what does Lassi have to say?'

'So far, nothing at all. He's in hospital, unconscious. The doctors don't know if he'll make it. The collision with a traffic light tonight didn't help. The stupid fools we have to deal with, every single day.'

'So he wasn't able to tell you anything about Danní? Or who the drugs were for?'

'We need to ask him about all this. He suddenly stopped texting the girl. It was the day before you found her. We just received the autopsy report, which states that she'd been dead for over twenty-four hours when you found her. That means she died around the time that Lassi stopped contacting her.'

'Do you think Lassi or those two guys knew what happened to her?'

'I doubt that they would have reacted to the message we sent from her phone if they'd known she was dead,' Marta replied. 'But I've run into so many bloody idiots in this profession.'

'You're telling me.'

'The coroner found no evidence of violence on the girl's body. According to him, she died of an overdose. But did she administer the drugs herself? That's the question. Or was someone else with her in the room? The two guys in the SUV? Lassi? Whoever it was that sent her after the drugs?'

'You mean that her death is linked to the smuggling? Because she didn't follow instructions and deliver the goods?'

'Who knows?' Marta sighed, taking a pack of menthol cigarettes from her pocket and hurrying out into the open air for a smoke.

24

Konrád hesitated for a moment before opening another folder. It had always been a mystery to him what his father was doing outside the slaughterhouse on Skúlagata Street that night, and he had given it a lot of thought when he was younger. The police had looked into that precise point, without ever finding an explanation. Konrád had come to assume that it was pure chance that his father had been stabbed there. In those days, that slaughterhouse had been in full swing. Lamb and bacon were smoked there in large ovens; frankfurters, sausages, singed sheep's heads and lunch meat were produced there, not to mention black pudding and offal, and carcasses were cut up and stored in spacious freezers.

Flipping through the police reports before being interrupted by Marta, Konrád had discovered that several of the slaughterhouse's employees had been questioned, but they all claimed not to have known the victim. The police believed that Konrád's father, given his past as a con artist and petty criminal, had possibly planned to rob the company and may have been scouting the location. The offices were on the second floor of one of the slaughterhouse buildings facing Skúlagata Street. That was where the money was kept, in a sturdy safe that was impossible to move and extremely problematic to open. The police speculated that Konráð's father had had an accomplice within the company, but that they'd had a disagreement, leading to a knife being drawn and ending in dramatic fashion. Konráð knew from his long experience as a policeman that assaults with knives were most often committed in fits of madness, and were rarely premeditated. That was even their main characteristic.

Konráð couldn't recall ever hearing his father talk about the South Iceland Abattoir in particular, either to him or anyone else. Much less that he'd dreamt of filling their home with products from its slaughterhouse. On the other hand, he always had more than enough fish, thanks to his connections with sailors down at the harbour, with whom he regularly did business. Konráð had always imagined that his father had only been passing by the slaughterhouse when he was stabbed. That he'd either just left his flat or was returning to it. It wasn't known if his attacker had been lying in wait for him or if he had encountered someone by chance, with it ending in tragedy. It was thought that the murder was committed shortly after midnight, a time of day when the streets are practically deserted, making it more likely than not that there were no witnesses.

The coroner had tried to determine what type of weapon was used in the attack, as well as how it was carried out. It was thought that the weapon was a medium-sized sheath knife, extremely sharp, with a wide, ten-centimetre-long blade. Konráð's father seemed to have been taken by surprise. The palm of his right hand had a shallow gash that was thought to have been made when he grabbed the knife as it struck a second time. The first blow must have caught him completely off guard, as there were no other signs of a struggle. An extensive search for the weapon had been made in the area around the slaughterhouse and on Skúlagata Street, as well as along the shoreline as far east as Kirkjusandur. The back gardens and rubbish bins of the Shadow District were searched, and then all the way down to the city centre, to no avail.

Over the years, Konrád's father had had a few run-ins with crew members of cargo ships from whom he bought contraband liquor or tobacco, but he tried hard to keep those people happy so as not to risk depriving himself of part of his income. The police knew about those dealings of his, having exposed them now and then over the man's long career. The sailors thought to have been involved in this contraband business at one point or another had been questioned about their whereabouts on the night of the murder. Konrád also recalled that his father had had good friends who worked on fishing boats, men who had come to visit and drank, played cards, and told stories of their adventures at sea. None of them were ever mentioned in the reports in connection with his father's death.

This wasn't the first time that Konrád had gone through the police reports and read everything they contained about his father and the murder investigation. At one time, the police suspected that the crime may have been committed by a close friend or family member. Statistical studies, not least those done abroad, showed that that was most often the case – that the victim knew his killer and that murders were seldom committed out of the blue, though it did of course occur sometimes.

The movements of Konrád's mother, who lived out east in Seyð-isfjörður, were scrutinised. At the time of the murder, she was in

Reykjavík, staying with her sister and brother-in-law, who had both confirmed that she was with them the night that it happened. The police had called her in for questioning. She was grilled about Konráð's relationship with his father, and under that barrage of questions, she admitted that it had been no bed of roses for her son to be raised by that man, but that Konráð wasn't the type who would ever resort to violence against anyone. She had tried hard to convince the police that her son was sweet-natured. Reading the transcript after all these years, Konráð could sense just how frightened she had been for him. Because of his closeness to his father. Because she had been forced to leave him with such a man. Reading these things reawakened painful memories in Konráð.

Questioner: 'How would you characterise your relationship with your ex-husband?'

Sigurlaug: 'We had no relationship.'

Questioner: 'When you lived together?'

Sigurlaug: 'It was bad. I left him.'

Questioner: 'Why?'

Sigurlaug: 'For various reasons. They don't have anything to do with this case.'

Questioner: 'Is it true that your ex-husband hit you?'

Sigurlaug: 'Who told you that?'

Questioner: 'Did it happen?'

Sigurlaug: 'I don't see what that has to do with this case.'

Questioner: 'Was it the reason you left him?'

Sigurlaug: 'I don't know why you're asking about this now. That's all in the past.'

Questioner: 'We have statements about it from more than one of your former neighbours. They mention seeing bruises on you, but that you tried to make light of them. Commotions in your flat. We also have it on record that the police intervened at your home following reports of drunkenness and violence. You yourself called for help because he was hitting you. Twice in 1955. The year you left him.'

Sigurlaug: 'He wasn't a good man.'

Questioner: 'Is that why you left him? And moved to Seyðisfjörður?'

Sigurlaug: 'Yes, that was one of the reasons.'

Questioner: 'How did your son react to the violence? Was he angry at his father?'

Konrád envisioned his mother squirming under the flurry of questions about domestic violence. She'd never spoken to anyone about it, not even her daughter, to whom she was closest. Having already read this transcript, Konrád knew that it would only worsen until it became nearly unbearable for his mother.

Sigurlaug: 'Konrád was so young. Why are you asking this?'

Questioner: 'Did he ever hit the boy?'

Sigurlaug: 'No.'

Konrád could hear the silence that punctuated his mother's reply.

Sigurlaug: 'It happened. But he was good to him, too.'

Questioner: 'Can you describe their relationship?'

Sigurlaug: 'Konrád would never have been able to hurt him, if that's what you're fishing for. I don't understand why you're asking these questions. We did nothing to him. Neither I nor my children. And you should know what sort of people he dealt with when he was smuggling and stealing and ... he had enemies everywhere. I thought you knew that.'

Questioner: 'Can you tell us about his relationship with Konrád in the weeks and days leading up to the murder?'

Sigurlaug: 'No, I hadn't been in contact with Konrád for some time.'

Questioner: 'But you came to Reykjavík to see him, didn't you?'

Sigurlaug: 'Yes, and to run some errands, meet my sister, and do various other things.'

Questioner: 'Where did you meet your son?'

Sigurlaug: 'At a cafe downtown.'

Questioner: 'What did you talk about?'

Sigurlaug: 'All sorts of things. I hadn't seen him for a while, as I just told you. I wanted to know how things were going for him.'

Questioner: 'Was he agitated? Relaxed? Did he say anything about his father?'

Sigurlaug: 'Konrád never loses his cool. He said nothing about his father.'

Questioner: 'You didn't talk about him?'

Sigurlaug: 'No.'

Konrád stared at his mother's lie. Of course they had talked about his father.

Questioner: 'You also have a daughter, Elísabet. How was her relationship with her father?'

Sigurlaug: 'Non-existent. She lives with me.'

Questioner: 'But when you all lived together?'

Again, Konrád could hear the long silences that punctuated the interrogation.

Sigurlaug: 'She was always closer to me.'

Questioner: 'Did she experience his violence first-hand?'

Sigurlaug: 'I don't see what that has to do with this case.'

Questioner: 'Just answer my question, please.'

Sigurlaug: 'It happened. Before I put a stop to it.'

Questioner: 'Put a stop to what?'

Sigurlaug: 'He had a monster in him, which I didn't know until too late.'

Questioner: 'Can you be more specific?'

Sigurlaug: 'I took her from him as soon as I found out.'

Questioner: 'Found out what?'

Sigurlaug: 'That he was going after her.'

Questioner: 'Do you mean sexually?'

Konrád closed the folder. He knew the next line.

Sigurlaug: 'Yes.'

25

While Lassi was kept sedated and on a ventilator in the intensive care unit of the National Hospital in Fossvogur, the police waited for the alcohol- and drug-induced haze to clear from the minds of Randver and his partner. They were being held in detention cells at police headquarters on Hverfisgata Street, with a doctor monitoring their gradual withdrawal from their days or even weeks of non-stop use. They were given medication to ease their cravings and hasten their recovery.

Randver was the worse off of the two. He had suffered a head injury and caused a commotion when he was first taken to the hospital for treatment, and then transferred to the holding cell. In the ICU, he put up a huge fight, knocking over tables and hospital beds before finally being subdued. His partner was much calmer. He also had a gash on his head, and a broken arm. Sitting on a bed in the ICU, he rocked back and forth and muttered things to himself, seemingly completely out of it.

Two days later, he'd more or less come to his senses. With his head wrapped in bandages and his arm in a splint, he was brought to the interrogation room. Placed in preventive custody, he would soon be transferred to Litla-Hraun prison, where defendants awaiting trial were held. The Drugs Squad was in charge of the interrogation. Marta monitored it from a side room, through the two-way mirror. The detainee's lawyer was next to him, but was rather discreet.

The prisoner claimed to have been unaware of the presence of Lassi in the boot of the vehicle. Randver had gone to the prisoner's place in his SUV and asked him to go for a ride with him. Before he knew it, they were at Nauthólsvík, picking up a bag of sportswear for a friend of Randver's. The prisoner didn't know this friend, but he must have lived in Breiðholt since that was where Randver headed next. But then they had their accident, and suddenly the police showed up and started barking orders and arrested them. That was when he first saw Lassi, when he rolled out of the SUV. He didn't think that Randver had done anything to Lassi – and as for him, he knew that wasn't the case. Somebody else must have put him in the boot, or else he got in there on his own.

The prisoner said he knew fuck all about that Lárus Hinriksson. If Lassi claimed otherwise, he was lying. Nor did he know anything about a girl by the name of Danní, and was flabbergasted to learn that the sports bag contained drugs not clothes. So ended his first interrogation.

The two defendants obviously hadn't had time to corroborate their stories, because Randver had a somewhat different one to tell, sitting there facing the investigators with a bandage around his head, a cracked lip, a bloodshot eye and a bruised face. His friend had suggested they go to the cinema, they'd seen a movie the name of which he'd forgotten, and then driven down to Nauthólsvík, where they'd found the sports bag. Taking it with them, they'd driven around until winding up in that terrible accident. Yes, he'd had a little to drink, and since a blood test showed that he'd taken drugs, he just may well have snorted a line or two, unless someone at the hospital had tampered with the blood sample, which certainly couldn't be ruled out. Like his friend, he couldn't explain Lassi's presence in the boot; he assumed that he'd crawled in there himself. When the investigators pointed out that the young man's injuries hadn't all been caused by the accident, but that Lassi had been beaten and tortured, Randver swore to high heaven that he'd had nothing to do with it. When asked how he'd read the text message sent to Lassi's mobile phone, he answered that he knew nothing about any message and repeated that he and his friend had found the sports bag purely by chance.

He didn't know anything about Danní. He was gobsmacked when told that the sports bag had been used to stash the drugs that were found at the girl's grandparents' home. He denied having been behind the smuggling, and hadn't heard about Danní's fate. No, he'd never set foot in Lassi's room. He didn't ask at all about the young man's well-being.

'We'll let them stew for a few days,' Marta had said when the interrogations were over. 'Let's see if detention softens them.'

Danní's mobile phone hadn't held any information of significance to the police. The girl seemed not to have been active on social media for the past few months, and nothing was found on the device about her trip to Denmark or her role as a mule, apart from two calls from Randver before she left. He seemed not to have tried to reach her by phone after she returned to Iceland. Lassi, however, had then tried in vain to call her several times and, soon afterwards, began sending her text messages to which she never replied. It appeared that he hadn't met Danní in his basement room in Breiðholt, because he'd kept trying to reach her after she was dead, according to the time of her death as determined by the autopsy. He didn't seem to be aware of what had happened to her.

Several numbers of girlfriends of Danní's were found on her phone. The one she called most was a certain Fanney, whom it turned out to be quite difficult to reach. The police were familiar with her, having had, on more than one occasion, to put out alerts for her in the media. She lived with her mother, and had started getting into trouble at a young age. She'd been placed in care homes for what were called problem teenagers, but had repeatedly run away from them and hung out in junkie squats, where she got drugs from guys who were twice her age and did all sorts of sleazy things to her.

The search for Fanney continued while Marta questioned another young woman who had recently been in touch with Danní. Her name was Hekla, a childhood friend of Danní's. Marta had called her in for questioning along with two other girls whom Danní seemed to know best, judging by the number of phone calls between them and her grandparents' remarks concerning Danní's friends.

Of the three of them, Hekla's testimony was the most useful. A psychology student at the University of Iceland, she was understandably shocked by the news about her friend. She asked Marta several times how Danní had died; she had heard that she'd been murdered and couldn't believe it. Marta replied that she could say little about the investigation, except that it was an exaggeration to say that Danní had been murdered. At this stage, the police were first and foremost investigating a drug-smuggling case involving Danní. Marta then asked Hekla if she knew a person named Lárus Hinriksson, known as Lassi. Hekla replied that she'd heard her friend mention him several times, always in a positive way.

'They were good friends, but both used drugs. Danní met him just when she was sinking into that hell which she never managed to get out of. It's unbelievable how quickly she hit rock bottom. A girl who was perfectly fine not so long ago.'

Hekla looked into Marta's eyes. The girl was a bit chubby, with dark, curly hair framing her smooth, childlike face. Her brown eyes revealed her utter incomprehension of the fate of her good friend.

'She hid it from us, her old girlfriends, that life of hers, until finally she stopped contacting us. She cut all ties with everyone except those who could help her get high. I think I was the last of our group who still tried to keep in touch with her, but it was no use.'

26

Pálmi, the ex-policeman whom Konráð had gone to see in Suðurnes, had told him that he could contact him whenever he wanted in regard to his inquiries into his father's death. He also said that he would appreciate it if Konráð let him know if he discovered anything new or important, and perhaps he could shed further light on it.

He was therefore quite surprised when Konráð called him late one evening to ask him more about the girl found drowned in the Pond, without even a word about his father. Pálmi repeated to Konráð that he'd had nothing to do with the girl's case; it was handled by one of his colleagues, Nikulás, and turned out to be his last. Nikulás had been quite old at the time, and then retired and died not long after. Pálmi recalled that Nikulás had had a reputation for being tough and inflexible. He'd been a patrol officer and had seldom had to deal with complex criminal cases.

'Shouldn't an autopsy have been done?' asked Konrád, who had found no report on it in the police records.

'Undoubtedly,' replied Pálmi. 'And maybe it was. I really can't say. I kept diaries at the time, and after you left the other day, I looked through them and saw that I'd spoken with Nikulás several times about the girl. He was convinced that it was a terrible accident. I don't think he ever considered any other possibility.'

Konrád told him about his visit to the teacher who had fished the body from the Pond; that he'd seen a man in a trench coat and hat nearby. He hadn't paid the man any attention, and didn't remember if he'd mentioned that detail to the police. He probably hadn't thought it mattered. In any case, the information wasn't included in the reports.

'A man in a hat?'

'Does it ring any bells?'

'No, unfortunately, but that doesn't mean much,' said Pálmi. 'I don't recall having heard of any other witnesses there at the Pond besides that young man. Did you say he's a teacher?'

'Retired. Leifur Diðriksson. You may have heard of him as a writer.'

'Leifur? No. Did he publish any books?'

'Poetry. A long time ago.'

'Maybe you could have a word with Nikulás's daughter,' suggested Pálmi, who had no interest in poetry. 'I believe she's still alive. She worked for the police, doing secretarial work, when headquarters was still on Pósthússtræti Street.'

Konrád wrote down the woman's name.

'Nikulás wasn't everyone's cup of tea,' Pálmi continued. 'Troublesome. You should go and talk to someone who worked with him at the Pósthússtræti station, and who could maybe tell you more about him and this case of his, if you're interested.'

'Troublesome?'

'Yes. I don't really want to go into that. Talk to someone who knew him better.'

'One other thing,' Konráð said. 'The mother, apparently, doubted it was an accident. What do you think?'

'What else would it have been?'

'I don't know.'

'Isn't that a perfectly normal reaction, that is, if it's possible to talk about normal reactions in such circumstances?'

'Maybe.'

Following their conversation, Konráð thought things over for a few moments, then looked up Leifur Diðriksson's number on the internet and called him from his old desk phone. The teacher picked up after a few rings, and Konráð apologised for disturbing him at that hour, but then came straight to the point: had Leifur got the feeling that Nanna's mother doubted her daughter's death was an accident?

'What else would it have been?' Leifur replied, exactly as Pálmi had done a few minutes earlier.

'Did she say anything about it? That it hadn't been accidental? That someone might even have deliberately drowned the girl?'

'Why . . . why are you saying this? Is that what happened? Have you found that out?'

'Absolutely not,' Konráð assured him. 'I heard that the girl's mother had such doubts, and I wondered whether you knew that. Whether she'd mentioned such a thing to you.'

'Not as far as I recall,' replied Leifur, 'but I only met her that one time. She said nothing about it. Not to me. I think I've told you everything I know.'

'Yes, thanks, I –'

'Apparently, she was good at drawing, the girl. Did I mention that?'

'No.'

'According to her mother, she loved to draw. I don't know whether . . . whether that can help you at all.'

'Oh, well, sorry again about the inconvenience. I didn't realise how late it is.'

At the same moment, Konrád heard a knock on his door, and he looked towards the hall.

'Actually, I was going to call you, because I've been thinking about the man I saw on Sóleyjargata Street that evening,' Leifur said. 'The evening I found the girl. I started thinking about him after you came here. To be honest, I hadn't given him any thought for decades.'

'The man in the trench coat?'

'No, the other one. The man on Sóleyjargata, whom I only saw vaguely.'

There was another knock on the door, louder and more insistent. The doorknob was shaken vigorously, and Konrád had a good idea who it was.

'I wanted to share with you a detail that I wrote in the notepad I had with me, where I used to jot down ideas I thought might be useful later,' said Leifur.

'Oh?'

'I think these were the last words I wrote before I found the girl.'

'What were they?' Konrád asked, looking again towards the hall.

'And the moon limps.'

'And the moon limps?'

'That's what I wrote,' said Leifur. 'I think I understand how I came up with it. I think it's connected in some way to that man. I think the man may have been limping. There was something about the way he walked that struck me, and now I realize that the two are connected, his gait and that remark of mine. And the moon limps. The moon hobbles. I think it's why I wrote that about the moon. He may have walked with a limp.'

27

No sooner had Konrád opened the door than his sister, Elísabet, rushed in and said she'd thought he was never going to let her in. When he pointed out to her that it was rather late, she asked him why, in that case, he wasn't already in bed. Then she asked if he was going to make her a coffee. She said she didn't understand the advice that people shouldn't drink coffee in the evening because it could screw up their sleep. She sometimes reminded Konrád of their paternal aunt, Kristjana, who had died at a very advanced age, after living her life alone up north. Kristjana, who was quite peculiar and had a rather archaic manner of speaking, Konrád remembered from the few visits she made to Reykjavík back in the day, dressed in layers of skirts and jumpers, and wore a beaten-up old hat on her head. Elísabet, who also lived alone, had worked at a library for many years, and although no one knew better than Konrád how kind and gentle she was at heart, she could be a harsh critic, pettish and intimidating, with her raven-black hair and piercing brown eyes. She was well read, especially in the old Icelandic sagas; no one could ask her a question about them that she couldn't answer.

'What's taking you so long?' she shouted towards the kitchen, where he stood by the coffee pot. 'Are you still hunting for ghosts?' she asked, looking at the articles spread out on the dining table.

'A man's got to have something to do,' Konrád replied.

More than once, he'd told his sister, who was never called anything other than Beta, that he wanted to determine what their father had been up to in the days and weeks before he was murdered, and had showed her the newspaper clippings now lying on the table. Beta had barely looked at them; mostly, she simply acted like their father had never existed. Once when Konrád had broached the subject, she'd replied that she had no interest in knowing what had happened outside the slaughterhouse, who had stabbed him and why.

Konrád brought out the coffee and told his sister about Eygló and the little girl who'd been found in the Pond, adding that Eygló had sensed her presence twice, years apart. He clarified that he himself didn't believe in such things, but that he wasn't accusing Eygló of lying either.

'Isn't that just something she read in the papers?' said Beta. 'Those people can be pretty shrewd. At least that's what I've heard.'

'Those people . . . ? She's not like that, Beta. And why should she entrust me with such information if she was just making it up? There's nothing in it for her.'

'Does she have some particular interest in you?'

'No,' answered Konrád. 'Quite the contrary. I always get myself in a bloody mess whenever I see her.'

He told Beta how he'd angered Eygló by mentioning his

suspicions about Engilbert, saying that her father may have wanted to do their father harm. Beta listened disinterestedly, as she did to everything touching on their father. She and Konráð weren't particularly close, though their relationship had evolved significantly over the past few years. They hadn't grown up together, and hardly knew each other when Beta moved back to Reykjavík after their mother's death. Beta was by then almost forty. Afterwards, it had taken Konráð some time to gain his sister's trust, and he quickly realised that she had no desire to talk about the years that they'd lived under the same roof. The years before the divorce. They'd seen each other when their mother made the occasional trip to Reykjavík with Beta, but for the longest time, the siblings had had almost no contact. He didn't even know that Beta was moving to Reykjavík until she came to see him one day at his office at police headquarters on Hverfisgata Street and asked him to help her with the move.

'I'm not surprised you're in trouble with that woman,' Beta said, 'if you go around accusing her father of being a murderer. That may not be the best way to get to know someone.'

'I realise that.'

'And you think he did it, that Engilbert?'

'No idea. No one ever looked into it. Not from that angle. But it's quite a significant detail, I think, that the two men were seen together at the time. That maybe they'd been collaborating again. That they might have had a connection, were cooking up something together. If I find that out, it could, well, help us understand what happened.'

'Do you think it's related to their former psychic swindle?'

'I don't know.'

'And this Eygló, what does she say about it?'

'She says it's absurd to think that her father could have stabbed someone, and she has no idea if the two of them were scheming together again. She's actually more interested in the girl in the Pond, and thinks I might be able to help her in that regard. She says the girl has a dark or unclean aura.'

'Isn't that typical psychic babble? Unclean. What does that mean? Unclean? How can anyone spout such nonsense?'

'The girl was more than likely holding her doll when she fell in the water, or she'd dropped it and was trying to fish it out, and Eygló thinks she wants it back. At least she wants to try to find it.'

'Konrád?!'

'Yes, of course, I know it's far-fetched, but this is something that . . . something she senses.'

'Who was this girl?'

'She lived in a Nissen hut on Skólavörðuholt Hill, just before they were all razed to the ground. Most of that neighbourhood's occupants had already left.'

'A Nissen hut on Skólavörðuholt? How old was she?'

'Twelve.'

'And had she been abused?'

'No, not according to the case reports. I believe there was no autopsy. The police must have felt there was no reason for one. Why do you ask that?'

'You know why Mum ended up leaving the old man.'

'Yes, I know what he did to her, and about his unhealthy interest in you. Though I didn't find that out until the day he died. I'd met Mum in town and she told me the truth. Those were things she'd never wanted to talk about. She lied when questioned by the police, telling them that we hadn't talked about Dad when we met. No doubt to protect me. I ran home and confronted him. We had a terrible fight. He said that Mum had made it all up. That she was crazy. Nuts. Off her head. I wanted to kill him. Next thing I knew, he was lying dead on Skúlagata Street.'

'He was a bastard, Konrád. He said he would kill Mum if I told anyone what he'd done. He wasn't going to kill me, but Mum, you see? She found blood in my pants and asked me if everything was OK, but all she had to do was look in my eyes to understand what was going on.'

'Yes, I know, you've told me this before.'

'There is one thing, now that you mention Skólavörðuholt Hill. That the girl was from there.'

'Yes?'

'Mum had certain suspicions about the old man's perversion, which she didn't tell me about until much later, shortly before she died. She never said much about him, having somehow managed to erase him almost entirely from her existence, but as strange as it might seem, there was one thing she felt she simply had to say, which had to do with the old barracks area on the hill.'

'What was it?'

'It actually just came out of the blue one day. Otherwise, we never talked about him, as I said. I was sitting at home with her, thinking for some reason about the time that he took me to the hill. I remembered it was cold, maybe even snowing. I also remembered two men in one of those slummy huts, how they looked at me as if they wanted to eat me; and that's all. When I told Mum about it, she started crying and cursing him to hell, and then told me about something she'd dreaded at the time. I could barely believe it – even though I thought him capable of anything.'

Konrád looked at Beta.

'And it had to do with your trip to the hill?'

Beta nodded. 'Mum knew I had no reason to go there with him.'

'And so . . . ? Why were you . . . ?'

'She didn't want me to tell anyone, and besides, it was just a suspicion. She didn't want the man's reputation ruined any more than it already was. As if that were possible. She knew that you had a soft spot for him, even though –'

'What did she tell you?'

'It never happened, but it was one of the things she feared when she left him.'

'What was it?'

'You have to keep in mind that she'd been in an abusive relationship with that man for years. When I told her about our trip up to the hill and the two men who leered at me, she said she'd feared at one point that he was going to use me to make money.'

'What do you mean?'

'By prostituting me to perverts.'

Dumbfounded, Konrád stared at his sister.

'I don't believe it!'

'No,' Beta said, 'but that's the way she thought of him. That it was something he could have done.'

'Did she know of such men there on the hill?'

'She didn't say that, but when you brought up Skólavörðuholt, I thought back to this nightmare of hers. That the creep could have left me with some bastards up there and taken money for it.'

28

She opened her eyes and stared at the peeling paint on the ceiling. In it, she could make out all kinds of shapes and colours that danced before her eyes and coalesced into images that played in the air, as if emanating from an invisible projector. A little white dog stood on its hind legs and played with two little kittens, reminding her of the curly-haired dog she once had, which was crushed by a car and lay there in the street with one paw raised. She'd had to look away – she had loved that dog, which her father had given her because she wanted it so badly. She was playing with it when it ran into the street and the car came and crushed it into the asphalt, first with its front wheel, then its back wheel, though it still had a little life left in it and it lay there twitching as if calling for help, which she couldn't grant it at all because it was dead as a doornail, smashed into the ground. The smear that was left of it spread over the peeling paint and the dog's paw shook and trembled at her from the ceiling and she couldn't tell if she was awake or if this was one of those horrid nightmares that she often had when coming down. She didn't know where she was, but felt as if someone was trying to fuck her, and she pushed him away and went back to sleep . . .

When she woke up some time later, she was drenched with sweat. The ceiling visions were gone and a man lay sleeping next to her. He looked twice her age, his trousers were unbuttoned and his fly unzipped. She thought he had given her some pills that morning. She guessed it was evening now, or maybe the next night. She still didn't know where she was, but remembered being told that someone had something or knew someone, and they'd gone to one of those basement ratholes, those squats, with filthy mattresses on the floor, a beaten-up old couch and a few chairs. The walls were covered in graffiti, symbols and images she'd never understood. Someone was holding the flame of a lighter under a spoon; she saw two syringes, and others were smoking. The music was nothing but a booming beat that filled her ears. One of the squatters handed her some pills, which she downed with vodka.

She pushed aside the guy sleeping next to her, pulled on her pants and tried not to think about what he'd done to her. She got up slowly, holding her head in her hands. She had a pounding headache and was nearly overcome with nausea. Light from street lamps shone through a window just below the ceiling. She thought it was just the two of them there in the room, she and the man. As she started looking for something to ease her headache, she tripped and fell, then got up and puked over the guy.

She needed air.

Suddenly, she fell head first and found herself lying prostrate on the street, without a clue what was going on. She sat up and realised she must have tripped over stone steps that jutted out onto the pavement, and saw that she was in the middle of Laugavegur High Street, but didn't know if she'd been heading towards the town centre or away from it. Having no idea where she was going, she just sat there on the street, staring down at the pavement, and it was night and she had heard that Danní was dead and didn't know what was in the pills the man had given her, knew only that she felt ill. She retched but nothing came up and she sat there quietly as a car passed by, and its lights shone in her eyes and someone took photos with a mobile phone.

An elderly couple knelt beside her and asked in English if she was OK. They helped her to her feet and she said, 'OK, OK,' and continued to walk unsteadily down Laugavegur. Then a big car stopped alongside her and a policewoman got out and shone a torch in her face, and she slapped the torch aside and tried to scratch the woman, who shoved her against a wall, knocking her face against the concrete, then a policeman threw her to the ground, pressed his knee into her lower back and twisted her arms behind her until she thought they would break, then handcuffed her. The entire time, she screamed like a stuck pig.

'We have her,' she heard the policewoman say into the radio after they'd secured her in the back seat of the squad car and driven off. 'Yes, it's her. We need to take her to the ICU. Bad gash on her head.'

The radio crackled.

'Yes, completely . . . out of it,' confirmed the policewoman, turning to look at her.

She opened her mouth to shout 'Fucking cop', but not a sound came out.

She retched. Drops of blood fell onto the floor of the police car, but she had no idea where they came from.

*

Marta learned of the arrest on the afternoon of the next day, after the girl had been left to sleep off her hangover at police headquarters on Hverfisgata Street. She asked that the girl be brought to her office, and a police officer escorted her there. She sat down and looked around as if she still didn't have a grip on reality. Her head was bandaged and her hands were bruised from her fall; her face looked haggard, her lips were cracked, and her eyes were lacklustre.

'Fanney?' Marta asked. She felt sorry for the girl. An alert had been put out for her three times over the last two years, and each time she'd been found lost in a haze of drugs and alcohol.

The girl nodded.

'How are you doing, young lady?'

Fanney shrugged and asked for a cigarette.

Marta informed the officer that she no longer needed him, and he left.

'All I have are these lousy menthols,' Marta replied, taking out her pack and a lighter. Then she opened the large window behind her, which overlooked the car park at the back of the building, and signalled the girl to sit next to her. She lit a cigarette for her and they both blew their smoke out the window.

'Do you have a friend named Danní?' Marta asked.

Fanney nodded.

'Do you know what happened to her?'

The girl thought for a moment.

'Isn't she dead?' she said. 'That's what I heard.'

'We think it was accidental,' Marta said, nodding. 'That she overdosed. Were you two good friends?'

'Yes,' Fanney replied reluctantly.

'I thought you might be able to help us find out what happened. Would you be up for that? Do you want to know for sure?'

Fanney had practically sucked down the menthol cigarette. She asked if she could have another.

'Did Danní have any reason to harm herself?'

'I don't know. I think about it sometimes.'

'About what?'

'Just . . . ending it all. Just getting it over with.'

'Did she do the same?'

'Of course. At some point. I don't know. She didn't tell me about it.'

'Did anyone else have any reason to hurt her?'

'I don't know. What do you mean? Was she killed?'

'Did you know that she was a mule?'

'I just know that she owed everyone money. Her grandparents would never give her any and she didn't want to live with them any longer. I know that she was going to Denmark, but I haven't seen her since. What are you getting at? What happened to Danní?'

'We don't really know yet. Any idea who she owed money to?'

'A guy called Randver for one. But don't say I gave you his name. I don't want any trouble.'

'Do you know a guy called Lassi?'

'He's her boyfriend.'

'They're a couple?'

'Yes, absolutely.'

'Did Danní have a boyfriend before him?'

'Yeah, a lot of them. She was always in some relationship, would get rid of one and find another. She was a fun girl. Funny. Always saying something clever. She'd read all sorts of stuff and was always telling others about it. Was always there to help when you were throwing up or shitting yourself or if someone hit you or . . .'

Fanney took her last drag on her cigarette and threw the butt out the window.

'She was a great girl. The guy who was with her before Lassi was called Stebbi, but . . . he was a pain in the arse. Have you talked to those old gits?'

'Old gits?'

'Her grandma and grandpa?'

'Why do you call them old gits? It's a bit rude, isn't it?'

'That's what she called them.'

'Danní?'

'She hated them.'

'Why do you say that?'

'Because it's true.'

'Do you know why?'

'She was mad at them. I asked her why once, but she didn't want to talk about it, or I just don't remember. Why are you asking me? I know nothing about it. I don't know anything. Just that she was furious and blamed them for something. For how she was. I don't know. I know nothing about it.'

'Could you –'

'Just talk to Lassi. He knows all about it. Talk to him. Just talk to him. She told him everything.'

29

Randver was no more cooperative during his second interrogation, when he arrived with his head still wrapped in a bandage, both eyes blackened and his chin covered in plasters. Marta couldn't even begin to feel sorry for him. She found him sadly comical, with his head all done up like that – it clashed with the surly, murderous expression on his face. She almost burst out laughing during the questioning at the sight of that comic discrepancy.

The head of the Drugs Squad, who was in charge of the interrogation, began by asking him again about Lassi, why the young man had rolled, closer to death than life, out of the boot of the SUV that Randver was driving. Given the seriousness of the young man's injuries, they couldn't rule out a charge of manslaughter. The lawyer tried to make Randver understand the seriousness of the matter, but to no avail.

The police hadn't been idle since the arrest of the two men. While searching Randver's flat, they'd found drugs, mainly MDMA tablets, a handgun and a taser, a fine machete and two baseball bats. His phone and email communications hadn't revealed much to the investigators, and he seemed to be careful not to leave much of a record of his online activities. His main benefit from the digital revolution seemed to be German porn sites. But he was registered as the owner of land in the Vatnsley-suströnd area south of Reykjavík. Two detectives from CID had gone there and found a work shed by the sea and, near it, the foundation for a summer cottage that had been dug a few years earlier. The shed door was locked, but the detectives had a warrant to force it open, and upon doing so, they immediately called in a Forensics team. What they discovered there was awful. Lassi's wallet, containing his driving licence, lay under the table. Fingerprints and bloody shoeprints on the floor connected Randver and his partner to the gruesome assault. Several items found at the scene explained the injuries inflicted on Lassi.

'Yeah, I don't give a shit if he dies,' said Randver during questioning. 'I didn't do anything to him. I didn't touch him.'

'Then what was he doing in the boot of your SUV?'

'I keep telling you, I have no idea. Maybe he was hiding there. What do I know?'

'We have evidence indicating that Lárus Hinriksson was held captive and tortured on land owned by you. How do you know each other?'

'I don't know him at all,' Randver replied.

'Then maybe you know a girl by the name of Daníela, who was a friend of Lárus?'

'Never heard of the cunt?' he retorted, giving his lawyer a grin that immediately gave way to a grimace of pain. Marta had a hard time imagining anyone being more moronic.

'What was Lárus doing in your shed at Vatnsleysuströnd?'

'Maybe he broke in.'

'And you, what were you doing there with him?'

'What makes you think I was there?'

'You left your fingerprints on the tools you used to torture him. Your shoeprints, made with his blood. We find him more dead than alive in your SUV. How do you explain that?'

Randver didn't answer.

'It doesn't look obvious to you?'

'What, so I'm guilty without a trial? It is obvious. I didn't do anything to him. Nothing. Don't try to pin it on me.'

'You say you don't know Danní, but that didn't stop you calling her twice before she left for Denmark just a short time ago.'

'It wasn't me,' Randver protested.

'Who else would it have been?'

'I don't know. Probably someone who used my phone.'

'Do a lot of people use your phone?'

'It happens,' said Randver. 'I don't mind lending it.'

'Who to?'

'I forget.'

The interrogation continued like this for a good while, without the defendant changing his initial testimony. Stubborn as a mule, he denied everything he was accused of and stuck to his story that he'd found the sports bag by chance.

Finally, he was taken back to solitary confinement, and the younger guy who'd been with him in the SUV was brought to the interrogation room. He was still living with his parents, and a search of his room uncovered a small amount of marijuana and a few ecstasy pills. No guns, knives or bludgeons were found, and his parents had been terribly surprised by this police operation. This was especially true of the mother, who had also tried to hide the fact that she was drunk. Yes, yes, the kid was into things he shouldn't be, like many others his age, but the parents didn't know that their son was in cahoots with drug smugglers and thugs. They had asked how soon he would be released.

With one arm in a sling and his face dotted with plasters, the kid limped into the interrogation room, thin and hunched, despite his young age. His nose was running and he sniffed constantly. He called himself Biddi. He was much more cooperative than the previous time, and when told that the police had proof that he'd been in the work shed with Randver and Lassi, he didn't deny it, like Randver, but tried his best to blame everything on his partner. Little by little, the police were able to reconstruct the string of events leading up to their accident on Breiðholt Road. Randver had flown into a rage when the drugs he was expecting weren't delivered after Danní returned to Iceland. He'd asked Biddi to go with him to find Lassi, which they did without difficulty. Lassi pretended to know nothing about the drugs and Randver had decided to take him to the shed by the sea, where he'd started beating and torturing him.

'I did nothing,' said the young man innocently, looking at his lawyer, who had floated the idea to the police that his client be given a reduced sentence if he confessed.

'Do you know why Daníela didn't deliver the drugs?'

'No. Randver told me that she was into drugs herself, and that it was always a risk using people like that.'

'When you were looking for Daníela and Lárus, did you go to his place?'

'Yes. No one was home.'

'When was that?'

'I'm not sure. I wasn't really –'

'How did you get in the building?'

'Someone opened the door for us, and the one in the basement wasn't locked.'

'That means anyone could get in, right?'

'We did.'

'Why did you have to treat Lárus as you did?'

'Randver is nuts. I thought he was going to kill him.'

'You took part in it, didn't you?'

'No, not at all. It was just Randver.'

'We found your fingerprints on various tools in the shed. Bloody fingerprints. Made with Lárus's blood.'

'Well, they were just things that Randver handed me. I really tried to stop him. I don't know how many times. He's a sadist. A real sadist,' said Biddi, looking at his lawyer.

'Did Lárus ever mention Daníela being at his place?'

'I don't think he knew where she was, but Randver was fucking furious about what Lassi said.'

'What was that?'

'Lassi said that she was going to do something to expose him. Post something on the internet.'

'To expose Randver?'

'That's what Randver thought.'

'And how did he react?'

'He freaked out. We barely understood what Lassi was saying given what Randver had done to him . . . he'd really hurt him, and Lassi was just spouting bullshit, just to say something, understand? I don't think he even knew where he was any more. Randver lost it and said he was going to kill Lassi. Then when the message came from Danní, he was all gung-ho about going to get the drugs and her and threw Lassi in the boot of the SUV and said he was going to put the little bitch and her boyfriend out of their misery and bury them both in the rubbish dump.'

30

Life hadn't been particularly kind to Nikulás's daughter. She was, however, reluctant to go into details with strangers such as Konrád. He didn't remember her from his time on the police force, and as it turned out, she had quit shortly before he began. She confided to him that her father had got her the secretarial job at police headquarters, taking advantage of his connections with superiors. When her father retired, it was as if the administration had less and less for her to do, and she was soon reduced to half-time and then dismissed as part of a departmental reorganisation, as it was called. She'd spent most of her working life as a secretary for various companies, and always enjoyed it.

She carefully avoided mention of certain details that Konrád had learned in his calls to former officers stationed at police headquarters when it was on Pósthússtræti Street. They spoke well of the woman, but said that drink had been her downfall. Her superiors had tried to reason with her more than once, and despite stable periods, things would always follow the same course. She even showed up to work drunk now and then. Sometimes she just didn't show up. Finally it became impossible to justify keeping her on. One of the officers thought she was a loner, a single woman living a dull existence in a flat in the Hlíðar neighbourhood.

Konrád had rung her twice. At first, she refused to let him come and see her at her place. During their second phone call, it was as if her curiosity had been aroused and she asked more about the girl found in the Pond. She ended up agreeing to meet him near her home, suggesting a bench in Klambratún Park where she liked to go and sit.

Klambratún was taking on its winter colours. Its lawns were yellowing and the trees bordering it had lost their leaves, for the most part. The birdsong was gone, and now all that was heard was the incessant murmur of the traffic on Miklabraut Road, which could be seen through the bare trees' twisted branches. In the summer, people came and lay here in the grass, idling away the time and enjoying life. Now, they turned up their collars, lowered their heads and hurried over the lawn.

Konrád found the bench that Nikulás's daughter had suggested, sat down on it and regarded the signs of the changing season before noticing a middle-aged woman who appeared between trees alongside Miklabraut and walked towards him. Her apparel reminded him a bit of his sister Beta – both looked like vagabonds from an Icelandic folk tale. She wore an anorak that had lost its lustre, a woollen hat, a heavy skirt, knee-length socks and tatty trainers.

'Are you Konrád?' she asked as she neared the bench. He nodded and she sat down next to him.

'Thank you for meeting me,' he said.

'I found it so odd that you . . . when you mentioned this case on the phone,' said the woman, whose name was Áróra. 'I didn't know . . . well, I was a bit shocked.'

'Why?'

'Well, why would you think I'd know anything about it? I had absolutely nothing to do with it.'

'I just wondered if you might remember it at all, since your father was in charge of the case,' said Konrád. 'The police reports on it told me practically nothing and, to be honest, it actually looks as if there wasn't even an investigation into the cause of the accident. Maybe because it involved people from the old barracks neighbourhood, I don't know. It was as if nothing important had happened, if you know what I mean. The news-papers barely covered the accident and, with all due respect to your father, it seems to me that his investigation wasn't particu-larly thorough. Then the bulldozers levelled the old Nissen huts up on the hill a few months later, and the case was pretty much buried.'

'But isn't that understandable, given the tragic circumstances? Particularly in those days. People talked about such things only in whispers, out of respect for the family.'

'Do you recall your father ever mentioning the accident?'

'No. Nikulás never talked about work. Never. And this hap-pened before I started working at the Pósthússtræti station, so I never heard anyone say anything about it there.'

'I was told he wasn't really a criminal investigator.'

'No, he subbed for them during their summer holidays, that sort of thing. He did take a course on that type of police work, as I recall, but he was always a patrol officer, and worked his way up to lieutenant. In fact, he had no interest in investigative work; he found it banal. Burglaries, thefts, assaults and fights pretty much explained themselves. They always involved the same people. Murders are extremely rare, fortunately.'

'Yes, fortunately,' Konrád agreed.

Most of those who had known Nikulás during his police career were now deceased. Pálmi was one of the few still alive who remembered him, but hadn't known him very well. He had advised Konrád to speak to a man named Arnór, who had worked with Nikulás for several years.

Konrád had rung Arnór, who was quick to tell him a number of things about his former colleague – among other things, that several women had complained about his behaviour when he responded to calls as a uniformed officer supposedly representing law and order. Apparently, he'd acted highly inappropriately, harassing the women verbally or molesting them, according to the complaints filed. His victims were mainly women on the downside of life, who were the easiest prey for men like him. The police had paid little attention to such reports until Arnór tried to get Nikulás fired from his job, after two women came to see him a few months apart and stated that Nikulás had sexually assaulted them. Arnór preferred not to go into details on the phone, but implied that in the first instance, Nikulás had forced the victim into performing oral sex on him, and in the second, he attempted to have sex with the woman. These incidents took place in the 1960s. Nikulás denied all of it and the women were reluctant to press charges. As so often in such cases, it was he-said-she-said, there having been no witnesses.

Konrád was hesitant to tell Nikulás's daughter about the things that Arnór had told him. On his way to see her, he'd pondered how he could bring this up without hurting her. He soon realised that he'd had nothing to worry about, since Áróra brought up the subject herself.

'You've probably heard that Nikulás didn't have a good reputation as a police officer,' she said.

'Yes, I . . .'

'Is that why you contacted me?'

'No,' said Konrád, 'that's not the reason, but I did hear something along those lines. I wasn't sure you would want to go into it.'

'Who told you?'

'Some ex-police officers whom I've spoken with.'

'Why are you interested in Nikulás? What is it that . . . what exactly are you looking for?'

'I want to get a clearer picture of what happened at the Pond,' Konrád replied. 'To find out if Nikulás told you or your mother about it. If it had been a source of concern for him. I don't have much information on it, and, of course, it all goes back a very long time, but –'

'Concern? Are you implying that it was no accident?'

'Yes,' said Konrád, reluctant to tell her about the clairvoyant, being uncertain of where he himself was headed by delving into this. Maybe he just had too much time on his hands since retiring. 'Actually, there's every chance that it was a terrible accident,' he said. 'I'd just like to learn more about it, if I can.'

'Was the girl related to you?'

'No.'

Áróra looked at the bare tree branches and listened to the constant hum of traffic on Miklabraut.

'It was one of the first things I learned when I started working at the Pósthússtræti station – a really nice workplace. There were some very fine people in the police in those days. And I guess there still are today.'

'What did you learn?'

'That Nikulás wasn't well liked. And I remember that I didn't give it much thought; it didn't really surprise me, I mean. I just felt like I understood better why he didn't like to talk about his job. At first he didn't want me to work there. Was uncomfortable about using his connections. It wasn't until he was asked if one of the people who had applied for the job was his daughter that he put in a good word for me.'

'So he didn't forbid you from applying for the job?'

'No, but I got the impression that he wasn't particularly pleased with my going for it.'

'Why didn't it surprise you that he wasn't well liked?'

'He could be unpleasant to be around,' Áróra replied. 'I knew that very well. But I don't really want to go into it here.'

'Did you know that women complained about him? Accused him of inappropriate behaviour and even –'

'Yes, I was told that.'

'It must have been hard for you to hear such things.'

'Of course it was. Especially thinking about those poor women.'

'I can imagine how surprised you must have been,' Konrád continued.

'Yes, a bit.'

'Only a bit?'

'Yes.'

'Because he was unpleasant to be around?'

'Yes. He was lewd. He treated my mother badly, too.'

'Was it hard to live with him?'

'He could be very difficult. When he drank. Which he did quite a bit. I don't really like talking about it. I also need to . . . I have a lot to do today.'

Abruptly, she made ready to leave.

'Of course, thank you very much for meeting me,' Konrád said. 'I notice that you always call him Nikulás, rather than my father or Dad.'

'Yes, it's an old habit,' said Áróra.

'I see.'

'Well, I need to get going,' she said, standing and zipping up her anorak. 'I learned early on not to call him Dad. They called him St Nikulás, did you know that? At the station. As a joke. Because he was completely the opposite.'

'No, I hadn't heard that.'

'These people knew all about him. You could probably use a lot of words about the late Nikulás, but "saint" isn't one of them.'

31

The hospital was quiet after the day's busy activity. Konrád stepped out of the lift and headed for the ICU. The corridor was practically deserted, apart from one or two orderlies or nurses who went about their work quietly, paying him no attention. He had planned to introduce himself as a family friend of Lassi's in case anyone asked him his business there, but it wasn't necessary. There were no police officers on guard outside Lassi's room, despite his alleged involvement in drug smuggling and being beaten to within an inch of his life by violent criminals from the drug world. Konrád assumed that the police didn't view him as being at any risk in hospital, besides the fact that the perpetual downsizing of the police force didn't allow for the extravagance of round-the-clock monitoring of petty criminals.

Konrád walked slowly down the corridor to the room where Lassi was kept sedated. He was showing signs of improvement and an attempt would soon be made to bring him back to consciousness, Marta had told Konráð, calling him in the early evening, as usual. She'd filled him in on what she'd learned about Danní and Lassi, and how one of Danní's friends had stated that she'd hated her grandparents.

'Oh, those nice people?' Konráð had replied in surprise.

'Her name is Fanney, the one who told us this. She may not be our most reliable witness. A decent girl, but, you know, a dopehead.'

'Shouldn't you ask them about it?'

'I imagine they'd been trying to persuade the girl to get her act together and it didn't sit well with her. It's the same old story. Those who want to help are always the bad guys.'

Marta told him about the interrogations of Randver and his partner – and how apparently, Danní or Lassi had threatened to post information about Randver's activities or other things about him on the internet.

Lassi lay there alone in his bleak room, an oxygen mask over his face and connected to various devices mainly unfamiliar to Konráð. Medications dripped into his veins and bandages protected the wounds that the doctors had had to suture. Konráð asked the orderly who was coming out of the room if the patient had had any visitors, but the orderly replied that he didn't know, he'd only just started his shift. He seemed to have no interest whatsoever in what Konráð was doing there in the room of the main witness in a criminal case.

Konráð hardly knew himself, apart from having felt the need to see Lassi and put a face to his name. He couldn't erase the mental image of the basement room where he'd found Danní lying among rubbish, with a needle in her arm. He thought of their debts, of Danní smuggling drugs through customs and of Lassi in the hands of those thugs, and couldn't help but feel sorry for those two newcomers to the world of crime. He imagined their descent down the drain, which was so typical of young people who got hooked on alcohol and drugs and couldn't or wouldn't stop and ended up on the street, out of their heads, outsiders, down-and-out. His experience as a police officer had taught him that in some cases, deep pain or anger lay behind their addictions, which the drug-induced haze temporarily alleviated. Those short respites were, however, often bought at a high price: violence, abuse of all kinds, and prostitution.

Konráð was looking at Lassi's disfigured face and thinking about the mechanics of life when he heard a noise behind him. A young man walked hesitantly into the room and asked if it was Lárus lying there in the bed. Konráð replied that it was.

'Damn, he looks awful,' remarked the young man as he drew nearer.

'Are you . . . ?'

'His brother,' said the man. 'Do you think he'll recover?'

'I'm not a doctor,' said Konráð. 'I knew his girlfriend a little. Danní.'

'The girl who died?'

'I found her at your brother's place.'

'Oh, OK. I didn't know her. The police told me they were good friends.'

'Yes, apparently.'

'He didn't deserve this,' the young man said, staring at Lassi. 'No matter how awful he was, lying and cheating and stealing from us. Nobody deserves such a thing. Just look at him! Some fucking bastards attack him and leave him in that state.'

'They say he double-crossed them in a drugs deal.'

'Yeah, I couldn't care less. They're barbarians.'

'Definitely.'

'I was talking with my other brother, about how we should lure them to our garage and beat – Sorry, who did you say you were?'

'A family friend of Danní's,' Konrád replied.

'Wasn't she all fucked up on drugs, too?'

'Let's just say she and Lassi were in the same boat.'

'It could have been her who had the prescription put under my name.'

'Prescription?'

'Lassi told me it was him, but I'm not sure. I think it was for an epileptic drug. I don't remember the name. Maybe Lyrsica?'

'Lyrica is prescribed for epilepsy. I guess that's what you mean?'

'Yes. I was at the garage and the phone rang. It was a pharmacy somewhere in Hafnarfjörður, calling to tell me that that epilepsy drug . . .'

'Lyrica.'

'. . . right, Lyrica, that it wasn't available, but they had an alternative and wanted to know if I'd be OK with that, or wait for the other. I had no idea what the woman was talking about, but she went over it all again and it turned out that a prescription for an epilepsy drug that I'd never asked for or needed to use had been filed under my name.'

'It's popular with drug addicts,' said Konrád. 'They squeeze some kind of high out of it.'

'I found out of course that Lassi or the girl had just put my name to a prescription for the stuff and got it that way. They probably used other names besides mine. Lassi admitted it when I got hold of him. He said they'd stolen a prescription ledger from some doctor and forged his handwriting, which wasn't legible anyway. He asked me not to tell anyone.'

'Addicts can be pretty darned resourceful when it comes to

getting their fixes,' said Konrád. 'From what I understand, they were very close.'

'I never met her. We haven't kept in touch much recently, me and Lassi, except when I called him about this. That's just how it is. All the scams and lies . . . Do you know what happened to the girl at my brother's place? That Danní?'

'They think she died of an overdose. Maybe accidentally. But maybe intentionally.'

'Suicide?'

'No one knows what she was thinking,' Konrád replied, looking at the equipment and tubes surrounding the patient. 'Except maybe Lassi here. He's probably the only one who can tell us.'

'If he survives.'

'Yes, if he survives.'

Marta had upset the elderly couple so much that she thought it best for her to leave and allow them to recompose themselves. She had dropped by their place on her way home from work to ask them about what the dopehead had said, that Danní had hated them. Marta had had trouble figuring out how to bring it up without shocking them, but failed – she was clumsy, as she could be sometimes. She tried as long as possible not to quote Fanney, who had called them old gits and said that Danní hated them and even blamed them for her situation, but the couple, especially the wife, had pestered her with questions and demanded to know what Marta was fishing for. They had asked her why she was tiptoeing around them like a cat around a bowl of hot porridge. Without mentioning any names, Marta replied that she'd spoken to some friends of Danní's, and one of them had said that their granddaughter harboured a certain antipathy – or rather, animosity – towards her grandparents. Marta wanted to know the reason for it, whether they could shed any light on their relationship with the girl and why she spoke so badly of them.

'Well, wasn't she doped up?' replied the woman. 'Can you really take such talk seriously? Doesn't it make sense that she directed her anger at us, who were always trying to make her understand that . . . ?'

The woman didn't finish her sentence. Marta looked around the living room. The couple had been sent numerous bouquets and cards expressing condolences, and had placed them wherever there was space.

'What exactly did she say to her friends?' asked the husband, knitting his brow.

'I'd rather not –'

'What? What did she say?'

'Well, first of all, that she hated you.'

'God . . .' groaned the woman.

'And that she blamed you in some respects for her situation.'

'Rubbish!' said the husband.

'I wanted to know whether you could explain those feelings of hers towards you,' said Marta. 'What prompted her to say such things.'

'This is all a bunch of bullshit!' said the man, looking worriedly at his wife.

'You must have felt –' Marta resumed, but the man immediately interrupted her.

'I can't believe that she said such things. It just shows how far gone she was. That's all. How deeply lost she was in that . . . that hell . . .'

'The poor child,' sighed the woman.

'Those friends of hers, are they also in the gutter?' the husband asked scornfully. 'They're probably not the most reliable witnesses, are they?'

'I should maybe come and talk to you again later,' Marta said. 'We're investigating Danni's death in connection with drug smuggling and her involvement with criminals, and I want to try to gather as much information as I possibly can about her.'

'What? You mean someone might have killed her?!'

'There are a number of pieces missing from the puzzle,' Marta said, taking care not to reveal too much. 'Danni's drug use made her some enemies.'

'Did they play a part in her death?'

'I don't know. That might have nothing to do with it.'

'We just want this to be over,' the man said. 'For this terrible story to end without you constantly upsetting us and hammering us with questions we can't answer.'

32

The room was spacious. Eygló's friend shared it with her little brother, Ebbi, who followed her like a shadow and didn't want to be left out. Eygló went to play at their house sometimes after school; she enjoyed their company and the siblings' mother always welcomed her warmly, gave them bread with butter and cheese or jam, milk to drink and biscuits, which she always had in plenty.

Unlike Eygló's mother, she was a homemaker, and her home was always clean and tidy. Sometimes when Eygló entered the flat, she caught a whiff of cleaning solutions. She liked going there with her friend after school, when no one was home at her own place. She didn't like being alone. Her father was always running around town and sometimes didn't come back for days. Her mother slaved away at the fish factory, and returned home exhausted in the evenings. Eygló would help with the housework before her mother fell asleep on the couch.

Her friend's flat was on the ground floor of a new block and was lovely and elegant, with paintings on the walls and something that her friend called 'parquet' on the floor. The three children drank fresh orange juice, which Eygló had never tasted before, and stirred chocolate powder into their milk.

'What's that you're wearing?' her friend's mum asked, noticing the string that Eygló wore around her neck.

'It's my house key,' said Eygló, showing it to her.

'Your house key? No one's at home to let you in after school?' the woman said in surprise. Eygló noticed how she stood there sometimes, cigarette in hand, staring longingly out the living-room window at the life beyond it. Later, when Eygló joined the women's movement, the melancholy memory of that woman standing at her window often came to mind.

But that wasn't the only reason she sometimes thought back with sadness to her visits to that block of flats. Once when she was over at her friend's they'd lost track of time and the winter darkness had settled over the city. Her friend's father had come home, dinner was on the table, and the mother asked if it was time for her to go home – unless she wanted to eat with them. She was welcome to do so. They didn't know that Eygló had fled to their kitchen from her friend's bedroom and didn't dare for the life of her return there to get her school bag and go home. She was rarely afraid of what she saw, even if it did happen sometimes.

'Is something wrong, dear?' asked the mum.

'Yes,' Eygló replied. 'I'm just waiting.'

'Fine, dear, but what are you waiting for?'

'For the woman,' said Eygló.

'What woman?'

'The woman in the black dress,' said Eygló.

The mum looked from her to her husband and back. The

husband shrugged as if this was something that didn't concern him. The mum tried reasoning with the child.

'There's no woman here but me,' she said. 'What woman are you talking about?'

'In the bedroom,' said Eygló. 'The woman in the black dress.'

'Did you see a woman in there?' the mum asked her daughter, who shook her head.

'Did someone come home with you?' she asked her husband.

He also shook his head, his expression suggesting the question was absurd.

'Come on,' said the mum. 'Show me.'

She took the girl's hand and Eygló resisted, terrified of seeing the woman again. But it was useless; her friend's mum was determined, and half dragged the girl behind her before throwing open the door to the children's room.

'What nonsense was that, my little Eygló?' said the mum. 'There's no one here. Go on, get your school bag. Your parents are probably worrying about you.'

Eygló inched her way back into the bedroom, keeping her eyes fixed on the floor. She grabbed her school bag and hurried out. She felt the presence of the woman, whom she'd seen standing in a corner of the room, looking at her. The woman's neck was broken, and her head hung limply on her shoulder. Her black dress was torn at the side. She'd probably been in a terrible accident. As Eygló hurried through the doorway, she glanced back to that corner and saw to her great relief that the woman was no longer there.

She calmed down immediately. It struck her as a bad omen, and she was immensely relieved that it was gone.

Most often, when Eygló was frightened by something she saw, but which was invisible to others, she would tell her father about it. He had encouraged her to do so, saying that she would feel better if she had someone she could share her experience with. She didn't discuss such things with her mother, realising quickly that she hated that her daughter had inherited that faculty from Engilbert. Her mother wished that she was just a normal daughter, free from supernatural visions and impervious to paranormal phenomena, ghostly visitations and all the rest of it. Engilbert could have it all for himself. Her mother would have preferred for Eygló to have no such deplorable 'gift'. She didn't believe in life after death and kept her nose out of her husband's activities. 'Death is the end,' she told her daughter, with the rationalism of a working woman who didn't have the privilege of being able to spend her time pondering the deep meaning of life. 'Don't imagine it to be anything else. We all end up in the grave and then it's over, and there's absolutely nothing afterwards. It's all just in your head, and the sooner you wean yourself off it, the better.'

She was treated completely differently by Engilbert. When, later that night, after her mother had gone to bed, she told him in whispers about the woman in the black dress, he was elated, as he often was when he heard stories from the beyond. He wanted to know exactly where in town this had happened, in what direction the woman was turned and whether she had said anything or hinted at who she was, or if Eygló knew what time period she belonged to. He asked if she'd ever seen the woman before and whether the people in the flat recognised her at all from Eygló's description. Eygló had replied that she didn't think so, because no one had believed her.

The fear that Eygló had felt upon seeing the woman in black continued to haunt her, and then, three weeks later, she heard the news at school and ran home in tears. For once, Engilbert was there. He smelled of alcohol and his eyes were glazed, as always when he returned from one of his drinking binges, and now he sat down with his daughter and asked her why she was crying.

'My friend's brother was in a car accident,' she said.

'No, what are you saying?!'

'A car hit him in front of his building.'

'The poor boy. Is he OK?'

'My friend didn't come to school this morning . . . and . . . I . . . our teacher told us there'd been a horrible accident.'

'How awful.'

'He said that we should pray for the family.'

'And that's exactly what we'll do, my love. We'll pray for them. But tell me, how is he?'

Eygló was unable to hold back her tears.

'Ebbi died in the hospital,' she sobbed. 'He's dead. Ebbi is dead.'

33

Konrád looked out at the rain as he listened silently and earnestly to Eygló speak of phenomena that could never be proven or explained. Few people actually believed in such things; most considered them to be superstitions, coincidences, or downright delusions or fraud. Eygló wasn't trying to convince him of anything, but told him about Ebbi's death just as she would have any other tragic event in her life. Admittedly, the event dated back several decades and the new century had long since begun, but Konrád could clearly see that this story continued to haunt her. She knew that Konrád doubted her, and it was as if she felt compelled to convince him that she was above board in everything she did and said.

They were in Reykjavík City Hall. The sky was heavy with clouds, and it had begun to rain shortly before their arrival. It was Eygló who had suggested they meet there, adding that an exhibition of aerial photos of old Reykjavík, from when the city was expanding at full speed just after World War II, was being held there, and she thought it might interest him. Taken from a bird's-eye view, the photos showed the farms where the districts of Háaleiti and Breiðholt would later rise, as well as the military camps that the British and later the Americans built all over Reykjavík during the war, from Grandi on the town's western edge all the way east to the Elliðaá River. They had meandered from photo to photo and regarded the city's development before sitting in the cafeteria, where Eygló told him the story of the woman in the black dress.

Konrád had finished telling her what he'd been looking at in connection with the case of the girl who'd been found in the Pond, mentioning how Nikulás hadn't been particularly careful in his investigation, or in his police work in general. He had a reputation for preying on women who looked to the police for help. Konrád said that he was also planning to contact Nanna's stepbrother and ask him about life on Skólavörðuholt Hill. And whether he remembered his stepsister's doll.

'Nanna was apparently very good at drawing,' Konrád said.

'I can't stop thinking about that doll. There's something about it that I don't understand, something . . .'

Eygló didn't finish the sentence.

'Of course, it was lost long ago,' she then said.

'Are you still in contact with that friend of yours?' Konrád asked after Eygló had told him the story of the woman in the black dress. 'The boy's sister?'

'No, we drifted apart and eventually lost touch,' said Eygló. 'I never went back to her home. I didn't have the courage. It was all so overwhelming to my young mind. I probably should have warned them of the danger, but I didn't understand it, and in any case, no one would have believed me. I was just a little girl.'

'Did that incident leave a lasting mark on you?'

'A year later I saw the girl during the birthday party, and I got the same feeling, that what I saw was a bad omen. I hated those visions, wherever they came from, whether they were the fruit of my imagination, conjured up from nervous impulses or intuition, ghosts from another world, or something entirely different . . . I didn't want to have anything to do with them. I told my dad that. Told him that I didn't want it. He tried to teach me to accept my visions, but I couldn't and it made me angry. I was also angry at him, and at my mum, who didn't understand me. I was furious at all of it, which is not a good feeling when you're young and naive. It's not a good feeling in general.'

'I can imagine,' Konrád said.

'Anger can never do any good.'

'And the woman you saw in that block of flats?'

Konrád sensed hesitation on Eygló's part.

'Is there any particular reason why you're telling me this story here at City Hall?' Konrád asked, glancing at the people taking in the photo exhibition. Outside, the rain pounded the surface of the Pond, which stretched towards Skothúsvegur Street. 'Why did you want us to meet here? Was it only to get a look at old Reykjavík?'

Eygló smiled listlessly, as if she wasn't sure she had the courage to face these unanswerable questions yet again.

'Do you know who she was? The woman in the black dress?'

'Come with me,' said Eygló. 'I want to show you something.'

They got up and Konrád followed her to a photo showing a military camp on the western part of town. The barracks were arranged in rows, with straight streets and intersections. Looking closer, cars could be seen driving down those nameless streets. Eygló pointed towards an intersection.

'There's where it happened,' she said.

'Where what happened?'

'Around thirty years after I saw the woman in Ebbi's room, I went down to the Office of City Planning. All that time, I'd wondered now and then who that woman might have been, but I had always shoved the question aside because the memory was too painful. I wanted to forget her, and knew that even if I tried to find information on her, it wouldn't change a single thing. So it took me all those years to go to that office and talk to people who knew this city's history, the demolitions, construction, the places that were now long gone and that most people didn't remember any more. Old intersections, for example – because it crossed my mind that the woman had been the victim of a traffic accident. I also leafed through old newspapers and was given access to police records on serious road accidents over a specific period. The reports gave the names and addresses of the victims. That's how I ended up finding the sister of the woman I saw in the bedroom.'

Konrád stared at the photo of the intersection at the entrance to the old military camp. The photo had been taken from a considerable height on a beautiful, sunny summer's day, and shadows projected from the buildings.

'The woman in the black dress was the girlfriend of an American soldier,' Eygló continued. 'They had been together for a few months, and were madly in love. Her sister told me how happy they both were, that they shared a perfect, beautiful love. One evening, they were driving home from a dance at the camp in an open jeep, but for some reason, they came to that intersection too fast and, tragically, it rolled over. The woman's neck was broken and she died instantly. The soldier had barely a scratch on him.'

Eygló wiped dust off the glass over the photograph.

'I spoke to a former soldier who remembered the accident quite well. An Icelandic-Canadian who came here during the war and worked for the military police. His name was Thorson, and he moved here for good after the war.'

'Thorson? I know who he is,' said Konrád. 'He died not so long ago . . .'

'Yes, exactly, I read that in the papers. He was a lovely man and extremely helpful when I went to speak to him. Would have done anything for me. He'd gone to the scene of the accident and remembered all the details. He told me that the soldier was utterly devastated, losing the love of his life in that manner. Three weeks after he rolled the jeep, he shot himself in one of the barracks.'

Konrád was beginning to suspect where this story was headed.

'Many years later, the site of the old camp was razed,' Eygló continued. 'After the poor of Reykjavík had been living in the old Nissen huts for more than a decade. When the authorities decided those huts were no longer habitable, they were razed and replaced with blocks of flats. One of the blocks was constructed on top of the old intersection. A young couple from Reykjavík moved into a flat on the ground floor. There they had two children, one of whom died in a car accident in front of the building.'

Konrád looked at Eygló, and saw that she was having difficulty going on.

'Can you explain that to me, Konrád?' she asked. 'I'd be curious to know how you would do so, if you can.'

34

Randver was again escorted to the interrogation room. He'd had the best medical care, the bandages around his head had been changed and he looked less ridiculous than before. His hostile attitude, however, hadn't dwindled, nor had his unwillingness to cooperate. Sitting next to his lawyer, he stared belligerently at Marta, who was leading the interrogation. She didn't let Randver's hostility bother her. She'd done this many times before, questioning bastards like him and getting obscenities spewed back at her.

After around half an hour of Randver's dithering, sarcasm and sly threats, she decided to stop wasting her time and closed the folder she had in front of her.

'Is that guy still lying there knocked out in hospital?' Randver asked. His lawyer had informed him of Lassi's condition. It was as if it amused him to know that the young man was still in intensive care. And for him, these interrogations were a welcome distraction from the miserable boredom of isolation. Marta had the impression that the loneliness was beginning to weigh on him, despite his swagger.

'He's in bad shape,' Marta replied. 'You certainly didn't hold back on him.'

'I didn't touch him,' Randver retorted with a smirk, revealing his yellowed teeth. 'I'm just telling you like it was. Didn't touch him. Don't even know who he is.'

'What were you afraid of?' asked Marta.

'Afraid? I wasn't afraid.'

'You were afraid of Danní.'

'What bullshit is this, you old bag? You should get fucked more often, then you wouldn't be so daft. I can help you if you want. Right now. Do you want to do it right now? Right here? No problem, sweetheart. Just ask.'

Marta looked at Randver's lawyer, who pushed his fashionable, black-rimmed glasses up his nose and shrugged, as if he was in no way responsible for his client's comments. Marta got the impression that the lawyer was afraid of Randver.

'What did she threaten you with?'

'Nothing. She didn't threaten me with anything. She couldn't threaten me. What would she have threatened me with?'

'I don't know,' said Marta. 'I know that she was going to post something about you on the internet. Will you tell me what it was?'

'I have no idea what you're talking about.'

'No? It didn't stop you from going into a rage and saying you were going to kill her and dump her body on the rubbish heap and Lassi's along with her.'

Randver thought this over for a moment, before suddenly realising where she must have got this information. He burst out laughing.

'Did Biddi tell you these lies?'

'What did Danní have on you to make you so angry?'

'Nothing. This is bullshit. You're just making up a bunch of fucking nonsense.'

'So it wasn't accidental? When Danní died?'

Randver didn't answer.

'Did she threaten anyone else? Threaten to air their dirty laundry on the internet?'

Randver said nothing.

'Do you know of anyone else who was as angry at her as you? Anyone else who may have freaked out like you? Any of your friends? Who are you smuggling the drugs in for? Do they know about Danní? Did Danní know who they are?'

'You shouldn't believe anything that Biddi tells you!' Randver barked. 'In the first place, it was Biddi who did that to Lassi. Lassi started calling him a mama's boy and a queer, and Biddi just snapped. He snapped, and I only just stopped him from killing Lassi.'

The lawyer cleared his throat, as if trying to signal to Randver that he should shut up. The detainee missed it completely.

'So you do know Lassi?' Marta said.

'Huh?'

'Were you with him in the shed?'

'Everything Biddi tells you is a lie!' Randver yelled, having momentarily forgotten that he was never supposed to have been in that shed with Lassi, whom, of course, he supposedly hadn't known. 'Don't believe a word of it! He's a fucking moron! Just a lying fucking moron!! Did he make a deal with you? Is that it? Are you going to cut him loose? Is the fucking bastard being cut loose?'

'Well, that's –'

'You can tell Biddi that I'll kill him as soon as I get out of all this bullshit! He's dead! Tell him that, bitch cop! Dead!!'

The lawyer was a young slacker who had barely managed to graduate from law school on his second attempt. Judging that it was time to intervene, he leaned towards Randver and whispered a few words in his ear, as he'd seen done in innumerable television series. Randver pushed him away so violently that the man nearly fell off his chair. His trendy glasses landed on the floor, and as he reached for them, his head hit the table and he let out a little whine that resembled the squeak of the sole of a shoe.

35

Konrád was coming in out of the rain when his mobile rang. He saw that, once again, it was Danní's grandmother, and after a moment's hesitation, he declined the call. Then cursed himself for his obstinacy. He had resolved to have nothing more to do with this matter, being unable to see how he could be of any help to these people. In his mind's eye he could see the woman in her desperation, trying to deal with the death of her grandchild. Nor did it help that the event had of course reopened old wounds, from when the girl's mother died in a car accident, which only added to the woman's burden of sorrow.

He'd said goodbye to Eygló down at City Hall, in the pouring rain. He didn't know how to respond to her story. She hadn't asked for his opinion. Simply laid her cards on the table. He respected her for that and trusted her, unable to imagine for even a moment that she would lie to him. They had sat there silently for some time, looking out at the Pond, until Eygló said she needed to go.

'Thank you for entrusting me with all this,' Konrád had said. 'I'm sure it isn't easy for you to talk about.'

'And I haven't done so for many years. Old Málfríður is one of the few people who know this story. I never told Ebbi's family exactly what I saw. My father said that I was right to keep quiet about it. Even though I didn't really understand it at the time, the idea of telling them what I'd seen seemed out of place. It wouldn't have eased their pain or changed anything. They moved out of Reykjavík soon afterwards.'

Eygló watched the raindrops trickle down the windows.

'I couldn't foresee the accident. There was nothing I could have done.'

'No, of course not.'

'I was just a child. I couldn't . . . I didn't understand it.'

'Naturally.'

Konrád detected a touch of regret in her words.

'And a year later, Nanna appeared to you?'

'I didn't ask for it to happen. I didn't want those visions, as I'm sure you understand now. I didn't try to find out more about her, and didn't know who she was until you called me the other day and told me about the girl in the Pond.'

'Yes . . . I doubt it's much fun for a child to be confronted with such things.'

'I'm not asking you to believe any of this,' said Eygló. 'I had good reason to stop holding séances. None of these things bring me any joy or satisfaction. On the contrary, these visions have only ever caused me pain, and I would much prefer to be rid of them.'

After stepping inside, Konrád was trying to shake the rainwater off his clothes when he saw Pálmi stand up, wave and motion for him to come and sit at his table. The two men had agreed to meet in a cafe in the city centre, and Konrád had hurried there through the downpour after his meeting with Eygló. It had surprised him when Pálmi had called earlier and asked to meet him to talk more about what they'd discussed the other day. Konrád hadn't known that Pálmi was interested in the case of Nanna's death. He'd visited the old man to ask him about his father's murder, but now Pálmi had said he really needed to see him about the girl who'd been found in the Pond.

They shook hands, and Pálmi said that he didn't often get the urge to make the trip from Suðurnes to Reykjavík, especially not in crappy weather like this.

'Did you speak to Nikulás's daughter?' he asked. 'Could she help you with the little girl?'

'A little.'

'And Arnór?'

'Yes, I spoke to him as well, and it was interesting. Nikulás was no angel. His daughter was actually quite open about it: he drank, was difficult at home, women accused him of sexual assault. His colleagues in the police department nicknamed him St Nikulás – did you know that?'

'Yes, but when you came to see me, I didn't want to get into that. I don't like to speak ill of people. I didn't know Nikulás very well, but enough to want to avoid him. He wasn't a good cop. Something wasn't quite right about him. Ever since, though, I've been thinking about that last investigation of his, about the girl, and something's really been bothering me. I ended up calling a friend of mine and asking her to go with me to the old coffin maker's workshop next to Fossvogur Cemetery, where the hospitals now store their records, to look through the old patient files and, more particularly, the old autopsy reports. She agreed to go after I told her about the girl who drowned. She found it quite exciting.'

'Don't you need special authorisation to consult those records?'

'She's a retired doctor and still has some clout, and she made up some excuse for needing to see her own file. In any case, she discovered that the girl's body was in fact autopsied, as you would imagine following such an accident. I would have been very surprised if it hadn't been done.'

Konráds mobile rang again, and he saw that it was Danní's grandmother, again, still trying to get hold of him. He declined the call and apologised to Pálmi for the disturbance. And silently cursed himself again for not answering.

'So I was saying that this friend of mine also went to the National Hospital in Fossvogur to consult the records archives. She told me that at the time of the accident, the autopsies were most often done by a doctor named Anton Heilman, a specialist in tuberculosis. He wasn't the only one to take on the task, but my friend thinks that Heilman could have been the one who autopsied the girl. She recognised his initials in one of the registers. She couldn't find the name of the doctor on duty that day anywhere, nor a record of who performed that particular autopsy, but she guesses it was Heilman.'

'She didn't find the autopsy report?'

'No, unfortunately,' replied Pálmi, 'not there in the archives. She found others dating from the second half of 1961. There were quite a few of them, most done for teaching purposes, in fact, and almost all by Heilman. Some on people who had died suddenly, heart attacks and that sort of thing. And to that operating room, little Nanna was sent. My friend found the morgue's register, a kind of logbook in which everything done there and in the autopsy room was recorded. The autopsy of a twelve-year-old girl is recorded in it. The child's name isn't given, but the date corresponds to that of Nanna's death. In addition, she's the only young girl to appear in the logbook at that time. The log makes reference to an autopsy report, which my friend couldn't find anywhere in the archives. Either it disappeared, was never placed in the corresponding folder, or was taken out, maybe for teaching purposes, and not put back. Sometimes old reports of that sort go missing. In any case, Nanna's is missing.'

'Did you know this doctor, Heilman?'

'No, as I said, my friend who helped me thought that he was a specialist in tuberculosis. It was before my friend started working at that hospital. He died around twenty years ago, and from what she understands, he was a well-liked and respected doctor.'

'So maybe she knew him or knew of him,' Konrád said. 'Nanna's mother. She worked in the hospital's kitchen and was probably familiar with the staff there. She may even have heard from him regarding her daughter's autopsy.'

'Yes, it's not unlikely, maybe, that they spoke to each other. Didn't you say the other day that Nanna's mother hadn't been entirely satisfied with the police findings? That she doubted it was an accident?'

'She went to the Psychical Research Society and asked for a recommendation for a medium. Those who spoke to her there got the feeling that she had some doubts.'

'And did she go and see a medium?'

'Yes, one named Ferdinand.'

'OK, but can you answer me this, then: is there any reason to think that the girl's drowning was anything other than accidental?' Pálmi asked gravely.

'No,' Konrád replied, after several moments of reflection. 'Actually, no. There's no evidence suggesting otherwise.'

*

It was still raining buckets when Konrád drove up to his house in Árbær and saw a woman whom he didn't recognise at first sheltering under the small awning over his front door. As he drew nearer, his eyes widened: it appeared to be Danní's grandmother. Drenched, bundled in a coat, she wore a plastic bonnet that did little to protect her blonde hair from the rain. He shut off the engine, hurried to her and invited her in, but she refused and started talking about the awful policewoman who had come to see her and her husband, that despicable, horrid woman who had behaved rudely and insinuated monstrous things.

'Won't you please come in out of the rain? I can't talk to you properly in the doorway,' said Konrád.

'I tried to call you. I wanted to know if you could talk to her. I'm so distraught about all of this. She said . . . said that Danní hated us. Can you believe that? To say such a thing? To say such a thing to us? As if we don't have feelings?'

'No, I . . . she must have her reasons, if she –'

'Her reasons? She has none! Lies told by junkies. That's all. Monstrous lies. Can you please talk to her? Why can't she leave us alone? Leave us to mourn our poor Danní? Can you talk to her and ask her to stop?'

Konrád didn't know how to respond.

'Why won't she leave us be? Why is she making these insinuations about us? Do you know what it is she's fishing for?'

'It's just part of the investigation, I should imagine. You shouldn't read anything special into it. These types of cases can be extremely difficult.'

'Who is she to judge us?'

'I really don't think she's ju—'

'Where is she heading with this investigation? Do you know?'

'All I know is that Marta is a very good policewoman,' Konrád replied. 'I'm certain that she wants to do her best to clarify the circumstances of Danní's death. You should try to be patient with her –'

'Patient?'

'Yes.'

'Could you talk to her? Or find out why she's doing this? We don't understand any of it.'

'No, it wouldn't be right. I think she would be furious if –'

'It wouldn't be right? Is it right for her to judge us? She said Danní blamed us for everything. And it was as if she believed that.'

'Please, won't you come in?'

'No, thank you. I thought you would be more helpful, but of course . . . of course you judge us as much as she does. I see that this was a mistake. I thought . . . no, goodbye.'

The woman turned on her heels and walked off through the pouring rain. Konrád watched her, wondering if she'd come by car or taken a cab. He saw her stop suddenly, and then she turned round and called out to him.

'We wanted only the best for Danní, you know,' she said. 'Always. Only the best.'

Then she tramped off through the rain, short-stepped and hunch-shouldered, the plastic bonnet over her hair.

36

He put the pot of porridge on the hob, then took a roll of liver-wurst from the fridge and cut a few slices from it. Once the porridge had thickened, he took the pot and sat down with it at the table, added a few of the liverwurst slices, then poured milk over it and stirred it in. He liked his porridge salty. He knew of people who wouldn't eat it without sugar and even cream, but the idea disgusted him. Porridge, to him, should be thick and salty, with milk in it, and best was if the liverwurst was cured, though he could only get it like that in winter, when delicacies for the mid-winter feasts were stocked in the food shops and supermarkets. He enjoyed the sour taste of those cured meats.

A burning smell wafted through the room, from the old splashes of porridge that he hadn't bothered to clean off the hob. He slurped his porridge and chewed on the liverwurst while listening to the midday news on the radio, an item about a man kept sedated in intensive care following a police pursuit of criminals that ended in an accident on Breiðholt Road. The two criminals taken into custody were suspected of involvement in drug smuggling. Eymundur listened distractedly. These sorts of stories appeared now and then in the news, but for him, they went in one ear and out the other.

He put his bowl in the sink and rinsed it with hot water, so that it would be ready for him at noon the next day. He did the same with the spoon. The room was windowless, like a large prison cell in size, with a sink and an electric hotplate with two rings. Out in the hallway were a toilet and shower, shared by the floor's tenants. There was also a shared kitchen, with a refrigerator, television and oven, but he usually just used the hotplate in his room. An old folding bed stood against the wall, with a table and chair at its foot, along with a little table for the hotplate. All provided by the landlord. He himself had no possessions there apart from his clothing and a few personal items that he kept in a box on the floor.

Four rooms on his floor were being rented by single men like him, who hardly ever interacted with each other. He had been there the longest, though tenants were constantly coming and going, with new faces appearing in the hallway and kitchen. Including some Poles who were looking for work. Even tourists, it appeared to him.

He never went out before noon, after he'd eaten and listened to the news on the radio. Then he would dress according to the weather and head eastward into town, in no big rush. In town, he would buy whatever food he needed, along with coffee and household products, limiting himself to what was strictly necessary, because he didn't have much to live on, especially since the rent for his room had risen so much. Sometimes he went down to the harbour to check what boats were unloading their cargoes and who was out and about at the pier. He'd worked at sea for many years and missed it.

That day, on returning to his building, he found a complete stranger sitting in the kitchen. The man was about his age, and asked him if his name was Eymundur. At first, he didn't answer, it being none of the man's business. 'Why are you asking?' he finally said, before admitting that his name was indeed Eymundur. The stranger said that he'd been told he was renting a room at this address and that he wanted to discuss a particular matter with him, if he didn't mind.

'And you, what's your name?' he asked.

'Konrád,' replied the stranger. 'I understand that you lived on Skólavörðuholt Hill around 1960. Is that right?'

'I don't see how that concerns you.'

'In one of the old barracks buildings up there,' said Konrád. 'You lived there with your father and his partner, who in fact owned the place, as far as I can tell. She had a daughter . . .'

'Yeah,' Eymundur replied, continuing down the hallway to his room. 'I've got nothing to say to you, and have other things to do.'

Konrád got up and stepped into the hallway.

'I wanted to ask you about your stepsister,' he called out after the man.

Eymundur didn't respond, but took out his key, opened the door to his room, went in and shut the door behind him. Standing there alone in the hallway, Konrád pondered his next move. Not wanting to give up so easily, he went and knocked on the man's door. When Eymundur didn't answer, Konrád gripped the door handle and found that the door was locked. He looked back down the hallway. Then he knocked heavily on the door and called out loudly that he only wanted to ask him a few questions about his stepsister and the accident at the Pond.

Konrád waited a moment, then gave up. He couldn't break into the room and force the man to talk to him. He had to be patient. He would come back later, and hope that Eymundur would be a bit more receptive to talking.

Focused on these things, Konrád was just about to leave the hallway when the door to another room opened, and a woman of around fifty asked what all the commotion was. Konrád apologised, saying that he hadn't meant to bother her.

'You came to see Eymundur?' she asked from behind her door.

'Yes, but it was nothing special,' Konrád replied, ready to go on his way and be done with this for now.

'What accident at the Pond?' asked the woman. 'What accident was that?'

'It was nothing,' Konrád said, surprised at the woman's nosiness. 'Nothing that concerns you.'

'What stepsister were you talking about?'

'Goodbye, ma'am,' he said.

'He's a creep,' whispered the woman. 'He's threatened me. Can't we get him thrown out of here?'

Just then, Konrád saw the door to Eymundur's room open, and the man stepped into the hallway and stared silently at them. The woman quickly shut her own door.

'What did you say to her?' asked Eymundur.

'Nothing at all,' replied Konrád.

'I don't want you talking about me to other people.'

'I'm not, not at all,' said Konrád. 'I would just like to speak to you for a few minutes, and then I'll be gone.'

'I have nothing to say to you. I just want you to get out of here and leave me alone.'

Eymundur was about to step back into his room, when Konrád drew nearer.

'Were you in Reykjavík when Nanna drowned?'

Eymundur hesitated. He looked at the woman's door.

'What are you talking about?'

'I'm talking about your stepsister.'

'My stepsister?'

'Yes.'

The man still hesitated, but then motioned for Konrád to follow him into his room.

'Why are you asking about her now?' said Eymundur, closing his door and pointing Konrád to the rickety chair.

'I was once a policeman,' Konrád said, sitting down. 'A friend of mine has asked me to look into that accident. I went through the police reports and saw your name –'

'What business of your friend's is it? And what friend?'

'My friend thinks she can help the girl find peace,' Konrád replied. 'She's a medium who sparked my curiosity about the accident. Having looked into it a bit, my curiosity has only grown deeper.'

Eymundur stared at him.

'What are you saying?'

'I would like to explore other possibilities regarding this case.'

'Other possibilities?'

'Yes.'

'You mean it wasn't an accident? When Nanna died?'

'I just wanted to ask you about that. If you've ever had any doubts about it.'

'No. None. Should I have done?'

'I think that the original investigation of the accident was neither careful nor detailed. It looks to me as if the police just immediately concluded that the girl had died accidentally, and left it at that. As I mentioned, the more I learn about it, the greater my curiosity. Did you have a good relationship with Nanna?'

'Good relationship? No, barely any relationship at all. There was a big age difference between us, and they weren't my family. I'd lost my mother, and Dad just moved in there – he had no other place to go . . . sorry, but I don't know why I'm telling you these things, to be honest.'

'And with your stepmother? Did you two get on well?'

'Yes. The little we saw of each other. She was always nice to me, but we were never close. I wasn't around much in those days.'

'It must have been awful for her to lose her daughter like that.'

'Of course.'

'Did she blame herself for what happened? For not having looked after her well enough? Or did she try to find someone else to blame? Do you remember? Do you remember her reaction?'

'I remember that she was devastated by the loss,' said Eymundur. 'As you can imagine. And it had an effect on her relationship with my father. He left her soon afterwards and I went with him, and didn't see that woman again. I went to work in the countryside and stayed for several years. Then I worked at sea.'

'What I mean is, did she question the conclusions of the police investigation?' said Konrád. 'Doubt whether it had been accidental?'

'I don't think so. Not that I was aware of.'

'Do you remember anyone there on the hill that the kids were afraid of? Said that they found scary or avoided?'

'Not really. There were all kinds of stories going around, as happens, but they weren't tied to that neighbourhood. Stories about creeps. Weirdos, as they were called. Those kinds of guys were everywhere.'

'Men that young girls should be particularly careful of?'

'You mean perverts of some sort?'

'For example.'

Eymundur shook his head.

'Do you know if Nanna's mother went to mediums for help following her daughter's death?'

'Mediums? No. I don't recall that, but if she had, she probably wouldn't have told me.'

'Among the people who visited your place, relatives or otherwise, was there anyone who had a trench coat? Or regularly wore a hat? Of course, I expect a lot of people dressed like that in those days. But a man wearing similar clothing was seen at the Pond around the time that Nanna drowned.'

Again, Eymundur shook his head.

'Or someone who had trouble walking, who limped or something like that?' Konrád went on, thinking of the poet's comments about the man he'd seen on Sóleyjargata Street.

'No, that doesn't ring a bell. I don't get any of this. I don't get any of these questions. Or your visit. What are you looking for? What does any of this have to do with you? It was an accident. We were told it was an accident. Are you suggesting something different, now, decades later?'

'No,' said Konrád. 'I have no reason to suggest that it was anything other than an accident, but still, when I began looking into the investigation, I found it somewhat slipshod or incomplete. I fully understand that it might be uncomfortable for you to recall these things, and I won't bother you again. Still, I would appreciate it if you would contact me if any details related to that incident come to mind. No matter what they might be. Anything at all. You can call me whenever you want.'

Konrád stood up and wrote his phone number on a newspaper before opening the door to the hallway, which was deserted. Eymundur, former occupant of an old Nissen hut on Skólavörðuholt Hill, stood there next to his electric hotplate speckled with traces of burned porridge.

'Have you threatened any of the others living here?' Konrád asked.

'Threatened? No. In what way?'

'I'd suggest you stop.'

'I've never threatened anyone. Was it that broad who said so? It's just a filthy lie.'

Konrád reiterated his advice to Eymundur to stop with his threats, and as he was closing the man's door, another question came to mind. He had almost forgotten the main question that he'd come there to ask.

'Do you remember a doll that Nanna had, and was found where she drowned?' he asked. 'Nanna's doll?'

'I remember a doll she played with. Terribly ragged old thing, but the only one she had. Her mother sometimes asked if she wasn't a little too big to be playing with it, but Nanna just ignored her.'

'Did you see Nanna play with it?'

'Yes, of course. The girl was a bit special, a bit simple, and kept all sorts of things in it. You could take off its head, and Nanna put this, that and the other in it. Sometimes something she'd drawn. She was really good at drawing, for her age, I think. Had a lot of talent. In any case, I saw her once fold up a little drawing and put it in the doll.'

'Do you know what happened to that doll?'

Eymundur shook his head.

'No, I don't know,' he said, 'but . . . I remember my father saying that he'd asked the kid to throw it out. Or, that's what I seem to recall. But I can't –'

'The kid?'

37

The words refused to materialise on paper, but that was nothing new. Sitting at his desk since noon with a few sheets of paper in front of him, Leifur had wrestled with the words well into the evening. The paper was old and thick, drank in the ink and had irregular edges. Leifur had bought it years ago, when he was still writing poetry. He remembered that it had cost him an arm and a leg and that he'd intended to use it only to make clean copies of his poems, but now, those sheets had no more value in his eyes than any other paper cluttering his desk, except that they carried faded memories of poems that had never made it onto paper and that he had once likened to children who never got the chance to grow and thrive.

He had paced the room and then gone out for a walk, which he'd cut short when it started to rain. He'd made himself a cup of coffee. He always drank it hot and freshly brewed. To him, coffee that was cold or reheated was undrinkable. He remembered one of his fellow poets, who had been vaunted by the cultural elite and who was, in his opinion, highly overrated – the man drank only cold coffee, finding it clever and priding himself on it, not to mention writing one of his worst poems on the very subject.

Leifur filled his pipe and lit it. He inhaled the smoke and blew it out through his nose, thinking about his struggle with the words. He found writing poetry hard. It had always cost him a great deal of effort, and during his studies at university, he'd even bought two handbooks on poetry in English. He never showed them to anyone, and felt ashamed of having them. Once again, he thought: I'm probably too demanding, which is handicapping me, unlike others who seem to be able to publish all sorts of rubbish and earn respect and admiration for it.

By late afternoon, he'd taken out a bottle and begun drinking, as he sometimes did when his heart was heavy. And at such times, he drank a lot. Tobacco smoke filled his study. He'd scribbled an observation or two, even two or three continuous lines of verse, when he found himself thinking again of the man who appeared on his doorstep after all these years and asked about the little girl, wanting to know what had become of her doll. If that wasn't enough to give him inspiration for a poem, he should probably just forget about writing altogether.

Again, he thought back to his visit to the former military barracks, as he'd done so often following the man's appearance. He recalled quite a few details after the man had gone and he'd let his mind wander back to hut number 9. Such as when he'd stood in the doorway, saying goodbye to the grieving mother, and a man walked up and pushed past him, asking rather brusquely what he was doing there, if he was collecting money for the storekeeper.

'This is the young man who found Nanna,' the woman answered wearily. 'He's no debt collector.'

'Oh?' said the man. 'Yeah, ugly business, that. All of it, bleedin' ugly. Have you seen the boy?' he asked, turning to the woman.

'Eymundur left early this morning,' she said listlessly.

'He didn't show up for work, the moron. I went to see him there and that's what those lads told me. The fucking slacker!'

'Don't talk about him like that.'

'What's that? I'll talk about him however I want.'

'I don't know what to do with this,' the woman sighed, the doll in hand. 'It was this wretched doll that she followed into the water. I don't want to see it any more,' she added, throwing the doll on the floor.

The man looked questioningly at the woman, before grabbing the doll from the floor and handing it to Leifur.

'Toss this out for us, mate,' he said.

Bewildered, Leifur took the doll. He didn't know what to think, but before he could say anything, the man had pushed him out the door and shut it behind him.

Leifur stood there awkwardly, holding the doll and looking around for a rubbish bin or skip, not daring to do anything other than what he'd been asked to do. A few metres away was an old petrol barrel that the neighbourhood's residents used for burning their rubbish. He went over to it, but instead of tossing the doll into it, he placed it gently on the cold ashes inside the barrel and then headed for home.

He hadn't gone far before doubts began plaguing him, and in his mind's eye, he saw the girl whom he'd fished out of the water, the doll floating under the bridge and the rest of that evening that had turned into a nightmare. That toy had been the girl's last companion. That doll. The last thing she held in her hands before death took her. Leifur stopped. His poetic sensitivity told him that there was something inappropriate about tossing the doll into a barrel like some common waste.

The bottle was almost empty. His pipe sat there in the ashtray, smoke ascending from it. Leifur looked up from the sheets of paper. He took what he'd written and read it over again, then winced, tore it up, and threw it into a wastepaper basket under the table. 'Rubbish,' he whispered. 'Nothing but rubbish. Goddamn fucking rubbish.' He took what was left of the empty sheets of thick paper and threw them into the wastepaper basket as well. In a locked desk drawer, he kept unpublished poems that he'd assembled into a collection. The drawer also held unfinished poems, observations, and lines that he'd never used. He looked around for the key to the drawer, which he found after fumbling around a bit, and emptied the drawer's contents into the wastepaper basket. Then he grabbed his lighter, determined to burn it all, but changed his mind, realising that it was probably dangerous to do so here, among all the study's books and papers.

So he carried the wastepaper basket into the living room and placed it in front of the fireplace, made from stylish stone. He was going to burn all these pages, and his old dream of becoming a writer along with them. To bid farewell to what had never become. A fire was soon burning briskly, and suddenly Leifur thought of his basement storage room, of what he had stored there, which was a permanent reminder of his broken dreams. Maybe he should never have kept it, because sometimes he felt as if all of his bad luck had started when he did. Started that evening, with that terrible event. Once, he'd saved it from destruction, and by doing so felt as if he were in a sad poem, but now he no longer saw any reason for keeping it. He descended the stairs, went into the storage room and moved a few boxes, reached for the top shelf and grabbed the doll, resolved to throw it into the flames along with all his poetic charlatanism.

He didn't really know why he hadn't told Konrád that the doll was in his storage room and had been with him all these years like an unwritten poem. Naturally, he didn't know the man at all, a former policeman, he had said, and who knows, maybe he'd started thinking that he had something to do with the girl's death. What did he know about how these people's minds worked? Besides, it wasn't any of that arsehole's business what he kept in his storage room, or where it came from. He didn't know him. Not at all.

38

Caught in a traffic jam on Miklabraut Road, Konrád regretted not taking another route to go and see the teacher. He couldn't see why the line of cars ahead of him had stopped, so he just sat there impatiently, thinking about his visit to Eymundur.

The man had made a surprisingly good impression on him, but Konrád may have shown him more respect than he deserved. He'd been careful to go gently on him, never mentioning in their conversation how he'd discovered that Eymundur had been given a prison sentence around two decades ago for an assault that resulted in its victim's permanent disability. He'd nearly killed the person, a woman he lived with and whom he'd accused of infidelity, which turned out to have had no basis in fact. It emerged during the trial that Eymundur had used the same pretext in the past to assault several of his former partners.

The woman on his floor said that he'd threatened her. Konrád had sensed that she was living in fear. Upon leaving Eymundur, he'd stopped briefly at her room to tell her not to hesitate to call the police if that man tried to intimidate her again. She said that she'd already done so twice, and was going to move out of there soon.

The traffic moved at a turtle's pace, and far in the distance, Konrád finally saw the flashing lights of police cars, suggesting to him that the traffic jam's cause was an accident. Hoping that it wasn't too serious, he edged forward a few metres. Eymundur had told him that the young man who found Nanna had been asked to throw the doll away.

'Do you mean Leifur?' Konrád had asked.

'I don't know what his name was. He was poking around there at the old barracks. She'd wanted to meet him, Nanna's mother. I don't know why.'

'And he was supposed to throw away the doll?'

'Yes.'

'You saw Nanna take off the doll's head to put things of hers in it? Drawings that she'd done?'

'Yes.'

'Did you see her do the same shortly before she died?'

'Yes.'

'Do you know what kind of drawings they were? Did you see them?'

'No, I only remember that she was really good at drawing, the girl. That, I remember.'

The fire was burning vigorously in the fireplace when Leifur came up from the basement, doll in hand. Sometimes, on dark winter nights, he would light a fire, then sit and watch the flames and listen to the crackling of the wood as it burned, alone with his thoughts. He kept firewood in a wooden crate by the fireplace, including branches that had broken off or he had sawn off trees in his garden – one of the only household tasks he did, either inside or outside the house. His ex-wife had seen to most of it, and said that he was a slacker when it came to actual work. Stupid biddy.

He began by tossing the sheets of paper he'd written on earlier that day into the fire. They were dry and crisp, and with a shower of sparks, the flames devoured them in an instant, reducing them to black flakes. He saw the words disintegrate into soot that wafted up the chimney. He took the collection of poems that no publisher wanted, tore the sheets out one by one and added them to the fire, thinking of his failed career as a poet and the little that he'd accomplished in his literary jaunt.

He'd opened a second bottle, from which he drank directly. He no longer grimaced while swallowing the strong liquor, but drank with increasing abandon, upset, angry, dismayed and full of self-contempt. The bottle fell from his hand and its contents splashed over his shirt and the hems of his trousers. He picked it up off the floor and set it down carefully, not wanting to waste what was left in it.

Eventually, all that remained was the doll, a reminder of unfulfilled dreams, the dreams of the girl in the Pond, the dreams of his own youth, when he had his whole life ahead of him. He hadn't taken the doll down from its shelf in the basement storage room since he and his wife moved into this house, decades ago. Before that, he'd kept it in the house he'd grown up in, having explained to his parents where it came from and telling them that he didn't want to throw it away just yet, out of respect for the little girl. His parents found it quaint, but they sympathised with their son, who had the soul of a poet. He had also told his wife the story of the girl and her doll, and she had been touched by his sensitivity.

He lifted the doll and looked one last time at its wispy hair, its mouth and chubby cheeks. The burning wood crackled and he thought that he should have got rid of this rubbish the moment he left the barracks, rather than lug it around all his life. Sunk in these thoughts, he heard a pop from the fireplace, and a few sparks flew out onto the floor. He didn't notice when one or two landed on his trouser leg – and the alcohol soaking it caught on fire.

Before Leifur could prevent it, both his trouser legs were aflame, and he sprang from the chair and threw the doll on the floor. Feeling the fire rush up his legs, he tried at first to put it out with his hands, but when he leaned forward, his shirt caught fire as well. He frantically ripped it off, tearing it apart as if he'd gone mad. He stomped his feet, trying to take his trousers off as he rushed towards the door. His shirt had landed at the foot of the living-room curtains, which, as dry and crisp as the paper in the fireplace, immediately caught fire. The next moment, the entire window was ablaze. From there, the fire spread throughout the living room and was quickly out of control.

After an interminable wait, Konrád finally passed the scene of the accident and the flashing police lights. It was a three-car crash that had caused the traffic jam on Miklabraut. He saw the drivers and their passengers talking in the rain. There seemed to be no serious injuries. As soon as he made it through the bottleneck, the traffic flowed smoothly again and he had just sped up to get to Leifur's as quickly as possible when his mobile rang. The number was very familiar to him.

'I know who she went to see,' Eygló said unceremoniously.

'Who?'

'Nanna's mother. She did consult a medium. At least once. You recall that Málfríður remembered her, and that she'd sent her to a medium named Ferdinand. After I spoke to her, she started digging around and discovered that Ferdinand wasn't a member of the Icelandic Psychical Research Society. For some reason, he hated the society. The man himself died many years ago, but his son said he would meet us. He still has his father's files.'

'Is he someone you knew?' asked Konrád. 'The medium, I mean?'

'Yes. In fact, he was an acquaintance of my father, and I remember him coming to our place –'

'What the hell!'

'What?'

'What in God's name is going on now?'

'What's wrong?'

'I'll call you later!'

Konrád hung up and called the National Emergency number, then pulled up to the terraced house and jumped out of his car. The living-room windows had shattered from the heat and flames leapt into the darkness of night. He didn't know if Leifur was trapped in the fire, but assumed he was. The front door was locked, and he drove his elbow through the ornamental glass next to it, reached inside and opened the door. As he entered the hallway, a wave of heat from the living room hit him, and he saw Leifur lying face down on the floor, shirtless and with the little that was left of his trousers, barely more than black shreds, down around his ankles. Leifur's legs were burned horribly, and he was unconscious as Konrád dragged him through the hall and out of the house, then laid him gently on the pavement in front of it. He was about to give him first aid, but realised that there was nothing he could do to help him. An unbearable smell of burning flesh filled his nostrils, and smoke rose from Leifur's mangled legs.

Konrád went back into the house, hoping he could salvage some valuables or do something to contain the flames. He admitted defeat as soon as he reached the living-room door. He was about to turn back when he saw an old, tattered doll lying on the floor a short distance from him, and, despite the heat being so intense that he could feel his hair singeing, he grabbed it and ran out.

As he emerged into the open air, fire trucks and an ambulance were pulling up to the house. Looking at the doll, the first thing he noticed was that, despite the heat and flames, which had consumed everything flammable in the living room, it was practically intact, as if protective hands had been held around it in the midst of the sea of fire.

39

His friend in Forensics wasn't exactly thrilled with his visit, and it took quite a bit of wrangling on Konrád's part to get the man to agree to help him – he'd had to explain all the ins and outs of the case to kindle the man's curiosity. The two men had worked together for years and knew each other well. Konrád was certain that if he could spark his interest, things would be much easier.

So he told the Forensics technician about the accident at the Pond in 1961, adding that he suspected the investigation of the case had been botched. A poor woman who lived in the old military barracks neighbourhood on Skólavörðuholt Hill had suffered a great tragedy, having lost her only daughter. He refrained from mentioning Eygló and her gifts of clairvoyance, knowing that the technician was more down to earth than that and would have laughed in his face. The man was a former hippie who had once been a great admirer of Mao and wanted to revolutionise the world. Nowadays, though, he drank nothing but cappuccino. He did, however, still have a bit of the revolutionary in him, and Konrád knew he took a strange pleasure in bending the rules and defying his superiors.

'And does this need to happen now?'

'I'm curious, but I don't want to make a big deal out of it. For the moment, I'd like to keep it just between us.'

'So this isn't an official investigation?' said his friend, after thinking it over for several moments.

'No,' Konrád admitted.

'You're not asking me to tamper with evidence, are you?'

'You can document it if you want. That way you'll have it on file if anything comes out of this.'

'Hold on now. What are you talking about?'

'I'm asking you to do me a favour.'

Konrád smiled sheepishly. They were alone in the Forensics lab, which was located in the Grafarholt suburb, on Vesturlandsvegur Road. He remembered the days when the department was on Borgartún Street, and was hardly more than one desk. Things were different now, and he regarded the ultra-modern facility with its state-of-the-art equipment. It was lunchtime, and they were the only ones there. The fire department had managed to control the fire at Leifur's house and prevent it from spreading to the neighbouring houses. Leifur had been transported unconscious to the hospital. He'd been badly burned and suffered smoke inhalation. Konrád had likely saved his life. If he'd been stuck a moment longer in traffic, he would have arrived too late to help.

The technician, whose name was Óliver, was dark-skinned and dark-haired. His grandfather was a Spaniard who had come to Iceland following the Spanish Civil War. Despite his cheerful, typically southern demeanour, Óliver struggled with an Icelandic melancholy during the dark days of winter, when he would head south sometimes, particularly as he grew older, to spend time with his relatives and allow the sun to warm him while it was coldest and darkest in Iceland.

Konrád handed a plastic bag to Óliver, who took from it the old doll that Konrád had found in the midst of the flames. Konrád was convinced that it was the doll he was looking for, Nanna's doll, but he hadn't examined it himself for fear of clumsily destroying evidence that could be useful. That was why he contacted Óliver and asked him to help. The technician put on latex gloves, removed the doll gently from the bag, laid it on one of the tables in the laboratory and pulled a bright lamp over it.

'What do you want to know about this doll?' Óliver asked.

'You should be able to remove the head,' Konrád said.

'Let's try it, then,' Óliver said, twisting the doll's head, with no result. 'Is there something inside it?' he asked, holding it up to the light as if to illuminate its interior. 'Maybe we should X-ray it?'

'I don't know,' Konrád said.

Óliver twisted the head again, but it wouldn't come off so easily. He tried pulling, twisting, and turning it, but nothing happened.

'I'd rather you didn't damage it,' Konrád said. 'I could just as well do that myself.'

'It's tough,' said Óliver, before placing his thumb under the doll's chin and pressing, as if opening a champagne bottle. The head popped off, fell to the floor and rolled under a chair.

'Hey, that's it!' Konrád said. He stepped over, picked up the head and placed it on the table.

Óliver held the doll's open body under the large magnifying glass attached to the lamp and peered inside as he slowly turned it.

'There's something in there,' he announced.

'What? What do you see?' Konrád asked.

'I see that I'm going to need some fairly long pliers,' Óliver replied, opening a drawer in the nearest table and rummaging through it until he found the right tool, before holding the doll under the lamp again.

'What is it?' asked Konrád.

'It looks to me like a little piece of paper stuck to the rubber where the belly sticks out.'

'Be careful not to tear it,' said Konrád.

Óliver stopped what he was doing and looked at Konrád, who gave him a sign that he wouldn't bother him again with completely useless remarks.

Óliver continued to grapple with the piece of paper for several moments, until it suddenly came free from the rubber and he was able to pull it out through the doll's neck and lay it on the table. It looked to Konrád like thin waxed paper.

'It looks like a folded note, which will probably be difficult to –'

'Is it a drawing?'

'– unfold without damaging it a bit. It could be a drawing; there's a scribble on it, visible through the paper.' He held the scrap up to the light. 'Hard to say what it is.'

He put the piece of paper back down on the table, and, with patience, managed to unfold and flatten it, revealing to them dull blue and yellow colours and a vague pencil squiggle that was indecipherable and useless.

'Is that all?' said Konrád, peering at the paper.

'Did you expect more?'

Konrád looked inside the doll, but saw nothing else. Clearly disappointed, he knocked it on the tabletop, shook it, and looked inside again, as if by some magic whatever he'd hoped to find there would appear, without him knowing exactly what it might be. The doll, however, was clearly not going to grant his wish.

'Was there anything else?' asked Óliver, secretly amused by his friend's frustration.

'Sorry,' said Konrád, 'I shouldn't have bothered you with this.'

He took the doll's head to reattach it to the body, but saw something inside it. He stared at it for a few moments, and then handed it to Óliver.

'What is that?' he asked.

Óliver took the head, peered through the magnifying glass into it, picked up his pliers, pushed them gently inside and detached a second piece of paper stuck to the rubber. Again, it was waxed paper, but in better shape than the first piece, and Óliver placed it on the table. Like the other one, it was folded, but he unfolded it easily, this time revealing a drawing of a girl. The two men leaned forward to get a better look at it. Although faded, the drawing was still relatively clear. It was skilfully done, and the girl's features could still be distinguished. Konrád immediately thought that the girl was crying. She wore a red dress and shoes with buckles. In the background was a vaguely outlined Nissen hut, or so it seemed to Konrád.

'Is this what you were looking for?' Óliver asked.

'Probably,' Konrád whispered, his eyes fixed on the girl in the picture.

'Is that the doll's owner?' Óliver asked.

'I was told that she was good at drawing.'

'So it's a self-portrait?'

'Very likely.'

'How old was she when she drew it?'

'I would say about twelve.'

'Can that be? Isn't she . . . look at her stomach,' said Óliver. 'It's as if she's . . . as if she's pregnant. Did she have a child at such a young age?'

'No,' Konrád replied, unable to take his eyes off the drawing. 'She didn't have a child.'

'What happened?'

'She died.'

40

Konrád's mother hurried past the windows of the Hressingarskáli cafe before opening the door, going in and joining her son, who was sitting in a corner, waiting for her. When she tried to give him a kiss, he turned away, considering himself too old for such things, not to mention how distant he'd grown from his mother over the years that had passed since she moved out with Beta. He knew that she'd arrived from the East a few days earlier and would soon be going back there. She'd sent him a letter telling him that she really wanted to see him, and had suggested this cafe. Konrád had never been to it before. He found the place too snooty, full of dilettantes who annoyed him and writers and journalists who sat chatting over coffee.

He hadn't told his father about meeting her, knowing he would object. His father never spoke of his ex-wife. A few times over the past months, Konrád had tried, especially if he'd had a drink, to talk about his mother, but had received only a tongue-lashing in return. Cheating bitch. That was the only reaction he got from his father.

She asked him how he was doing and he mumbled a few words under his breath, but otherwise remained silent for the most part while she tried to make conversation. It had been almost a year since they had seen each other, and he suddenly noticed that age was beginning to mark her face. Her wrinkles had deepened, her skin had lost its lustre and a few grey hairs had appeared on her head. One time, he'd asked her how she'd met his father, and she'd told him about a dance at a nightclub during the war. Some soldiers showed an interest in her but she wanted nothing to do with them, and was in a bit of an awkward position when Konrád's father fended them off in a gentlemanly way. He had come across as a confident man of the world. One thing led to another, as happens with young people, and she moved in with him and became pregnant with Konrád. They were married hastily. She never really knew what he did for a living, nor got to know him very deeply, his inner man, as she worded it. Sometimes they were visited by soldiers, with whom her husband did some wheeling and dealing. Sometimes sailors from cargo vessels, with whom he had other sorts of deals. He held séances at their home – yet another venture. Gradually, she realised that it was all the same to him how he made his money. He didn't care if anyone was hurt by his schemes. She tried to stay out of it, but doubts crept in about whether she'd made the right choice in marrying him. A suspicion that she'd been a bit too hasty in her decisions. Then Beta was born.

'Wouldn't you like to come live with me in the East Fjords?' she asked after a long pause, during which they just sat and listened to the cheerful chatter of the Hressingarskáli patrons.

'I prefer to live in Reykjavík,' Konráð replied, aware that he wasn't making this meeting of theirs easy for her at all. Nor did he know where his aversion to this place and this moment came from, or why he felt anger simmering inside of him. He'd drunk heavily with his mates the previous two nights and wasn't in the best form.

'Why don't you rent a room? You don't have to live with him,' she said. 'You're old enough to fend for yourself.'

'Maybe I will.'

'You shouldn't wait too long before –'

'Don't meddle in my business. I'll do what I want, when I want.'

'Of course. I didn't mean to be pushy.'

They sat silently for several moments.

'You seem so . . . is everything OK?' she finally asked.

'Yes, everything's fine,' he replied. 'And with you? Is everything OK with you?' he asked in return, haughtily and contemptuously.

'Konráð? What's wrong?'

'Nothing.'

'Yes, there is. Why are you angry? Are you angry at me?'

'I'm not angry.'

'What's wrong, Konráð?'

'I don't know what you two were thinking,' he said. 'Why you had me. Or Beta. It's complete bullshit. We're just accidents. Bad luck. We don't matter. What were you thinking?'

'That's not true, Konráð.'

'Then one day, you suddenly disappear. Poof, you just run away from the whole charade.'

'It wasn't like that, Konráð. I didn't just leave.'

'Yes, you did. What else would you call it?'

'I couldn't be with him any more.'

'Yes, that's right. You couldn't.'

'And there was a reason for it.'

'No doubt.'

'Listen to me, Konrád. There was a reason for it.'

Konrád stared into his coffee cup.

'I haven't been able to explain it to you before because children have trouble understanding such things. Your father never did anything to you and could even be good to you, and I know that you're close to him even though you can see his faults. But now may be the time for you to know the truth.'

'The truth? You mean you're going to start telling me lies about him.'

'No. I would never lie to you, Konrád.'

'He blames you for how it all went,' said Konrád.

'I know that.'

'He says that you betrayed him. Cheated on him. Says that you'll invent anything about him to hide those facts and that I shouldn't pay attention to anything you say.'

'It was for Beta's sake,' said his mother.

'Beta?'

'He hurt her.'

Looking up, Konrád saw that his mother was fighting back tears.

'What do you mean? How?'

'I had to get her away from him.'

'Why?'

'He hurt her as only men can hurt little girls.'

Upon returning home, Konrád stormed through the door and rushed at his father, attacking him without a word. Accustomed to fighting, his father didn't let the boy catch him off guard, but managed to wrestle him to the floor, where he held him and asked him what the hell he was doing and if he'd lost his mind.

'You fucking pervert!' Konrád shouted, crying with rage and cursing his father. 'Goddamn filthy scum! You fucking monster!'

41

Marta sat smoking at the window of her office, listening silently and earnestly to Konrád. He had come to see her immediately after leaving the Forensics lab, and started telling her the story of the girl from the former military camp who had been found drowned in the Pond in central Reykjavík in the early 1960s. The girl had lived with her mother in a dilapidated dwelling on Skólavörðuholt Hill, along with the mother's boyfriend and his son. A young junior-college student had discovered her body while crossing the Skothúsvegur Bridge. The police investigation had concluded that the girl's death was due to a terrible accident. The body had been autopsied, but the autopsy report could not be found. In her last moments, the girl had been holding her doll, which was found floating in the Pond. The doll had something of a peculiar history as well, and was still in the possession of the man who had found it. This man had been saved from a fire the day before, and was now in the hospital. Inside the doll, a drawing had been found, very likely by the girl it had belonged to – a kind of self-portrait. Judging by the drawing, it was as if she had seen herself as pregnant.

'How old was she?' Marta asked, putting out her cigarette.

'Twelve,' Konrád said, handing her a photocopy of the drawing found in the doll's head. He had asked Óliver to store the doll and the two drawings as if they were evidence in a criminal case. 'Biologically,' he added, 'it's not impossible.'

Marta took a good look at the image.

'What a strange way to draw herself,' she finally said.

'Yes.'

'How do you know this is the girl?'

'She was supposed to have been very good at drawing,' said Konrád, 'and there's no reason to think this isn't a self-portrait.'

'But not of her mother, for example, or a friend?' said Marta.

'Her mother had no other children.'

'So, what does this drawing tell you?'

'That the girl was abused. That she was sexually mature at a young age. That someone may have wanted to silence her.'

'The one who did that to her?'

'Possibly.'

'Did she show any signs of being pregnant when she was found? Or even before that?'

'There's no evidence for that. Probably not.'

'Did someone tell you that she was sexually abused?'

'No.'

'But you suppose that she knew what was happening in her body and drew a picture of it? Is that how you see it?'

'This would be an obvious conclusion, but there's another possibility. She may have been aware of one of the consequences of sexual abuse and drew an image of it.'

'Are you convinced that she was abused?'

'I think we have to try to determine that.'

'And you think that her body was autopsied, but the report can't be found?'

'Yes.'

'What do you want to do about it?'

'Go to the cemetery. Exhume her. Determine if she was pregnant.'

'When you have nothing to go on but this drawing?'

Konrád looked silently at Marta.

'Is this all you have?'

'I think it's more than enough. As far as I know, the girl has no relatives who could object. All I need is your consent to look into this.'

'Although the girl may have drawn herself in this way, it doesn't necessarily suggest that she was pregnant,' said Marta. 'We simply don't know. We don't even know if the picture is of her. That's just an idea of yours. Nothing says it's a self-portrait. Her body was autopsied, according to you, and even if the report has gone missing, the police would obviously have been made aware of the girl's condition if it had been as you think. But we have no evidence that suggests anything abnormal was found when her body was examined.'

'I think the investigation was botched,' said Konrád.

Marta shrugged, as if she needed something more concrete to go on than Konrád's speculations.

'So you're not going to do anything?'

'There's nothing I can do, Konrád, and you know that.'

'I thought you would understand this better than most people,' Konrád said, disappointed.

'I don't know where you got that idea,' Marta concluded.

He walked slowly down the cemetery path, looking at the headstones and crosses to both sides and all around him, many adorned with candles or flowers left by family and friends. Some of the decorations were recent, while others were older, not having been refreshed for a long time. A few sparsely maintained graves had none.

Konrád had gone onto the Association of Icelandic Cemeteries website, entered the girl's name and date of death, and was provided with the location of her grave. He was in no hurry. He had plenty of time, the sun gleamed on Fossvogur Bay, the air was rather warm and nothing disturbed the cemetery's tranquillity apart from the low murmur of traffic on Kringlumýrarbraut Road.

It wasn't long before he came to a grave marked only with a number, which he checked against the one he'd noted down. This grave had no cross and no headstone, no name or date of death, only the sparse, yellowed grass beneath which the girl slept.

Maybe Marta was right. Maybe he was wrong, and he was reading too much into the drawing. He really hoped that he was. He'd thought a lot about his mother recently, and as he stood there over the grave, he again recalled their meeting the day that his father was murdered, shortly after they'd clashed. Konrád immediately understood what his mother was implying about his sister, and that she was telling the truth. Seeing him turn pale with anger, his mother warned him not to do anything stupid, otherwise she would be sorry for having confided in him. Konrád also understood that he'd been unfairly resentful of her all those years. She took no pleasure in confessing those horrors to him once she felt herself compelled to do so. He knew, too, that she had done the only thing she could think of when it became clear to her what was going on: which was to get Beta out of that house and try to persuade Konrád to join them later. He was no less angry with himself for having accepted what the old man said when he berated his ex-wife and accused her of infidelity, allowing himself to become complicit to his evil, his hatred and contempt.

Staring down at the grass, Konrád remembered an old prayer his mother recited to her children every night, making the sign of the cross over their hearts to protect them during the night. He thought he'd forgotten the words when, suddenly, it came back to him from the depths of memory, and he recited it in his head. And even though Konrád wasn't a religious man, he did as his mother had done and made the sign of the cross over the grave.

It wasn't entirely devoid of ornamentation. Someone had recently placed a red rose on it, in memory of the young girl who had been found years ago alone and abandoned in the Pond.

42

From the cemetery, Konrád could see the National Hospital in Fossvogur, and he decided to drop by there and check on Leifur. Marta had informed him that the teacher had been admitted to the ICU, where his burns would be treated and he would remain over the few next days. Leifur had been very surprised to learn who it was that had pulled him out of the burning house, and said that he would very much like to see his rescuer. His arms and legs were badly burned, but it seemed that he was able to put out the flames on his trousers before smoke inhalation laid him out.

Konrád tried to banish the cynical thoughts he had of the advantages of this proximity to the hospital as he made the short drive. Instead, he focused on the twists of fate, how it had happened that two total strangers who had made their way into his life via two completely unrelated cases ended up in the same hospital, with equally serious injuries.

Although he'd been given strong painkillers, Leifur was

conscious. His arms and legs were wrapped in thick bandages, and an oxygen canister was placed next to his bed to aid his breathing. As there was no longer any reason to keep him in the ICU, which was sorely lacking in space, he had been moved to a three-bed ward.

'You're here! Thanks for looking in on me,' Leifur said in a slurred voice when he saw Konrád in the doorway. 'The police told me that it was you who pulled me out of the fire.'

'You seem to be doing much better than anyone expected,' said Konrád.

'Entirely thanks to you.'

'Sounds like you're in decent spirits.'

'More like doped up,' Leifur said, looking down at his bandages. 'I came that close to losing my life. Had you come to see me about something specific? When you rescued me from the fire?'

'Yes, about the doll. I heard that it had been given to you, back in the day.'

Leifur gave him an enquiring look, and Konrád told him about his visit to Eymundur.

'I don't know what came over me,' Leifur said, looking at Konrád like a repentant sinner. 'Of course, I should have told you about it. I haven't . . . haven't really been myself lately.'

'Everyone has his own demons.'

'Where's the doll?' Leifur asked. 'Burned to a crisp, I suppose. Is that right?'

'No, in fact. I'm trying to have it used as evidence in the case of the girl's death, but it's not going so well. It's in the hands of the police, who aren't really interested.'

'Evidence?'

Konrád told him what Eymundur had said about Nanna's

artistic abilities, and how at one point, he had seen her putting drawings that she'd done into the doll. Removing the doll's head had revealed two small pieces of paper that were currently being examined by the police. He didn't tell Leifur anything else despite the latter's intense curiosity, deflecting his questions by saying that the police were looking into this, and that it was too soon to say whether anything would come of it.

'OK, but why should the police . . . wasn't it an accident?'

'I've been doing a bit of digging around in this case and there's one thing that I'm curious about and wanted to ask you last night. Why did you keep the doll all these years? Why were you obsessed with it?'

'Obsessed? I don't know if I would call it that. It came into my hands for some strange reason, and I couldn't bring myself to throw it away.'

'Right, maybe I shouldn't be talking to you about this, considering your condition.'

'About what? Talking to me about what?'

'Why didn't you tell me about the doll?'

'I felt . . . felt that it was none of your business, to be honest. I didn't know you. It was a private matter.'

'But it's as if you have something to hide.'

'What, because I have a private life?'

'You're the only witness in the case. There was no one else on the scene. You were alone.'

'And the man in the trench coat?'

'You mentioned him. But you're the only one who saw him. Do you understand? We're pretty much forced to believe whatever you say about the incident.'

'What do you mean? That I had something to do with it? With

what happened to the girl? How? Do you think I made it all up? I didn't know her at all. I'd never seen her before.'

Leifur was quite agitated. He grimaced with pain as he tried to sit up in bed, glaring at Konrád.

'Where did you keep the doll?'

'In my basement. I hadn't touched it in ages.'

'Then why was it lying in the living room when I found you?'

Leifur hesitated.

'I'd taken it out.'

'Why?'

'I wanted to have a look at it,' Leifur replied.

'Is that why you lit a fire in the fireplace? Were you going to burn it? Was that it?'

Again, Leifur hesitated. He was clearly in no mood to discuss this, and had a hard time hiding the discomfort it was causing him.

'I was burning some papers,' he said. 'Old papers that I didn't want any more. I was . . . I wanted to get rid of various things that had been burdening me, things from the past, including the doll, yes. I was going to burn it. Are you happy now?'

'None of this makes me happy,' Konrád said. 'If that's what you think, you're mistaken.'

'I guess that's why I didn't tell you about the doll. I was afraid that you would make some kind of crazy accusation. Why had I kept it all this time? What weird obsession did I have?'

'I didn't mean to upset you. I'm just stating the facts. There aren't many witnesses in this case.'

'What about . . . that stepson?'

'What about him?'

'I just remembered something. He didn't show up at his

workplace the day after the girl died. Did you know that? His father was pissed off about it. He was going to go and meet him there, or something like that, but the guy had skipped work.'

'Eymundur?!'

'Yes, is that his name . . . ?'

43

Eygló was working in her garden at home in Fossvogur when Konrád went to see her after leaving the hospital. He didn't want to wait any longer before telling her about the fire, the drawing he found inside the doll and his suspicions about the girl's condition at the time of her death. The garden was small but well maintained, the lawn cut short and the trees neatly trimmed. Eygló grew heather and other autumn flowers which stretched towards the sun. Expecting no visitors, she was slightly startled when Konrád suddenly showed up. A glass table and garden chairs with soft cushions stood next to the wall of the house and she invited him to have a seat, then went inside and returned with two glasses and a carafe of water with slices of lemon in it. While filling their glasses, she remarked on the beautiful weather, adding that the forecast said that it was to continue.

'Well,' she said after they'd had a few sips of the water, 'now that we've made ourselves comfortable, you can tell me why you're so serious on this lovely day.'

'I found the doll,' Konrád said in a neutral tone.

Eygló looked at him obtusely, as if she'd never expected to hear those words.

'Leifur kept it all these years. He was going to throw it into his fireplace, but his clothing caught fire, and then his house.'

Suddenly, as if realising the implications of what Konrád had just said, Eygló sprang to her feet.

'I can't believe it!' she said, flabbergasted. 'Is this true? It . . . it still exists?'

Konrád nodded.

'But what . . . what did you say about Leifur? What . . . his clothing caught fire?'

'I've just come from visiting him at the hospital. He'll recover from his injuries – incredibly, considering the state he was in when I pulled him out of the fire.'

'What were you doing there?'

'I'd found out that he'd taken the doll all those years ago. But he didn't tell me that when I went to see him the other day. He felt that it wasn't any of my business, and he was of course perfectly right.'

'Aren't you happy? This is . . . this is great news. Are you sure it's the right doll?'

'Yes, unfortunately.'

'Why unfortunately? Where is it? Do you have it with you? Can I see it?'

'The police have it for now. Forensics. We found something in it that puts everything in a new light. A drawing that I think is a self-portrait of Nanna. It's in decent condition. Both Leifur and Eymundur said that the girl was good at drawing, which is clear from the picture. As strange as it may seem, it shows a girl who's pregnant. Who's with child.'

Eygló stared at Konrád.

'So she was abused?'

'It's hard to say. There are various possibilities. One of them is that she was sexually abused.'

'But she could also have been drawing someone else?'

'Yes.'

'Or imagining things, as kids do?'

'Yes.'

'Now I know why she wanted her doll,' Eygló went on. 'Why she was looking for it. This is the reason. The doll is important.'

'I tend to think it was a coincidence that –'

'Wasn't the man going to toss the doll on the fire?'

'Yes, but –'

'But set his own clothes on fire?'

'Yes, that's –'

'And the doll? Was it damaged?'

'No.'

Eygló looked at Konrád as if there was no need for any further discussion.

'The drawing is of her,' she said. 'Nanna was raped. When the consequences of the rape became clear, she was murdered. Drowned in the Pond. By the one who raped her, of course.'

'No such conjecture appears in the case files.'

'You yourself admit that the investigation was poorly done. We need to dig up her coffin. Find out if there's anything to this. Seriously. You can't just sit there and do nothing.'

'I've spoken with former colleagues of mine in the police. What we've found isn't enough to warrant an exhumation and examination of the remains, or to reopen the case. We have no tangible proof. None.'

He looked at Eygló and saw that she wanted to head immediately to the cemetery, tear up the turf, dig up the ground, pull up the coffin and bring the truth about Nanna to light. He was of the same mind, in fact, but also knew that Marta was right. What they had wasn't enough to justify such an action.

'I need to speak to Eymundur again,' he said. 'And see if he can answer my questions about sexual abuse. We need more evidence. We need to dig deeper.'

'Don't you think her mother would have known?' asked Eygló.

'Known what?'

'If Nanna was pregnant?'

'There's nothing about it in the records. But she may have known about the abuse and what condition her daughter was in, without it having had any connection to the accident. In any case, she didn't mention it to the police. Or to Leifur. Maybe she just wasn't a good mother. Maybe she was drinking. Maybe just indifferent.'

'Or just at a loss,' said Eygló. 'Things were different then.'

Konráð shrugged.

'I went to her grave,' admitted Eygló.

'Yes, I guessed that. Did you put the rose there?'

Eygló nodded. 'I spoke to the cemetery staff. No one has asked about that grave in all these years. No one has visited it, as far as they know. It's been lost and forgotten. Except by you and me. We've got to do something.'

'You mean exhume the body? Ourselves?'

'I doubt the girl would object,' Eygló said, as if she found the idea no worse than any other.

The porridge splashed out of the pot and burned on the hotplate, creating smoke that wafted out the door and into the hallway. Slices of liverwurst lay on the table, waiting to be added to the porridge.

The hallway was deserted, but the door of the woman who had been listening in during Konrád's visit was ajar. Konrád had advised her to call the police if the tenant at the end of the hallway threatened her again or gave her the slightest bit of trouble.

The stench of burned porridge carried down the hallway and into the woman's room, which was the same size as the one at the end, but whose window faced an untended back garden. Dirty curtains covered the window and the room was dark. It was furnished with a divan and a table, upon which were a few toiletries and a box of different types of microwaveable food. On the floor lay a grocery bag, from which several items had spilled. The room smelled faintly of cheap perfume.

From the woman's room came her muffled cries of pain as her attacker's steady blows pounded her face.

Then there was silence. A few moments later, Eymundur stepped out of the room, closed the door carefully and walked down the hallway to his room. He tossed back the lock of hair that had fallen over his forehead. With bloody hands, he lifted the pan off the hotplate, scraped what hadn't burned too much onto a plate, and sat down at the table and ate the porridge and liverwurst, resuming what he'd been doing as if nothing else had happened.

44

Marta was speaking with a doctor outside Lassi's room around dinnertime when she received news of a serious assault in the western part of town. A middle-aged woman had been attacked in a tenement close to Framnesvegur Street. More dead than alive, the woman had managed to crawl out of the room she rented, where the assault took place, and alerted another tenant. Her injuries were so severe that the assault could certainly be called attempted murder. One person was in police custody, a middle-aged man who lived down the hallway from the woman. She had been able to identify him. The man had a police record for violence against women, and had done time for it. His name was Eymundur. He was in his room when the police arrested him, and he was then taken and placed in a detention cell at the Hverfisgata Street station. He hadn't resisted arrest, and in fact had admitted attacking the woman.

'That fucking bastard!' Marta exclaimed.

'But he refuses to tell us what happened,' said the detective who'd called her.

'Well, fuck him!'

'He refuses to talk to us, but says he's willing to meet Konrád.'

'Konrád? Why?'

'He gave no explanation.'

'Why does he want to talk to Konrád?'

'No idea. He won't say.'

Marta went into Lassi's room and sat by the bed. The doctor had called her to let her know that he was probably regaining consciousness, and she'd rushed to the hospital and sat by his side for three-quarters of an hour, waiting for him to wake up. The doctor said that his condition was still worrying, but he'd opened his eyes that afternoon and seemed to be fairly cognisant when asked simple questions.

She waited a little longer and then called Konrád, who picked up after a few rings.

'Am I bothering you?' she asked.

'Actually, yes,' replied Konrád. 'I'm a bit busy at the moment.'

After promising not to be too long, Marta told him about Eymundur's arrest and asked how he knew him.

'He's connected with the case of the girl I told you about, and which you've decided to ignore,' said Konrád. 'He was her stepbrother.'

'Have you seen him recently?'

'Yes. What's going on? Why was he arrested?' Konrád asked, suddenly getting a very bad feeling.

'For assault and battery. He attacked a woman who rents a room in the same hallway as he does. He nearly killed her.'

There was a long silence on the line.

'Konrád?'

'That fucking scum.'

'What's going on between you and this Eymundur?'

'Fuck! I spoke to that lady, and told her to contact the police if Eymundur bothered her in any way.'

'She didn't have the chance. In any case, he wants to meet you, this man. Do you happen to know why?'

'He wants to meet me?' Konrád asked in surprise.

'He's down at headquarters, if you have time. I'd be curious to know what he has to say to you, even though I generally object to granting the requests of such people. They don't deserve any special treatment.'

'Why me?'

'I don't know.'

'Well, I actually have some more questions for him, so –'

'Fine, we'll set it up for tomorrow. I need to get going.'

Marta was quick to conclude their conversation when she saw Lassi fidgeting. His breathing changed slightly and, opening his eyes just a touch, he saw her at his bedside. She put away her phone and introduced herself, saying that she was a police detective in charge of investigating his case, his kidnapping and the battery to which he'd been subjected, and then asked if he felt up to answering a few questions.

'Da . . . nn . . . í?' Lassi whispered.

Marta hesitated.

'Danní . . . ?' Lassi whispered again.

'She's dead,' Marta said gently. 'I'm sorry.'

Lassi closed his eyes and grimaced with pain.

'Ho . . . oww?'

'She was at your place. Overdosed. That's the most likely explanation. Suicide. Either intentional, or due to clumsiness.'

Lassi shook his head. Fearing that he was slipping into sleep again, she remembered something that Biddi had told her during his interrogation.

'Was she going to post things about Randver on the internet?' she asked.

Lassi didn't answer.

'Is that what made him go berserk? Could she have threatened anyone else with the same? Someone who then went to your room and left her there for dead?'

The young man appeared to have lost consciousness again.

'Someone from the drugs world, who she was going to expose?' Marta continued, hoping that he could still hear her. 'Someone bigger than Randver?'

'Not . . . Ran . . .' Lassi whispered. 'Grand . . . the grand-mother . . .'

'Yes?'

'. . . knew . . .'

'The grandmother? Danní's grandmother? She knew? What did she know?'

Marta's questions rained down in vain, as Lassi no longer heard them. He had fallen back into a deep sleep, gone to a place where there was no pain and no answers, and where bereavement could wait.

45

Following his conversation with Marta, Konrád switched off his phone and went back to the office where Eygló sat chatting with the man who had invited them to meet him at his place of work, adding that he would be there until late that evening. Eygló was convinced that it was an excuse, and that for some reason he didn't want them to come to his home. Konrád said that he didn't see why that should be, and took the liberty of pointing out her constant suspicion of others.

The office was cluttered with papers, invoices and old purchase orders, all jumbled together and overflowing from bookshelves. The man, named Theodór, ran a small publishing company in a former industrial building in the Skeifan area. He introduced himself as a genealogist, was around fifty and rather chubby, and had a white goatee that he stroked mechanically whenever he had meaningful things to say.

Eygló had contacted him and got Konrád to meet her in

Skeifan. The latter, having dropped by his house after their conversation in Fossvogur, was a bit late, and Eygló introduced him as an ex-detective. Theodór tried to act impassive, but Konrád noticed the man's slight hesitation – which was usual whenever someone discovered his former profession. Everyone had something to hide.

Theodór told them about his father, who had been a member of the Icelandic Psychical Research Society but hadn't made the advances that he'd hoped to do, become frustrated and quit. He'd been a practising medium for a number of years, most active during the 1960s and 70s. After that, his interest in the supernatural largely dwindled, and then he died in the year 2000. From an early age, he'd kept a diary, though a large number of the notebooks had suffered water damage after his death, when the basement where they were kept flooded. Theodór had thrown most of them away, but kept the ones that the disaster had more or less spared in his office, he explained to Eygló and Konrád as he got up and went into a small storage room at the back of the office, in which there were filing cabinets, cardboard boxes and more bookshelves. Konrád thought he saw biographical dictionaries of people from Skagafjörður and other books of that sort.

'This is why I asked you to meet me here,' he explained from inside the storage room. 'I brought the diaries here.'

Konrád looked at Eygló as if to indicate that she had had no reason to mistrust the man. She showed no sign of changing her opinion.

'That said, I haven't had any time to read them all properly,' continued the genealogist, lugging two cardboard boxes out with him. 'Maybe you can find something in these. I've sometimes thought that I should write a book based on these diaries, or even publish some of them. They're full of ghost stories. He knew Engilbert, your father,' he said. 'I remember him talking about Berti sometimes. Especially about what happened to him. Wasn't it an accident?'

'Yes,' said Eygló. Sometimes it surprised her how many people remembered her father. 'It was an accident.'

'It was a pretty simple scam, on their part,' said Theodór, 'and not really unique. People can be so gullible. Apparently, Engilbert became very popular very quickly during the war. His partner ensured that,' he said. 'He knew the people who participated in the séances and gathered information on them in various ways. A lot of it was simple genealogy. Apparently, he paid a genealogist to look up the name of a deceased grandfather or grandmother. A deceased wife, a brother who died in an accident, a mother who died after a long, painful illness. That's how he got the right names, the right connections, the right events.'

'I see,' Konrád said.

'Look at this,' Theodór continued. 'Many of these entries are from the 1960s. I understand that's the period you're interested in. Unfortunately, I can't lend them to you, even though we should be able to trust the police,' he added with a smile, revealing his sturdy-looking teeth behind his beard. 'These are my father's personal archives, which I may use later, and I don't want them falling into just anyone's hands. But you're welcome to look through them here in my office.'

Konrád thanked Theodór for his cooperation and reiterated that he was no longer a detective, before asking him if he'd inherited any of his father's clairvoyant abilities. The man stroked his beard and shook his head, saying that, to be completely honest, he didn't really put much stock in psychic abilities. Despite his father having been a medium. He looked at Eygló as he said this, but she was impassive. Then he turned back to Konrád and added that he didn't remember his father speaking of any particular cases of his that were any more unusual than others. Theodór had viewed it all as little more than humbug, and had never understood why his father had fallen out with the Icelandic Psychical Research Society.

'However, I do remember him sometimes speaking of the woman who came to see him because of her daughter, the one Eygló told me about on the phone. My father was a sensitive man and she was memorable to him because she'd lost her daughter, her only child, in that terrible way and was looking for answers. My father remembered the accident at the Pond, but didn't know anything more about it, and I don't know if he helped her in any way or did anything to make her life more bearable.'

Immersed in the diaries, Eygló had heard nothing the two men said. She'd taken out a few of them, dating from 1961 to 1965, each volume apparently covering a quarter of a year. They were thick notebooks of ruled paper, each entry headed with the date. The handwriting was very clear and elegant.

Eygló continued browsing the diary entries. Knowing roughly what she was looking for, she scanned the pages quickly: descriptions of the weather, notes on the news, short reports of daily activities and accounts of séances that the diary's author had either held at his home or attended elsewhere. Sometimes an entry was only two concisely worded lines on the weather, presumably because nothing else notable had occurred. Other days were more substantial, with their entries occupying an entire page, but seldom much more than that.

She was rather startled when, in one notebook, she suddenly came across her father's name.

. . . when Engilbert came to see me, drunk as usual, and we discussed the Society and its treatment of me. I think he came mainly to sponge liquor off me, agreeing with everything I said and then asking if I had any. What a terrible sot he's become . . .

Eygló continued to flip through the pages, one after another, pausing briefly if something of interest caught her eye. In that way, she got through several volumes. As she was browsing through one, covering the first quarter of 1963, one entry in particular caught her attention.

This evening, a young woman from Keflavík came to me and asked if I could hold a séance for her. Málfríður had mentioned her to me once, saying that she'd been struck by tragic misfortune and had come to the Society for help. So now here she was, poorly dressed, and hungry-looking with sunken cheeks. I immediately invited her in and gave her something to eat and strong coffee to drink. She was very forthcoming, telling me that she'd lived in the old barracks on Skólavörðuholt Hill, that she'd lost her daughter in the Pond and was afraid that she hadn't looked after her well enough. I admitted that I'd heard of her and was aware of the accident and . . .

Eygló turned the page, but the rest of the entry was illegible due to the water damage. She tried to decipher it, but the ink had run. She thought she could make out a word or sentence or two, but nothing that was useful. Eygló grabbed the next volume and ran quickly over its first few pages, but didn't see anything about the woman from Keflavík or the private séance. She continued to leaf through it, finding nothing of interest except for a sentence about her father that the diary writer had added following a short description of the weather.

Awful, what happened to dear Bert. RIP.

'I can't find anything about the séance,' she said to Theodór, who was explaining all the secrets of genealogy to Konrád.

'No, much of what's in the diaries was ruined, unfortunately,' he replied.

'Do you know how the séance went?'

'According to my father, it went quite well. That doesn't mean the girl made an appearance. That's not how it was, but he had the impression the woman left feeling a bit calmer. Too bad you can't ask Engilbert,' Theodór said, shaking his head as if to say he couldn't help her any further.

'What do you mean? My father?'

'Apparently, he was there. By complete coincidence.'

'Engilbert?'

'Yes, and that partner of his. They stopped by that night. My father was a good friend of Engilbert's and liked him very much.'

'And they met that woman? Did they take part in the séance?'

'Engilbert was at the séance, my father told me. I don't know if the other man was, too.'

'Who was that?' Konrád suddenly asked.

'Who?'

'What partner of his was it?' Konrád said. Until now, he'd kept out of the conversation. 'Who was it that accompanied Engilbert?'

'My father found it remarkable, and brought it up quite often,' said Theodór, 'because both of those men passed into the great beyond shortly afterwards. First, one of them was stabbed, and

then the other drowned. I mean Engilbert,' he said, looking apologetically at Eygló as if he'd been tactless.

'Stabbed?' said Konrád.

'In front of the slaughterhouse on Skúlagata Street,' replied
Theodór. 'Stabbed – fatally. Murdered.'

46

As she parked in front of the house, Marta recalled the first time that she'd come there to inform the occupants of the death of the girl who had gone astray in life. She remembered the grand-mother's expression when she told her the news – how the spark of hope was extinguished when she learned what had happened to her granddaughter, how a veil of sadness settled over her face and her eyes became dull and lifeless. Marta had felt so sorry for her and tried to do her best to lessen the shock, but knew that it was useless. Such visits are never forgotten.

And she may not forget this one either, Marta said to herself before ringing the doorbell and waiting. When no one answered, she rang it a second time and finally saw movement, a dark shadow pass behind tinted windowpanes. A moment later, the woman opened the door, and Marta could see that she'd been napping and wasn't fully awake.

'I'm sorry for disturbing you so late,' Marta said, looking at her watch. It was going on eight o'clock.

'Oh, that's all right,' the woman replied, inviting Marta in. 'What time is it?'

Marta told her and apologised again for disturbing her, before saying that she'd made note of a few things concerning Danní that she wanted to ask her about. In return, the woman asked when she and her husband could begin making arrangements for Danní's funeral, to which Marta replied that she wasn't able to answer that yet. The examination of the body would be finished sometime over the next few days, she thought.

The woman led her into the living room. To Marta, she appeared to have aged several years since her first visit, and somehow grown smaller, shrunk: her shoulders were drooping and she'd lost her former dignified bearing. She was downcast and uncaring of her appearance, unkempt, her hair unbrushed, as if she no longer deserved the place she previously occupied in life.

Marta felt as if the woman would have preferred to go back to sleep, having finally managed to catch a wink, thanks perhaps to sedatives that she'd been prescribed.

'I've got nothing to offer you,' the woman said quietly and apologetically. 'I wasn't expecting you, so . . .'

'Don't worry about it. Is your husband at home?'

'No, he's gone out. He doesn't feel well. Goes for long drives. Neither of us feels well. Of course we don't feel well.'

'No, of course not,' Marta agreed, wanting to ease into her questions. 'I've been thinking about Fanney's comments about your granddaughter. In my opinion, we should take into account what she says, and no matter how you interpret her remarks, it seems to me that there are two things we need to address. Why did she say that Danní hated you, and why did Danní blame you for what happened to her?'

'I don't know this Fanney and don't know why she told you those things. Danní was fine here with us.'

'Your granddaughter's case is no exception,' Marta said. 'Unfortunately, we deal with many young people like her, though, luckily, they don't all end up dying prematurely. Girls lose their footing in life. Boys too, of course. One of the things these kids often have in common is that they have quite a few difficulties in their lives.'

'Why are you telling me this? Here with us, Danní wanted for nothing.'

'Some of these kids come from very good homes. Others from very bad ones. Some become addicted to alcohol and drugs and soon find themselves in trouble. Others use these substances a bit like an anaesthetic. To forget reality, even if only momentarily. It's usually those ones who've had difficult pasts.'

'Yes, I don't know why you're telling me this. Maybe we'd better wait for my husband. He can tell you, as I do, that Danní wanted for nothing under our roof.'

'For many of these young people, something sets off a process they can't easily tear themselves free from. Their parents' divorce. Bullying. A death in the family. Hanging out with the wrong crowd.'

The woman said nothing.

'Danní lost her mother, of course?' said Marta.

The woman shook her head. 'I think we should wait for my husband,' she said.

'She was too young to remember when it happened, wasn't she?'

'Yes, but naturally she always knew about her mother, and . . . and how important she had been in our lives. We did everything we could to keep her memory alive.'

'Was she bullied? At school, or . . . ?'

'No, nothing like that. Danní was always happy in school. But as she grew older, she drifted away from her classmates and started spending time with people we didn't know. She never invited them home. Like this Fanney. None of those people.'

'I see,' Marta said, feeling that it was time for her to get to the heart of the matter. 'It has been suggested by her friend – Lassi – that she was aware of certain things and was going to post what she knew on the internet, or something like that. Do you understand what I mean?'

The woman shook her head, and Marta repeated what she'd just told her.

'We thought, and we still think, that she was going to expose the people behind the drug-smuggling operation she was involved in. The ones who sent her overseas and used her as a mule.'

The woman gave her a blank stare.

'When I asked Lassi about this, lying there in the hospital in Fossvogur, he hinted that what Danní knew had nothing to do with the drug scene, but something else. Do you have any idea what it might be?'

'No,' the woman replied hesitantly, as if she still didn't understand what Marta was talking about.

'Lassi said that you knew what it was.'

'What what was?'

'The secret that Danní was going to post on the internet.'

'I don't know what you mean,' the woman said. 'I don't know what it could be.'

'If something comes to mind, would you mind contacting me? You have my number.'

'Of course.'

Marta gave her an encouraging smile, got up, said goodbye and went to the door. She'd communicated to the woman what she had intended to, and would follow up on it later.

'Miss,' Marta heard from behind her, as if the woman were calling for a waitress at a fine restaurant.

Marta turned round.

'I just wanted to tell you how Danní . . . how Danní was always a lovely and cheerful girl, how she could be such a pleasant child. So smart, imaginative and . . . she was a dream child. Just like her mother. She was our jewel and always will be. She was our dream child and I wish I could have done more for her before . . . before it was too late.'

Marta nodded and walked out the door. She suspected that her visit hadn't been for nothing.

After the detective was gone, the woman sat silently by her phone for a long time, before dialling a number and waiting as one ring after another sounded in her ear.

'The police have been here again with new information,' she said agitatedly and hurriedly, as soon as someone picked up at the other end. 'Now they think that Danní was going to post something on the internet. Did you know about that?'

The voice on the phone told her to stay calm and say exactly what she meant.

'That friend of hers. Lassi. He knows. She told him. He's regaining consciousness, and soon he'll tell the police everything he knows. You can be certain of it. And what we know. What I know.'

'I'm going to hang up now,' the voice said. 'We'll discuss it later, after you've calmed down.'

'But that's what he's talking about . . . how it all was, how it all happened. Isn't that what Danní was going to post on the internet?'

Again, the voice on the phone told her to calm down; everything would be fine.

'Did you know? Did you know she was going to do that?'

She received no reply.

'Tell me you didn't know anything about it. Tell me!'

The voice on the other end suddenly became loud, angry.

'Don't threaten me like that,' said the woman. 'Stop . . . stop it . . . stop it . . . for God's sake, stop it, stop . . .' she cried into her phone, before violently slamming it down.

47

At police headquarters on Hverfisgata Street, Eymundur was escorted from his cell to the interrogation room. As he was calm and collected, it was deemed unnecessary to handcuff him. He smelled quite strongly, having neither washed nor changed his clothes for several days. He was wearing worn jeans, an Aran jumper and a grimy overcoat. When the police arrested him, he put on a knitted cap, which he stuck in his overcoat pocket on his way to questioning. All night, he'd sat in his cell whistling an Elvis Presley song, which, to the guard, sounded like 'Heartbreak Hotel'.

Konrád was waiting for the detainee in the interrogation room. Although opposed to people such as Eymundur being given preferential treatment by the police and having their requests granted, Konrád had agreed to sit down with him because he needed more information about Nanna, and thought that Eymundur was one of the few people who could provide it.

Konrád noticed stains that he assumed were traces of blood on the sleeve of Eymundur's jumper sticking out from his overcoat. Marta had told him that it would take the woman a long time to recover. Eymundur had hit her mainly in the face, to cause as much damage as possible. He'd broken her jaw and her cheekbone, and she had a haemorrhage in her right eye and was at risk of losing sight in it. She'd suffered a concussion and lost four teeth, two of which were found up her attacker's sleeve.

'Do you feel any better?' Konráð asked as soon as Eymundur had sat down.

The guard remained outside in the corridor. Konráð regretted not having given the woman a clearer warning about Eymundur or trying to prevent the attack, although it was hard to see how he could have done so. He wasn't worried about sitting there alone in this room with the man. Experience had taught him that men who attack women are generally cowards.

'Better?' said Eymundur.

'I mean, now that you've attacked a defenceless woman and nearly killed her. You must be feeling better. Must be almost . . . satisfied.'

'Think what you want.'

'What in the hell did she do to you?'

'She gets on my nerves,' said Eymundur.

'Oh? Who doesn't?'

'She shouldn't poke her nose into things that don't concern her.'

'What might that have been? Her only mistake was renting a room under the same roof as an idiot like you.'

'You don't know her.'

'Neither do you, for that matter. Why did you want to talk to me?'

'Why were you asking me about the girl?'

'We've already gone over that. What do you want from me? Why didn't you go to work the day after Nanna died?'

Eymundur wasn't prepared for this question.

'What do you mean?'

'You skipped work that day! Why? What prompted you not to go to work the day after the girl died?'

'Who told you that?'

'Your father mentioned it. He went to see you there, but you hadn't shown up. Why not? Where were you?'

'My father?'

'What sort of relationship did you have with the girl?'

'We didn't have any. I hardly knew her. I don't remember skipping work.'

'No, of course not. Did you mess with her? Is that it? Did you rape her and then drown her in the Pond?'

'Rape? What are you talking about? Wasn't her death an accident? Why are you asking me if I raped her? What really happened to her?'

'Are you sure you don't already know that?'

'Do you think I killed her?'

'Have you changed at all? Aren't you still doing exactly the same thing? Abusing women? Abusing those you can easily handle? Abusing those weaker than you? Why did you ask to meet me?'

Eymundur sat there silently, thinking over Konrád's remarks.

'I remember a man who came to our place once or twice,' he finally said. 'Maybe more often. I tried to be there as little as possible. It was someone my stepmother met at the hospital. She worked at the National Hospital.'

'I know that. And?'

'He'd had tuberculosis. That man. I remember my stepmother saying that he'd stayed at the Vífilsstaðir sanatorium. Because of his tuberculosis. I don't know if he worked at the National Hospital or if my stepmother just met him there because he'd come there for help.'

'Help?'

'He had TB in one of his legs.'

'And?'

'He . . .'

Konrád suddenly understood what Eymundur's words implied.

'Did he walk with a limp?'

'I thought you might want to know about him, since you told me that a man had been seen at the Pond the day the girl died, and that he'd had a limp.'

'Do you know who it was? What his name was?'

'No.'

'Why are you telling me this now?'

'Do you want to know it or not?'

'I think you're –'

'I don't care what you think of me. I didn't do anything to the girl. I started going over this after your visit. I saw that man later. That limping bastard who came to our place on Skólavörðuholt Hill.'

Konrád motioned for him to continue.

'I drank a lot in those years, so my memories aren't very clear, and I never would have thought of this if you hadn't started talking about a man with a limp. I was with some mates of mine down on Austurvöllur Square when he came by, and after he was gone, one of the lads said that he was a fucking bastard and knew of some girls he'd messed with. Kids. Said that he was a fucking child molester.'

'And you don't know his name?'

'No.'

'Was he an older man? Younger?'

'He's probably dead, if that's what you're thinking. A fucking scumbag, and he limped away like a miserable wretch.'

'Did they say anything more about him, your mates?'

'Probably. But that's all I remember.'

'What was he doing at your place?'

'I don't know. I didn't care.'

'If Nanna had been abused, don't you think her mother would have noticed it? Did she know about it? Did she just let it happen, maybe?'

'I don't know. She was more or less a wretch herself. A drunk, did I mention that? Still, she managed to keep her job at the hospital.'

Eymundur leaned forward in his chair.

'I want you to talk to them,' he said, nodding towards the door. 'Tell them that I've helped you. Done you a favour.'

Konráð shook his head, making it clear that that was out of the question.

'Haven't I done you a favour?' said Eymundur.

'You haven't done me any favour,' said Konráð.

'Isn't that the man you're looking for? Didn't you say that the girl had been raped? Wasn't he seen by the Pond?'

'Aren't you just diverting attention away from yourself, and trying to get something out of it at the same time?'

'You don't believe me?'

'In my eyes you're nothing but an imbecile, Eymundur,' Konráð replied, shaking his head. 'And will never be anything else. A daft imbecile.'

Eymundur smiled coldly, as if nothing that Konráð said could ever touch him. He was missing two bottom teeth, and when he spoke, the air hissed a bit through the gap.

'Same thing my dad always said. As far back as I can remember.'

48

Konrád watched as Eymundur was escorted out of the interrogation room and back to his cell. He had asked the thug question after question about the man who limped due to tuberculosis in his leg, his relationship with Nanna's mother and his visits to the former barracks on the hill, but either Eymundur knew nothing more or he was withholding information, intending to use it as a kind of bargaining chip for more lenient treatment following his assault on the woman in his tenement. Little of note was gained from what he said, apart from the man's connection with the old TB sanatorium at Vífilsstaðir.

Before a specialised unit dealing with sex crimes was created within the police force, Konrád had occasionally investigated such offences, but couldn't recall any offenders matching the description provided by Eymundur. It would take forever to compare the sanatorium's medical records with the police reports on cases of sexual abuse, if any of the man's victims had actually filed a complaint. In fact, Konrád didn't expect that Marta would agree to a request for a court order granting access to the medical records, besides the fact that she didn't have the personnel for such a comparison to be done, particularly in connection with a long-forgotten case with which Konrád, and only Konrád, was obsessed. At the very least, she would need something more substantial in order to justify such an operation.

If this all wasn't just a heap of lies on Eymundur's part. Konrád had no reason to believe a single word of what Eymundur had said, apart from the fact that he'd pointed out to him where the doll was to be found.

As he stood there in the police station's detention wing, pondering his next steps, his mobile rang. It was Eygló. She asked if he could meet her, and he promised to stop by her place before going home.

'It's OK if you come late,' she added. 'So it turns out they were in cahoots again, after all.'

'Looks like it,' Konrád replied, aware that she was talking about their fathers.

'And they met Nanna's mother.'

'Yes, when she was at her most vulnerable,' said Konrád.

'Are you suggesting they took advantage of it?'

'They wouldn't have hesitated to do so when they were working together during the war,' Konrád said.

'No, probably not,' agreed Eygló, reminding him to stop by to see her on his way home.

He knew that she needed to talk about what they'd discovered, the fact that, at a certain point, their fathers had crossed paths with Nanna's mother.

Konrád put his phone back in his pocket and paced the floor of the corridor, thinking over his conversation with Eymundur. No matter how often he pondered the different possibilities, he always returned to the same disagreeable conclusion. He tried to come up with alternatives, but found none. He went back to his car, got behind the wheel and headed for the westside of town. He'd long known the address of the man he was going to see and assumed that he hadn't moved since the last time he'd dealt with him, in the late 1980s. Konrád didn't know if he'd had any scrapes with the law since then.

The man had inherited his house from his parents, a run-down wooden one clad in dilapidated corrugated iron. It had small windows, and its door was painted black. The walls were sprayed with graffiti that Konrád couldn't decipher, and it looked to him as if they'd been painted to cover older tags. In the end, the owner had probably given up fighting against these acts of vandalism.

There was no nameplate at the door, and when Konrád pushed the doorbell, it didn't ring inside the house. So he knocked, softly at first and then a little harder, without anyone responding. He walked back out onto the street, saw a gleam of light from inside, went to the back of the house and saw a lamp in one of the windows. He picked up a pebble and threw it at the window, but nothing happened. He did it again and saw a shadow cross the light. A face appeared in the window and looked out, sullen and pallid. Konrád stood there as the man stared at him for a few moments before disappearing again from the window. Konrád assumed that the man had recognised him.

He returned to the front of the house and noticed that the door was ajar. He waited a few moments, then pushed the door open and stepped inside.

'Shut it behind you,' he was instructed from within the house.

Konrád complied and waited for his eyes to adjust to the

darkness. He'd come to this house once before, to arrest this man and bring him, handcuffed, down to the Hverfisgata Street station. That time, he was charged with having sexually assaulted two boys in the town of Selfoss. Such cases had long been treated quite negligently, and habitually suppressed. Because of that, the man had managed to continue working with children and adolescents, without anyone ever intervening. Sentences for sexual offenders were minimal, and those charged weren't supervised.

'I heard you'd retired from the force.'

The shrill, weak voice came from somewhere beyond the living room, and Konrád saw the man's silhouette in the dim light from the bedroom. He was standing next to a tall, glass-fronted bookcase. After Konrád's eyes had adjusted to the half-light, he saw a sickly old man, with hunched shoulders, a wispy beard, washed-out eyes and thick, tangled hair that reached to his shoulders. The man was dressed in a dirty bathrobe and seemed to have difficulty breathing. Konrád thought that he must be ill and that his days were numbered.

'That's right,' said Konrád. 'And you? Are you retired?'

'What do you want from me?' the man asked.

'I didn't mean to drag you out of bed,' said Konrád. 'Is everything all right? Would you like me to call a doctor? You don't look well.'

'No. It's nothing you need to worry about. What do you want from me?'

As he said this, the man was shaken by a long fit of coughing, after which he had difficulty catching his breath. Finally recovering, he went to his armchair and settled into it with a heavy sigh.

'What do you want from me?' he said again.

'I'll try to be brief,' Konrád replied, not wanting to linger longer than necessary. 'It crossed my mind to ask you about something.'

'Ask me?'

'About a man I'm interested in who may have had the same . . . how shall I put it? . . . the same inclinations as you. A paedophile, like you.'

The man sat there silently in his chair, surrounded by darkness. Hearing his heavy breathing, Konrád suspected that the man had heart disease. It was as if he were in respiratory distress.

'Well, I think you'd better go,' the man replied after a few moments. 'I have nothing to say to you. So . . . you should just clear off.'

'He had a disease, that man,' said Konrád. 'Tuberculosis. In one of his legs. Walked with a limp because of it. Does that ring any bells?'

The man's breathing grew even more laboured and he reached for something that turned out to be an oxygen tank, connected to a mask that the man groped for but couldn't grasp properly. He was on the verge of suffocating from lack of oxygen. Konrád watched him for a moment, then walked over and handed him the mask. The man clutched it with eager relief, put it over his nose and mouth, and sucked in the oxygen until his breathing stabilised.

'You're probably enjoying seeing me in this state,' the man said as soon as he'd recovered.

'Would you like me to take you to the hospital?'

The man shook his head.

'Do you know who he is?' asked Konrád. 'The tuberculosis patient?'

'Why are you looking for him?'

'It's in connection with an old police case. Do you recall anyone matching that description?'

'What case?'

'Do you know who he is? Can you tell me his name?'

'What case?'

'A twelve-year-old girl drowned in the Pond many years ago. She may have known this man.'

The man had taken off the mask, but now he put it back on and sucked in the oxygen. Two minutes passed without the two of them saying anything. The man didn't take his eyes off Konrád and the silence was broken only by his efforts to breathe. Finally, he took off the mask again. Konrád saw the expectation in the man's face and knew what he was going to ask next.

'What did he do to her?'

'It doesn't make any difference. Nothing says that he did anything to her. What makes you think he did something to her?'

'Why else would you be asking me about him? Was she murdered?'

Konrád didn't answer. He was beginning to regret coming to this house. He didn't feel well. The air in there had an unpleasant odour whose origin he didn't know. The man leaned forward in his chair, and Konrád could see that life had quickened in his watery eyes.

'Was she raped first?'

'I told you it doesn't make any difference.'

'Was he the one who did it?'

'Will you pay attention?'

'How?'

'How what?'

'How did he defile her?'

Konrád grimaced.

'I never said that she was raped,' he said, trying to maintain his composure. 'Do you know who he is? Can you tell me that? If you can't, I'll go and leave you alone with your misery.'

The old man stared at him for several moments, then leaned back in his chair.

'Fine,' he whispered. 'We'll have it your way. Sorry, but it's been a long time since I've had such a . . . visit.'

'What? Have what my way?'

'Tell me about her mother,' the man said. His breathing was stable. The oxygen mask lay in his lap. His eyelids had sunk over his colourless eyes. Konrád thought he was falling asleep.

'The girl's mother?'

'What did she do?'

'She lived in hut number 9 on Skólavörðuholt Hill and worked at the National Hospital.'

'What did she do there? At the hospital?'

'She worked in the cafeteria.'

'In the cafeteria,' the man repeated. 'Was she married?'

'She lived with a man whom I know little about. He had a son who's still alive. His name is Eymundur.'

'Had this woman worked in the hospital for a long time?'

'I don't know. For some time, I think.'

'Did the man whose leg was affected by tuberculosis go to the girl's home?'

'Yes. At least once. Who was he? What was his name? Can you tell me?'

'What do you know about this Eymundur?'

'He was a sailor on cargo ships. He lives alone. He's a brute.'

'What do you mean? Why do you say he's a brute?'

'He's in jail at the moment, for assault and battery.'

'Does he attack women?'

'Yes.'

'Defenceless women?'

'Yes.'

'Has he raped them?'

'No. Not that I know of.'

'What sort of relationship did he have with the girl?'

'He says he didn't have much of a relationship with her. Almost none. That he hardly knew her.'

'Was he older than her?'

'He was sixteen years old.'

'Do you believe him?'

'I don't know what to believe.'

'And the stepfather?'

'As I said, I know almost nothing about him,' said Konrád.

'Did the police investigate the girl's death?'

'Yes.'

'Who was in charge of the investigation?'

'A man called Nikulás.'

'St Nikulás,' the man whispered. 'When the mother went to work, did she take her daughter with her?'

'I don't know. Probably every now and then. Why do you ask?'

'Did she like her job?'

'I haven't heard otherwise.'

'Did she have evening shifts?'

'I don't know.'

'Was the girl healthy?'

'I think so.'

'Was she . . . was she sexually mature?'

'Possibly.'

'So young?'

'We don't know for sure. Why did you call Nikulás by that name?'

'He was an extremely disagreeable man. Corrupt. All you had to do was slip him a few coins and he would close his eyes to anything. When the girl went with her mother to the hospital . . . did she resist? Did she not want to go? Or was it all the same to her? What did she do? How did she act?'

'I don't know,' said Konrád. He wasn't at all pleased with this interrogation. 'I don't know if she even went with her mum to the hospital.'

'Well, you don't know much, do you?'

'Why do you think I've come here?' Konrád snapped back. 'I need information. Do you think that this is a courtesy visit?'

It was as if this remark offended the man.

'I remember your father, Konrád,' he said, opening his half-shut eyes. 'He wasn't an easy person to deal with. Any more than you are. Did you two have a good relationship?'

'Are you going to tell me who this man was –'

'Was he a good father?'

Konrád didn't answer.

'Was he good to his little boy?'

'Do you know the name of the man I'm asking about?'

'Am I right in remembering that you have a little sister?'

Konrád wasn't sure if he'd heard the man correctly.

'A pretty little girlie who was sometimes alone at home with her daddy?'

Konrád stood up.

'I'm not going to listen to your bullshit any longer,' he snapped.

'Did I hit a nerve?' the man said, sucking in air with difficulty. He grabbed the oxygen mask. 'I went there once. To your basement flat. Did I ever mention that to you, Konrád?'

'Shut up!'

'So wonderfully pretty she was. I believe your father called her Beta?'

'Shut the fuck up!'

Konrád wanted to get out of that house before losing control. He was afraid he might hurt the man. He longed to rip off that oxygen mask, shove it down the man's throat and watch him suffocate. His desperate search for answers didn't justify his having to listen to the venom that welled from the man's mouth.

'Was the girl pregnant, or what? Is that why she went with her mother to the hospital? Because someone got her pregnant?'

Konrád walked towards the door.

'Konrád!' the man called out. 'Is that the reason, Konrád? Was the girl pregnant?'

He heard the door open.

'Konrád! Answer me!'

He sat up in his chair.

'I'm sorry, Konrád! That was uncalled for! I shouldn't have mentioned your father!'

The man stood up. He was tall and thin, and his robe was tied loosely enough to reveal his pale, bony body.

'Find Luther! Dig through the medical records!' he tried to shout, but his voice cracked and became a shrill whisper.

The door slammed shut. The old man muttered something to himself as he slumped into his chair, placed the mask over his face and sucked in the oxygen as if each breath were his last.

49

Konrád drove aimlessly around Reykjavík, barely paying attention to the traffic. He thought about going back to that despicable bastard and doing what he longed most to do when he was there and watch him suffocate in his own foulness. He gripped the wheel so hard that his knuckles whitened, trying to forget what the man had said about his father and Beta. He hoped with all his heart that he'd only said that to unsettle him. To toy with his emotions. Make him angry and spiteful. Still, the man knew his sister's name. He had called her Beta.

Konrád pounded the steering wheel, furious, brimming with despair, regret and self-loathing. It wasn't for nothing that his mother had fled their home with Beta and never returned. How could he have been so blind to his father? All those years, until he finally turned his back on him and stormed out their door, the day the old man was found murdered? Konrád had often wondered what had prompted him to try to understand that man. He had listened to him complain that the world was hostile to people like him, and believed what he said when he presented himself as a victim of circumstances, of his upbringing, his environment, the police, society, Konrád's mother, or people like Svanbjörn. Konrád should have understood that the only victims were the people who had had the misfortune to cross his path and that all he said and did was only to serve his own twisted ego.

He was on his way home when he remembered that he'd promised to look in on Eygló at her place in Fossvogur. Despite being in no mood to visit her, he headed there.

She was quick to notice that he wasn't in his normal state, but didn't bring it up. He sat down on the couch in the living room, silent and serious, and responded to her curtly. Acting as if nothing were out of the ordinary, Eygló shared what she'd been thinking since their visit to Theodór, where they'd got confirmation that their fathers had resumed their old war-years acquaintanceship. She had speculated on the nature of their relationship and wondered if they had once again conned people with sham séances, as they had done in the past. She said that she didn't dare to think that Nanna's mother might have been one of their victims. That she'd fallen into their clutches.

'I wouldn't be surprised if they had lied to her,' said Konrád, 'and conned her out of what little she had.'

'We know nothing about that,' said Eygló.

'It's no use trying to defend them,' said Konrád. 'At least not my father. You should assume the worst, when it comes to him.'

'Konrád, is something wrong?'

'No, everything's fine.'

She didn't press him, and instead told him that over the past few days, she had tried to remember whether Engilbert had ever mentioned Nanna's mother or that Nanna had drowned in the Pond, and whether the image of the girl who was looking for her doll had in that way become imprinted in her mind. In her subconscious. She had no recollection of him having done so. It was also possible that she'd overheard her parents talking about the case, and the image of a girl looking for her doll had remained, without her knowing where it came from.

'There's also what you told me about Engilbert and your father,' said Eygló. 'That it could have been Engilbert as much as anyone else who attacked him near the slaughterhouse.'

'If I were you, I wouldn't worry about it too much,' said Konrád. 'Try not to dwell on it.'

'But that's what you do,' said Eygló. 'What happened? Why are you so down?'

'You should forget about it. Forget about my fucking father.'

'Why? Why do you talk about him like that?'

'Because he was a bastard,' said Konrád. 'He was a despicable bastard, and I should have faced it, instead of turning a blind eye to it.'

'Wasn't that just your strategy for living with him?'

'He wasn't good to my sister Beta,' Konrád confessed, 'and that's as polite a word as I can find.'

'Oh.'

'I didn't learn that until much later, and now I regret having swallowed all his lies.'

'It isn't good to harbour anger about things you have no control over.'

'No. I'm aware of that. Erna said the same thing. But I can't help it. I'm constantly reminded of how he was and how he treated his family. It has always haunted me and I'm tired of it. When I was on the force. Now, when I'm retired. It's something I can't get rid of. Ever.'

His phone started ringing and he saw that it was Marta. He told Eygló that he needed to answer it, and asked her to excuse him. Marta was at home, and was even more talkative than usual. When she asked if she was disturbing him, he said that he had dropped in on someone in town and couldn't stay on the phone too long.

'Huh, stopped to see who?' asked Marta, as curious and direct as ever. She knew that Konráð had few friends, and seldom visited people. 'Is it a woman? Is there a woman I don't know about?'

'I'm talking to a woman I know. Her name is Eygló,' Konráð replied, realising that Marta had had a few drinks. 'She's the one who put me on the case of that girl you're refusing to help us with.'

'So we're calling that a case now?'

'I am, and it's a big one. I need to talk to you about a few things –'

'Save it until tomorrow. I wanted to tell you that I just came from Danní's grandma, and there's some odd stuff going on there,' said Marta. 'Apparently Danní was going to post something on the internet before she died. Randver got all stressed when he heard about it, as if he thought it was about him and his smuggling chums. He denies it all, though we can hardly ever believe what that moron says. Still, Lassi hinted to us that the grandmother knew something about it.'

'Were you able to speak to Lassi?'

'He said just a few words, then went back to sleep and hasn't woken since.'

'So what Danní wanted to post on the internet may have had nothing to do with Randver and his partners. Randver just assumed it did, in his drug-induced haze?'

'Exactly,' Marta said. 'Then I went to see the grandmother, who is, needless to say, in a very strange state of mind. I told her about it, but she seemed utterly flabbergasted, and started saying things about her dream child and jewel. The poor woman! I feel sorry for her.'

'So you think Danní was going to expose something about her grandparents? Make it public?'

'Why not?'

'Some family secret?'

'Is that so odd? The woman was in politics. Very elegant. Prominent in parliament. Constantly on TV. Highly principled. The most respectable person in the room at all those bloody cocktail parties. She calls me "Miss"! Who does that nowadays?'

'And what? Are you saying that she and her husband are responsible for the girl's death? Isn't that –'

'Am I not allowed to ask myself that question?'

'But –'

'Why do these kids end up in the gutter, Konrád? Can you tell me that? Why do they fall so hard?'

'Because they had difficult childhoods, for example?'

'Growing up with those two, Danní never wanted for anything. She said that twice, the grandma. She was their dream child and jewel. Except their little flower hated them. Their dream child hated them with all her heart. How does that square with what the woman is telling us? Can you explain that to me?'

'I don't know . . . what are you thinking?'

'I'm thinking of abuse. Is the idea absurd? That the girl was going to expose it, post it on those MeToo web pages that are full of stories of rape and sexual abuse suffered by women. Does that seem absurd to you?'

'What did the grandfather say? Was he there?'

'No. He's basically left his wife to fend for herself in this.'

'Are you going to call them in for questioning?'

'Then all the shit would hit the fan, for sure.'

'For sure.'

'You should get some sleep,' Konrád said.

'Get some sleep yourself!' Marta snapped, before hanging up.

Konrád put his phone in his pocket and went to the kitchen, where Eygló was making them tea.

'This will calm you down,' she said, handing him a cup.

'I need to go through the old medical records of the Vífilsstaðir sanatorium,' he said. 'See if I can find anything in them about a man named Luther.'

'Right now?' she asked, sensing his impatience.

'Yes,' answered Konrád. 'It can't wait.'

50

The old Vífilsstaðir sanatorium stood like a castle on its hill, the last defence in the war against a deadly disease. It had been built out of urgent necessity in 1910, at the height of the tuberculosis epidemic, then the leading cause of death in Iceland. It was meant to provide the best conditions possible for housing and isolating those who were victims of that endemic disease. In those days, the building was located well outside the city proper, but was now near one of the capital's main arteries. Below the sanatorium, to the south, there was once a beautiful lake, now dry, and to the west of the main building was the old arcade wing where the patients sat in rows on fine summer days to take in the view and the fresh air. At the height of its activity, the agricultural production of this sanatorium was equivalent to that of any large European farm. There was a large cow shed and barn, a chicken coop, a dairy, a woodshop and everything that allowed the establishment to operate self-sufficiently.

After tuberculosis in Iceland was controlled, the sanatorium continued as a medical facility until the start of the twenty-first century, when it became a retirement home. Konrád drove slowly up to the building and parked his car. There was light in only a few of the building's windows, most of its residents having gone to bed. Everything was quiet. Konrád envisioned the place as it was in the days of the epidemic, when attempts were made to stem the tide by quarantining those infected. He thought of the stories of love, of victory and death that had taken place within the sanatorium's thick walls. The building had suffered from an obvious lack of maintenance due to budgetary restrictions, and had even stood empty for a couple of years, until the lack of space in the city's hospitals was remedied by its reopening.

Earlier in the day, while looking up information about the old sanatorium and the archives of the National Hospital, Konrád had discovered that although most of the medical records of both institutions had been consolidated in the old coffin workshop of Fossvogur Cemetery, a few files were still to be found here and there in their various care wards. He had called an old friend of his named Svanhildur, a doctor at the National Hospital who had sometimes done autopsies in connection with police investigations. She was on a golfing trip with some friends in Florida and was surprised to be asked about medical records while under the blazing Florida sun. At first, she didn't understand what Konrád was after and said that all queries regarding medical records had to be directed to the archivist at the National Hospital in Fossvogur. Then, when he repeated his question concerning the likelihood of his finding information about tuberculosis patients if he went straight to Vífilsstaðir, she replied that it wasn't out of the question. She vaguely recalled an archive room in the building's basement. She reminded Konrád that he would need permission to access the records, which he would have to get from the Fossvogur hospital. Then she said she needed to get back to her golf game, and Konrád hurriedly asked if she had heard of a doctor named Heilman, who had worked at the hospital in the 1960s and 70s and been in charge of autopsies. She replied that the name rang a bell, but that was about it.

Inside the building, all was quiet, and despite never having been there, Konrád had no trouble finding the basement stairs. After descending them, he soon came to a door marked 'Archives'. It was locked. The door was old and its lock tired and worn, like almost everything else in the place. Konrád didn't want to do any unnecessary damage, but all he had to do was push hard on the door before the lock gave way.

He shut the door behind him, turned on his phone's light and saw that he was in a spacious office containing rows of filing cabinets, both newish, made of grey metal, and much older wooden ones, which to Konrád looked as if they might have been from the early days of the sanatorium. Several of the drawers were open and empty, others held a few papers, while still others contained hanging files yellowed by time and arranged in alphabetical order. He flipped through them randomly, armed with his phone's torch. He stopped to set the torch on low power, then took out one folder and looked at the name. Sigurgrímur Jónsson. The folder contained a few documents on the patient. A brief biography and medical history. Konrád looked quickly over the papers. Originally from Barðaströnd County. Pulmonary tuberculosis. Two operations. Removal of ribs. Died 14 December 1949. Konrád took out another folder. Katrín Andrésdóttir. Born in 1936. Pulmonary tuberculosis. A two-page-long medical history. No major surgery. Several hospitalisations starting in 1947. Final recovery in 1950. Physician: Bergur Lúðvíksson. It was around that time, Konrád thought, that therapies effective against tuberculosis were developed.

He looked through one drawer after another until he found the files of the patients whose names began with an L. The name Luther wasn't common in Iceland, and it didn't appear on any of the folders. He went through all the filing cabinets, both the old ones and the newer metal ones, but found no Luther.

Konrád's phone torch had begun to dim by the time he started going through the loose pages in the filing cabinets. Many files had been removed, no doubt having been transferred to the Fossvogur archives. Discouraged, he was about to give up when he saw Luther's name in the low light. Grabbing the three sheets and holding them under the light, he quickly scanned their contents. Luther K. Hansson. Bone tuberculosis in the left leg, below the knee. Amputation unnecessary. Born in 1921 in Reykjavík. Currently staying at Vífilsstaðir . . .

The physician's name was recorded and Konrád stared at it until his phone lamp went out, leaving him in complete darkness.

A. J. Heilman.

51

Danní's grandfather drove down into the Hvalfjörður tunnel, decelerated to the speed limit and then switched the cruise control on. He'd been in the habit of using this technology ever since buying his first car equipped with it. It was around the same time that the tunnel was opened, and he found it comfortable to use it. He'd also bought a toll tag, which allowed him to pass without stopping through the gate to the tunnel, thus avoiding the lines that formed at the tollbooths. He constantly tried to make his life more comfortable in any way possible.

He'd never been afraid to drive through the tunnel, unlike his wife, who always expected disaster every time. A collision with another car. A fire. Or worst of all, that the tunnel's walls would give way and the fjord's water would submerge and drown them.

He was thinking of these things while driving. It was his way of pushing from his mind all the embarrassing and painful memories that bore down on him with all their weight when Danní was found dead. The days since that happened had been unbearable, particularly when he met his wife's gaze and the accusations flew both ways. They blamed each other for what had happened to Danní.

It was nothing new. They had become accustomed to it over the years as they helplessly watched her gradually lose her footing in life. Turn away from school and her friends, and especially the two of them, her grandmother and grandfather. They had watched her come home drunk, time after time, and put up with her invectives. They had worried about her when she didn't come home at night. Tried to talk sense into her when she asked them for money so that she could get her fix and endured her yelling at them in return. She didn't listen to anything they said to her or asked her to do, but was bellicose and rude to them. Hateful. Angry and hateful.

His wife had called him as he was driving along the foot of Mount Esja, and he had hesitated before answering. She was very upset and he couldn't calm her down. But he hardly tried. He no longer had the strength. She'd been upset like that for a number of days, thinking that that policewoman, what was her name – yes, Marta – was slowly but surely approaching the truth.

He drove up out of the tunnel and continued onward to Borgarfjörður, trying not to think of his wife or Danní, but something entirely different. He'd driven this road so many times that he knew every hill, every mound, the outlines of the mountains and the farms that he passed. His phone began ringing again and he saw that it was his wife again. He decided not to answer, and instead, switched the phone off. He had turned off the radio and, out of habit, checked the speedometer every time he approached a place where he knew there were speed cameras.

About half an hour later, he drove up to the guest house, parked the car and went inside. He had no luggage with him. The young woman in reception smiled at him, and he asked if she had a room for him.

'Yes,' she replied, looking at her computer screen to check the reservations, despite knowing that several rooms were free. It had been a rather quiet week. 'For one person?' she added.

He nodded.

'One night?'

He nodded again.

'Do you have a room with a bathtub?' he asked. 'I would prefer to have a bathtub.'

The young woman replied that most of the rooms had showers, although a few did have bathtubs to cater to those who appreciated that comfort. With a smile, she said that she herself was one of those. She was cheerful and talkative, clearly at ease around people she'd never seen before in her life.

'Will you have breakfast?'

'No, thank you, I . . . won't be needing it.'

'No problem.'

She found a room with both a shower and bathtub, checked him in and handed him the key, then pointed out where the room was and said that if he needed anything, all he had to do was ask. She was a lovely young woman. Blonde, like Danní.

The room was nice, and the tub that the young woman had promised was there. Avoiding looking at himself in the large mirror above the bathroom sink, he returned to the main room and sat down on the bed. Looked at his watch. Waited. Without actually knowing what for. He went back to the bathroom and opened the tub's tap.

Then began unbuttoning his shirt.

It was Italian.

He'd always opted for comfort, beyond all else.

52

Despite the lateness of the hour when Konrád came home, he decided to call his sister. He wanted to know how she was doing and whether they ought to see each other soon. She wasn't bothered by his calling so late in the evening, and Konrád told her what he'd been up to and about his visit to the man with the oxygen mask, what the man had said about their father and that he'd mentioned Beta by name. She had the right to know, and he didn't want to put off telling her about it. To his relief, Beta had no idea how the man could have known her name; she didn't recall him coming to their home when she was a child or any other visits by men of his kind, visitors who could have done her harm. Nor, for that matter, a tuberculosis sufferer who limped.

Konrád had left the archive room of the old Vífilsstaðir sanatorium and gone back to his car without anyone noticing him. He had tried to close the door properly, but knew that the next time someone entered the room, his crime would be discovered. If the police were contacted about the break-in and it reached Marta's ears, she wouldn't be long in putting two and two together.

He and Beta had quite a long conversation, during which he told her how he had found the doll in the fire, when the man in whose possession it was nearly burned himself alive. Found in the doll was a clue that the girl had possibly been abused, and Konrád wanted to exhume her body. Marta, on the other hand, was opposed to doing so, saying that she needed more evidence. Beta encouraged her brother to find it, and he told her what he had discovered at the old sanatorium. The doctor of the man who had a reputation for abusing children, visited Nanna's home, and was named Luther was the same doctor who had autopsied the little girl's body.

'And what, what does that mean?' Beta asked.

'I think that Nanna was pregnant. Luther had been in her home. He knew the girl's mother from the National Hospital, or something like that. The doctor, that Heilman, had by then left Vífilsstaðir and started working at the National Hospital. He autopsied the girl but decided to keep her pregnancy quiet. Why? Were they friends? Did the doctor know about that . . . inclination of his, that perversion?'

'So Luther rapes the girl, finds out she's pregnant, and drowns her to hide his crime, and the doctor covers it up for him? Is that your theory?'

'Yes, more or less.'

'But you don't know if she was really pregnant?'

'No.'

'And everything depends on that?'

'Yes.'

'And this is nothing but an idea of yours? You have no tangible proof?'

'That's why we've got to get into the grave,' said Konrád. 'But Marta won't allow it. According to her, this is just some fantasy of mine, as you suggest, too. And Marta is right, in a way. It's an old case. It was never fully investigated. Those involved are dead. I have nothing tangible to support the idea that the girl was raped. And I won't have any until I can open her coffin. These are all just suppositions. Nothing but guesswork.'

'Where is she buried?'

'At Fossvogur Cemetery.'

'Thanks for telling me about that creep with the oxygen mask,' said Beta. 'Don't worry about him. Now go to bed.'

Konrád lay awake until well into the early hours. He tossed and turned in bed, thinking of his father and Beta, the girl in the Pond and girls like Danní who were lured into the world of drugs, and abusers of defenceless children. It wasn't until his thoughts turned to Erna that the storm subsided and the salty air of Nauthólsvík Bay filled his nostrils, he heard the distant echo of children's laughter from long-past, happy days and fell asleep to the sea breeze with her kiss on his lips and words of love written in the soft sand.

The next day, as Konrád drove into the car park behind police headquarters on Hverfisgata Street, he saw Marta talking with two uniformed policemen. He parked quickly and walked towards them. The two policemen knew him and said hello, before getting into their car and driving away.

'I'm going to call Danní's grandparents in for questioning,' Marta announced. 'I think there's no need to wait.'

'Of course not,' said Konrád.

'I think that asking them to come down to the station will make a strong impression. Show them how seriously we view this matter.'

'Yes,' Konrád said, his mind elsewhere. 'You probably have enough on your plate as it is, so I'll keep this short. You need to exhume the girl's body. Her remains have to be examined properly. The sooner you do it the better.'

Marta looked at Konrád. She knew that he wouldn't insist like that unless he was dead serious, and she knew from experience that when he was serious, it was better to listen to him. It started to rain, and they went into the station, where Marta took out her pack of cigarettes. Then she stood at the door and blew her smoke outside as she patiently listened to Konrád explain yet again why he thought it necessary to open Nanna's grave and determine whether she had been abused.

'You know as well as I do, Konrád, that you don't have enough evidence to justify such an operation,' Marta said after he presented his arguments to her. He told her about Luther, saying that he'd probably raped the young girl. He said that the doctor who had treated Luther at the sanatorium had also performed the autopsy on the girl's body and possibly covered up his former patient's crime. 'It's all just bloody speculation,' she added. 'Our request for an exhumation would be denied immediately. I would like to help you, but I can't.'

'It may have been a murder case,' Konrád insisted. 'It's not improbable.'

'Yes, but you have nothing to prove it.'

'That's simply not true.'

'Let me think about it,' Marta said. 'I'll bring it up with my colleagues here and see what they say, and then I'll let you know. There's little else I can do.'

'Of course there is.'

'No, Konrád. You know that as well as I do.'

'It could take weeks, if not months, to get people moving here,' Konrád said.

'What are you going to do? Dig her up yourself?'

'I was hoping you would do it for me.'

'In that case, you'll need to bring me something tangible, and not just wave some bullshit in my face.'

By now, Marta was furious, and she tossed her cigarette into the car park and stormed off down the corridor. Then she suddenly turned round, marched back towards him and glared at him angrily.

'Did you say the sanatorium?'

'Yes, that Luther, he was there,' Konrád said, hoping that he'd finally managed to pique Marta's interest and get her on his side.

'At Vífilsstaðir?'

'Yes. He was at Vífilsstaðir.'

'Don't tell me . . . was it you?'

'What?'

'I saw in the report this morning that someone broke into the archive room at Vífilsstaðir last night. Where medical records from the old tuberculosis sanatorium are still kept. A very peculiar case. Nothing was stolen and no damage was done, except to the door. Someone simply entered that room, which is in the basement of the building, then got out of there, without disturbing anything or making any noise.'

Konrád had expected this, but didn't know what to say. He didn't want to lie to Marta.

'Was it you?'

Konrád kept silent.

'Are you completely out of your mind?!' she said.

'I know I'm right,' he said.

'Jesus and Joseph!' Marta exclaimed, before turning on her heels and disappearing down the corridor.

Standing in the doorway, Konrád stared out at the rain, thinking that Marta wasn't entirely wrong. After several moments, he went to see Olga in the records department. As gruff as ever, she asked him if the police would ever get rid of him. They both knew how jaded that joke was.

Finally, Olga allowed him to consult the records. He'd confided in her the events at the Pond, and although some might have said that Olga had a heart of stone, Konrád knew that she was a warm, passionate person deep down. He'd caught a glimpse of that warmth when she'd hit on him once at the annual policemen's ball, admittedly under the influence of quite a lot of alcohol.

It took only a few minutes for Konrád to discover that there were no police records on Luther.

53

Lassi's mother was sitting at his bedside in the hospital, reading a book. She had managed to wangle two days of sick leave from her employer to deal with a serious family situation. Her manager hadn't been particularly sympathetic towards her until she suddenly burst into tears and said that she absolutely needed to be with her son, whose chances of survival were slim. Their relationship hadn't always been good, but now he needed her. 'Fine, then,' her manager had said, rather sullenly. 'I'll give you two days.'

She'd borrowed the book from the hospital's library: a dated translation of a Norwegian romance novel, which she read aloud because the doctor had told her that Lassi could still hear her despite his condition. Finding the story boring, she took breaks from it quite often, sometimes falling asleep in her chair and starting in surprise whenever someone came in or there was a noise in the corridor.

Lassi didn't move. His doctor assured her that he would wake up before too long. He'd briefly regained consciousness three times and then gone back to sleep, and in fact, it was best for him to sleep as much as possible. His wounds were healing well and he was on his way to a full recovery.

She hadn't been in contact with her ex-husband, but their two other sons had told her that he'd flown to Reykjavík, spent a few hours at Lassi's bedside and spoken to his doctor. Lassi's brothers had also visited him, so he wasn't entirely alone in the world. His mother was happy to see that the whole family supported him despite everything, and gathered around him in his time of need. His brothers told her gently that surely, after this horrible experience, Lassi would think things over and start making some changes in his life.

The police said that the case was under investigation, and that Lassi's attackers had been remanded in custody. It wasn't yet known why her son had been abducted and subjected to such violence, unless it was in connection with drug smuggling involving large sums of money, and that the smuggled drugs hadn't been delivered as instructed. Complicating matters was the girl who had been discovered in Lassi's room, with a needle in her arm. Lassi's mother asked the police specifically about that, and was told that, in all likelihood, her son had had nothing to do with her death. On the other hand, the girl and Lassi were suspected of having worked together in the smuggling operation, and Lassi would be questioned by investigators in connection with that offence. It would therefore be better for him to cooperate fully with the police once he regained consciousness, and help them shed light on the case.

For the past few days, she'd been thinking a great deal about her son and the situation he was in. She wondered why he'd always got himself into so much trouble and sunk into addiction at such a young age, unlike his brothers, who had had the same upbringing. She had no answer for it. Lassi had been no different from the other kids, except that he hadn't done well at school and had been bullied. She knew that, even though he didn't talk much about it. He'd changed schools once, without it doing any good, and had stopped his studies at the end of compulsory schooling. By then, he'd been drinking for a long time. So young. He always owed people money. Was always in some bloody debt to people who treated him badly.

Lying there in his hospital bed, he seemed peaceful; it was a peacefulness that she hadn't seen in him since he was a child. She cursed his fate and hoped with all her heart that his brothers were right, that he would put this awful experience behind him and find his way out this hell. She didn't want to be forced a second time to watch her son fight for his life in a hospital room.

She looked up from her book to see a doctor of a venerable age, wearing a white lab coat and with a stethoscope around his neck, walk past the door. With Lassi still sleeping peacefully, she decided to go and have a cigarette break. A charming young lady in white clogs had stopped in and asked if she would like coffee, then brought her a cup and smiled beautifully at her. She asked the young lady if there was a place for her to smoke on this floor, perhaps out on a balcony. 'Smoking is strictly prohibited throughout the hospital,' the young lady replied. She would have to go down to the car park.

'Of course I could just quit,' she said to the young lady, taking the coffee cup with her. 'But, so it goes.'

She'd been gone only a few minutes when a doctor came into the room and looked at the patient. He glanced over the machines and devices connected to Lassi, and, having consulted the patient's file, knew the drug doses that he'd been administered. Everything was in order. The prospects for the patient's recovery were good. Soon he would regain consciousness.

The doctor was in Lassi's room for only a few moments before leaving and heading down the corridor, without anyone noticing him.

54

One of the names that Konrád had written down in the basement at Vífilsstaðir sanatorium was Katrín Andrésdóttir. He knew that she was over eighty years old now, and after some digging, he thought he'd found the right woman. Her age fitted, in any case. He called the number he'd found in the phone book, and the woman confirmed that she'd been at the sanatorium in the 1940s. She said that he was welcome to visit her. She didn't have many visitors, so it would be a nice change.

She was a widow and lived in a block of flats for the elderly. The block had a caretaker who dealt with various small problems encountered by the residents, as well as a cafeteria for those who wanted it. With a smile, Katrín told Konrád that she was still fully capable of preparing her own meals and didn't need the cafeteria. After inviting him in and offering him a chair, Konrád asked the woman how it was living there in that block, and she said that she had nothing to complain about. Talkative and cheerful, she said that she remembered her days at Vífilsstaðir very well and could not begin to describe how kind the staff of the sanatorium had been, how helpful and considerate, whether it was the nurses, orderlies or doctors. She'd stayed there three times and was one of the first patients to undergo the new tuberculosis treatment, which cured her for good.

'Those lovely people did all they could to make our stay there more pleasant, but obviously it was no picnic,' the woman said. 'Many patients suffered a lot, because it was an absolutely horrid, debilitating disease whose outcome was often death. It hit young people hard. That was the worst. I was eleven years old when I went there first, for my lungs . . . yes, the worst part was all those young people there.'

'Do you remember a man named Luther?' Konrád asked. 'He was a patient there. Suffered from bone tuberculosis in one leg.'

'Luther?'

'He was much older than you. Luther K. Hansson, born in 1921.'

The woman thought this over. She had white hair and a round face, and was quick to smile. Her flat smelled of freshly baked bread. She shook her head.

'No, I can't –'

'He walked with a limp. His doctor was a man named Heilman.'

'I simply have no recollection of the man.'

Konrád didn't know how far he should go in trying to jog her memory, or how he should word what he needed to know about Luther.

'The reason why I'm asking about this Luther is because he may have behaved somewhat, how can I put it, indecently, if you know what I mean.'

The woman looked at him quizzically.

'Abnormal behaviour. Towards young girls,' he said. 'Girls who were your age.'

The woman seemed suddenly to understand the real reason for this visit. On the phone, Konrád had told her only that he was seeking information about life at the sanatorium, and she had assumed that he was a journalist. Konrád had only given her his name, without specifying his profession.

'Didn't you say you're a journalist?' she asked.

'No, I didn't, in fact,' said Konrád. 'I used to be a policeman. But I'm retired now.'

'And . . . this Luther . . . why are you asking about him?'

'Do you remember him?'

'A friend of mine, unfortunately deceased . . .'

'Yes?'

'Why are you asking about this? Does it have to do with the police, somehow?'

Konrád saw the concern that filled the woman's eyes when she realised that this was no courtesy call, but that this was an ex-policeman, come to ask her about abnormal activity at the sanatorium a lifetime ago. So he decided simply to tell her what he knew, but asked her to keep it entirely to herself, if she would. He then told her about the accident at the Pond, that the young girl who had drowned there may have known Luther and that he had possibly raped her.

'Almighty God!' she exclaimed.

'These are all just speculations and hypotheses. There's no certainty that these things happened, but I would like to know if they were possible. To be honest, this girl's case has been haunting me so much that I hardly have a moment's peace.'

'I can understand that perfectly,' said the woman. 'The poor child . . . if what you say is true.'

'You were going to say something about your friend?'

'Yes, it might not matter much, given the context. It doesn't have to do with that . . . whatever you called him.'

'Luther.'

'Yes. I don't remember him. On the other hand, I remember quite well that doctor. Heilman.'

'Oh?'

'One day, the friend I mentioned came from Reykjavík to visit me, and pointed him out.'

'Why was that?'

'I never had any problem with him. He was always polite to me. Anyway, my friend had come to visit, and when she saw him in the entrance hall there, she stiffened up and acted very awkward. She said I should watch out for him. She was considerably more developed than me and whispered that he had had a practice in town, in Reykjavík, I mean, and once when she had gone there for an examination, he touched her where he absolutely should not have done. She told me that she would never go to his practice again. She had told no one about it but me, there at the sanatorium. She was terribly ashamed of it. At the time, people never spoke about such things. Unlike now.'

'And it was the same doctor?'

'Yes. His name was Heilman. Anton J. Heilman. She said . . . I've never forgotten it because she never talked like that, in general, and he was a respectable doctor et cetera. She said that he'd been horrid to her . . .'

55

Like most ordinary citizens, Danní's grandmother had never been inside police headquarters on Hverfisgata Street. Disconcerted and hesitant, she was escorted into the interrogation room where Marta was waiting for her with a serious expression on her face. She'd sent uniformed officers to pick up the couple, to worry them a bit and impress upon them the gravity of the situation and their position as witnesses. Only the woman was at home, and she went with the police to their car.

Since she wasn't being arrested, she could have refused to go with them. She could have contacted a lawyer. She did neither, but just stared at the two officers obtusely until they repeated that they would like her to come with them to the police station. She asked them to excuse her while she put on her coat, and then asked if she could call her husband, who had been unreachable for a while. She took out her mobile phone, rang his number and waited, and when no one answered, she accompanied the officers to their car.

The uniforms and the ride in the police car had the desired effect, because the woman was more or less in shock when she entered the interrogation room, exhausted from lack of sleep and disorientated. Marta knew that the events of the past days had taken a heavy toll on her. She felt sorry for this woman, but was convinced that the courtesy visits to her weren't doing any good.

'Do you know where my husband is?' the woman said after shaking hands with Marta, who asked her to have a seat.

'I expected to see him here with you.'

'I haven't heard from him for quite some time,' the woman said worriedly. 'It's not like him to just disappear without a word. To be honest, I was about to contact you.'

'Do you think he disappeared purposely? Would he have reason to do so?'

'No. Actually, I don't know if disappear is the right word. This has been so hard on him. All of it. On both of us, as I'm sure you can understand. He told me he was going for a drive and now I can't reach him. He didn't come home last night and I really don't know what to do.'

'He'll come home before long,' Marta reassured her.

'Why did you bring me here?' the woman asked, looking around the room, at the worn tabletop between them, the voice recorder, the harsh neon light hanging from the ceiling. It was a cold place.

'I'm still gathering information on Danní,' Marta replied, 'and I'm not sure you've told me everything you know.'

'I don't understand what you mean by bringing me here,' the woman said. 'You know who I am. This will be sure to arouse curiosity. I hope you've exercised discretion.'

'Do you think that's more important than the truth about Danní?'

'What truth about Danní? I've told you everything. Everything I know.'

'Are you sure you don't know where your husband is?'

'Yes, of course I'm sure. I called him yesterday and we talked for a bit, but that was the last I heard from him.'

'What did you talk about? When you called him.'

'This and that. I asked him when he was coming home.'

'And what did he say to that?'

'He said he was on his way, but I haven't heard from him since then, and I must say that I'm beginning to worry.'

'Yes, of course. We need to speak to him, too, and should maybe put out an alert. Would you want that?'

The woman didn't answer.

'Do you want us to put out an alert for your husband?'

'I think you should wait a bit with that,' said the woman, as if she feared attracting even more media attention to it. As if that was always her first concern.

'We have reason to believe you're not telling us the whole truth,' Marta continued patiently. 'We have evidence that Danní was going to post information on the internet, sensitive information, in all likelihood, and that you and your husband, or at least you, knew about that and what the information was. We'll be able to find out more when her friend regains consciousness, but I wanted to give you the opportunity to tell us everything you know and if you think it may have played a part in Danní's death. Do you think I'm wrong?'

'Well, I don't know what . . . honestly, I don't know what you're talking about. I simply have no idea. I can't believe that you think my husband and I bear some responsibility for Danní's death. I don't understand how you can come to such a conclusion.'

'I don't know if you're responsible for anything, but I have the feeling that you and your husband, and especially you, aren't telling us the whole truth,' Marta insisted. 'I think it's important that it comes out. Don't you agree?'

'Of course.'

The woman was silent for a few moments, as if pondering her situation. For quite some time now, Marta had had the feeling that she wanted to open up and tell the truth, but that something was stopping her. It was as if she lacked the courage to take that critical step. Marta hoped that she would be able to help her do so.

'When I was trying to reach my husband, I called his brother,' the woman finally said. 'I thought my husband might have gone to see him. I don't know why. They don't get along well . . . not at all.'

'Your husband's brother?'

'Yes, he's a doctor and . . . We thought we could trust him.'

'Trust him?'

'Their father was also a doctor. They dropped his name. The family name. They only use the patronymic. They think that family names are snobbish. Or that's the explanation my husband gave me, anyway. I don't know if it's true. I hardly know what's true any longer.'

'What do you mean, they only use the patronymic?'

'Well, they don't go by Heilman,' the woman said, running her hand over the worn tabletop, at which thieves, rapists and murderers had sat before her. 'As they should, maybe,' she continued. 'They go by Antonsson.'

'So they're, what, the sons of . . . ?'

'The sons of Dr Anton J. Heilman. And Gústaf is also a doctor, like his father.'

'Gústaf?'

'Gústaf Antonsson. My brother-in-law. He works as a doctor at the National Hospital in Fossvogur. He's highly respected.'

Just then, Marta's mobile rang, and she asked the woman to excuse her, then got up and went into the corridor to answer it. When she returned moments later, her face was scarlet with anger. She said that she had to stop this interview now, and that the woman would be taken home. They would talk more later.

'Oh, why?' the woman asked.

'I've got to take care of an urgent matter, unfortunately. Thank you for your help, for the time being.'

As she rushed down the corridor, Marta lifted her phone again and called Konrád.

'What have you done now?' she hissed, as soon as he answered. 'Are there no limits to how far you're willing to go to unravel that fucking case of yours?'

'What? What do you mean?' said Konrád, who was just leaving the block where Katrín lived.

'You know perfectly well.'

'What?'

'Are you saying that it wasn't you who did it?'

'Did what, Marta? What have I done? Why are you so angry?'

Marta said nothing, and Konrád could hear his friend's heavy breathing.

'What am I supposed to have done, Marta?' he asked.

'We just received a call from Reykjavík Cemeteries.'

'And?'

'They're reporting the desecration of a grave in Fossvogur Cemetery.'

'The desecration of a grave?'

'Yes, Konrád, a desecration! Don't act so ignorant,' said Marta. 'I know you.'

'What are you talking about?'

'The grave has been opened,' said Marta. 'Of the girl you've been obsessed with. Someone exposed the coffin and left the grave open, just as you wanted. Don't you find it a fucking strange coincidence?!'

'Marta –'

'Don't tell me you had nothing to do with it.'

'Marta, I –'

'Don't lie to me, Konrád! Don't even try!!'

56

The cemetery workers hadn't noticed anything out of the ordinary until late in the day, when they discovered that a grave had been dug where no burial was scheduled. The two men whose responsibilities included digging the graves and who first saw the mound of earth knew that neither of them had dug there. One of them called his supervisor, and it wasn't long before confirmation came that there should be no open grave in that location.

When their supervisor called back, the two men were looking down into the grave, at what was left of the little coffin that had been put together from cheap wood. The grave was unusually shallow and the coffin hadn't endured its time in the ground very well: the boards had given way, the lid had broken and collapsed, letting dirt in. The grave's perimeter was riddled with footprints, probably made by work boots like the ones they were wearing. However, the men did notice immediately that the work had otherwise been done well and methodically, leaving the grave as tidy as possible considering the circumstances, with care having been taken not to damage any of the neighbouring graves. The police had been informed and the cemetery workers had received instructions not to touch anything, including the beautiful bouquet of flowers that had been placed on the coffin's broken lid. A solitary rose lay next to the grave.

Before they knew it, more cemetery staff arrived and a police car drove slowly down the path towards the grave. Grave desecrations were extremely rare.

Marta arrived soon after being notified. After her endless conversations with Konrád about the girl in the coffin, she felt as if she were on familiar ground – literally. She shone the torch she had with her into the coffin, but didn't see the girl's remains. Konrád had got what he wanted, but the way he'd dared to do it sat badly in Marta.

'There have been a number of inquiries about this girl lately,' admitted an employee of Reykjavik Cemeteries, who had come to the grave and introduced herself to Marta. 'But for this to happen . . . it's . . . it's absolutely unbelievable.'

'Do you know who they are?' Marta said. 'The people who asked about her?'

'No, we don't keep any records of such things. We only point out the graves when appropriate and try to assist people.'

'I think there were at least three people involved,' said the Forensics technician who had stopped Marta when she shone her torch at the coffin, saying that she was contaminating the scene. 'It looks to me as if the footprints here are from three different pairs of boots.'

'It would have been after our shifts yesterday,' said one of the workers who found the open grave.

The Forensics technician had asked the two men to show them

where they had stepped when they came to the grave, so that he could rule out their tracks. Remaining were shoeprints or boot-prints of three rather small-footed individuals. He guessed immediately that one or all of those involved were women.

'Women?' Marta said, watching Konrád come walking down the path towards them.

'If I were to guess,' the technician said.

'I should arrest you this instant,' Marta said, turning to Konrád as soon as he got close.

'I didn't do this,' Konrád said, staring in shock at the open grave. 'I swear I didn't do this. I wasn't responsible for it, and I have no idea who was.'

'He thinks it was three women,' Marta said, pointing at the Forensics technician. 'But that doesn't mean you didn't know about it or organise it.'

'They left behind a bouquet,' Konrád said. 'This wasn't done out of disrespect. Those who did this want to draw attention to the girl's case. The attention of the police.'

Marta, who was still seething, glared at him. He knew that her anger was directed entirely at him, making him reluctant to bring up the decision that she would obviously have to make before too long. But then he decided just to go for it.

'Are you going to cover it over, or –'

'Or what?'

'Do as I asked you, and examine the remains,' said Konrád.

'What do you think I'm going to do?!'

After photographs had been taken and the investigation of the grave was concluded, they all watched silently as the coffin was lifted from the earth, placed in the bed of a trailer and driven care-fully up the slope to the car park. It was then placed in a police vehicle, which drove Nanna's earthly remains to the morgue on Barónsstigur Street.

Konrád drove along behind the police vehicle as it made its way slowly through the afternoon traffic. While driving, he called Eygló, who finally picked up after numerous rings. He asked if she had been in Fossvogur Cemetery the day before, after the cemetery staff had gone home. Eygló said no, and he told her that Nanna's grave had been opened as tidily as possible and a bouquet laid on top of the coffin. A long silence followed his words.

'Who . . . who could have done such a thing?' Eygló finally asked.

'I thought it was you,' said Konrád.

'Me? I could never do anything like it. Never.'

'Are you sure?'

'Yes, of course I'm sure. It wasn't me. Absolutely not. And what . . . what are the police going to do about it?'

'Marta is furious and is blaming me for all of it, but she's going to have the remains examined,' said Konrád. 'So, that's a positive step. We may be nearing the goal . . .'

As he watched the police car pull into the morgue's car park, he suddenly realised who had been at work in the cemetery.

'The poor girl,' said Eygló. 'The things she endured. She could never rest in peace.'

Konrád's phone call had woken Eygló from a deep sleep, and the dream she'd been having stayed with her upon waking. Feeling tired, she'd lain down on the couch with a book and soon fallen asleep. She couldn't tell how long she'd been sleeping when her phone started ringing. In a drowsy haze, she got up and looked at the clock hanging on the kitchen wall, and saw that she'd been dozing for nearly two hours.

Following the phone call, Eygló stood there motionless, somewhat muddle-headed after all that sleep, as well as the news that Konráð had just delivered to her. Feeling slightly dizzy, she supported herself on the living-room table that she'd used for her séances.

During the few moments that it took her to recover, she thought of her dream, which was about the girl in the Pond.

She was standing by the bridge on Skothúsvegur Street in her worn dress and buckle shoes, and was suddenly illuminated by vehicle headlights hurtling towards her at full speed. Just before the vehicle hit her, the beams of light disappeared, leaving Eygló overwhelmed with confusion and sadness, as always when the girl came up in her mind.

57

Beta stared blankly at her brother for a long time, waiting for his reaction. She had told him what she and her friends had done, on their own initiative and without any regrets. He had remained stony-faced as she recounted their trip to Nanna's grave.

The three women had waited for the day's burials and funerals at Fossvogur Cemetery to be completed and the staff to finish their work day and go home. They had parked the old clunker belonging to one of them on the westernmost side of the car park next to the church. There, the car stood for a while, with its dented front bumper and rusty doors, as the women finalised their plans. They knew that once they were in the cemetery, there would be no turning back.

A few moments later, the car doors opened and the three women stepped out and went to the boot. They were all dressed as if for doing gardening work, wearing work boots, gloves, old trousers and thick jumpers. One of them opened the boot and took out two shovels and a light pickaxe, which she handed to the other women. Had there been any hesitation on their part up until then, it was gone when they headed together into the cemetery.

They were in no hurry, and didn't notice anyone else in the area around the girl's grave. There had been only two other cars in the car park. They hadn't checked on the other entrances to the cemetery. There wasn't a breath of wind, but a gentle drizzle settled on their clothes and dampened the ground.

Beta had gone to the Stígamót counselling centre to see two of her good friends and persuade them to join her. They were all the same age, all victims of sexual abuse, and it was through their work there, advising victims of violence who turned or were referred to Stígamót for help, that they had become friends. Beta had asked them to meet her at the centre. She had a story to tell them.

They knew stories that no one should have known and that should never have existed, but that happened almost every day. Stories of rape and other forms of assault, stories of children, girls and boys, stories of women trapped in abusive relationships, stories of men's harassment of them, threatening them and their children with violence. Stories of daughters, mothers, friends, female relatives and sisters. Stories of wives who feared being punched in the face with no warning.

Now they heard Nanna's story. They weren't surprised in the least to hear about the pervert who had come to her house, the drawing she had made and hidden in her doll, and her death by drowning in the Pond. Or when Beta told them that the police investigation had been incomplete and that the results of the autopsy performed on the girl's body were unknown because the report had disappeared and none of its conclusions appeared in the police records. Or when she added that the police didn't consider it necessary to carry out an exhumation and examine the girl's remains. 'If it turns out that she was abused,' Beta had concluded, 'it could also very well be that she was murdered. A twelve-year-old girl.'

'What do you want to do?' said one of them.

'Go to the cemetery,' said Beta. 'Open her grave.'

Her friends exchanged glances.

'If we hesitate,' Beta resumed, 'feeling as if we have no right to do this, we have only to think about what was done to us, and about the justice that was never ours. We have only to think of the children who have crossed our paths and have been so unhappy because of the neglect, humiliation and mistreatment they have suffered.'

'We did it as a sign of respect for the girl,' she explained to Konrád, when he was slow to respond. 'No one can claim otherwise. So that her case gets due process. I'm relieved that Marta's decided to have her remains examined. If nothing comes out of it, it will be good to know that she was done no harm. Otherwise . . .'

'. . . the investigation will have to be reopened,' Konrád concluded, finishing his sister's sentence. 'I hope I didn't go too far by telling you about Nanna. Marta isn't entirely wrong. You know that.'

Beta nodded. 'Still, I think we did right,' she said.

Konrád heard a message notification alert from his phone. The short message was from Marta, asking him to meet her at the morgue on Barónsstigur Street.

'We'll soon find out,' said Konrád, sending a message back to Marta that he was on his way.

58

Marta was standing in front of the morgue, smoking one of those slender menthol cigarettes of hers. Glancing at the pavement at her feet, Konrád saw that she'd smoked several in a row. Holding her empty coffee cup, she was much calmer than she'd been at the cemetery, and in fact seemed almost exhausted. He knew that weary look from when they'd worked together and Marta got tired of her job. When she'd had enough of what she saw, heard and experienced every day. Enough of the tossers she had to contend with and arrest, enough of the insults hurled at her and the stories she heard. Her expression suggested that if she were offered a job as a binman and told that she would have to work for free, she would happily accept the offer and quit the force on the spot.

'You've stopped smoking, of course, haven't you?' she said, stubbing out her cigarette with her foot.

'Almost,' said Konrád, who sometimes allowed himself a cigarillo when the urge for tobacco became too strong.

'Did I ever tell you that I never actually wanted to be a cop?' said Marta, taking out another cigarette and lighting it. She blew out the smoke and watched it dissipate into the darkness.

'Yes. More than once.'

'It's a shitty job.'

'Tell me about it.'

'A poorly paid, unbearable, shitty job. I don't know why I do it. I still don't know why I'm a fucking cop.'

'Because you want to do good.'

'Oh, leave off.'

'It was worth a try. Isn't it just something you get used to and after a few years you realise it's what you know best and don't know what else you can do? Isn't that how it is with most jobs?'

'I sometimes thought it would be fun to be a guide, taking tourists around the country, but to tell you the truth, I know nothing about Iceland. Absolutely nothing. I've never known anything about it. I don't know the names of the fjords or mountains. And I hardly ever step foot outside this bloody town any more.'

'Well, I –'

'I think it might do me good to get out of here for a little while. Just leave it all.'

Konrád didn't know how to respond to his friend's bad-tempered remarks.

'We finally got the results of Danní's toxicology test,' Marta said after a long silence. 'Somehow, they screwed up and only sent them to us now. She didn't inject herself with MDMA, but Fentanyl.'

'Fentanyl? Isn't that a prescription drug?'

'Yes, it is. A very powerful opioid. Some junkies manage to wangle prescriptions for it, and it's relatively easy to get hold of.

You can buy it on Facebook, like so many other drugs today, and it's stronger than shit.'

Again, there was silence, until Konrád cleared his throat. He felt compelled to confess to Marta what he knew. Beta hadn't said that he couldn't.

'I know who opened the grave,' he said. 'It was my sister. I told her about the girl in the Pond, and the story lit a fuse in her. She's also familiar . . . familiar with these issues of abuse and rape. She has friends at Stígamót. Two of them went with her to the cemetery, and don't regret what they did. They don't feel the slightest remorse.'

'Why should they?'

'What do you mean?'

'I should probably apologise to you.'

'What did you find out?'

'That you were right,' Marta replied, throwing away her half-smoked cigarette. Konrád sensed that her earlier anger was completely gone. 'I should have listened to you. I managed to persuade a doctor here at the hospital to do a preliminary examination on the remains. The girl had been pregnant. The remains of a foetus were found in the coffin. The doctor who performed the autopsy at the time would have seen it immediately, if he'd really done his job. The doctor here told me the autopsy was completely bungled, and he started looking to see who had done it. It took him quite some time to find out. He didn't find the old autopsy report, but that's not particularly unusual.'

'Was his name Anton Heilman?' Konrád asked.

'That's right,' Marta said, looking at him quizzically. 'Which is strange, because this is the second time I've heard that name today. A name that I'd never heard before, and that I can't get rid of now.'

'Where did you hear it before?'

'Anton Heilman was Danní's great-grandfather.'

'What?'

'This Anton had two sons. One of them is Danní's grandfather.'

'You're sure of that?!'

Konrád was stunned. It took him a moment to realise the implications of what Marta was saying about Heilman and Danní.

'Why are you so surprised?' Marta asked when she saw his reaction. It wasn't often that she managed to dumbfound him. 'Everyone here's related somehow.'

'Can it be?'

'What?'

'Hold on. Wait a minute. Anton Heilman was the doctor who performed Nanna's autopsy, and no one has ever seen his report. He was also the doctor of a man named Luther, a child abuser, according to Eymundur. An old scumbag I went to see suggested the same. Luther had been to the home of Nanna, who sometimes went with her mother to the National Hospital where she worked. Anton Heilman also worked there. Anton knew the child molester Luther from when he was his doctor at Vífilsstaðir. Luther may have been seen at the Pond the night when Nanna drowned. Anton Heilman autopsied the girl's body, and . . .' Konrád stared at the cigarette butts that Marta had crushed on the pavement. '. . . and to top it all off,' he muttered, 'Nikulás was a completely worthless cop.'

'Are you saying that this Luther raped the girl and the doctor covered it up for him when he did away with her?' Marta asked. 'Why would Heilman have done that? What interest did he have in –'

'Have you requested a DNA analysis of the foetus?'

'Obviously.'

317

'Maybe Luther wasn't the father,' Konrád went on. 'Maybe the child wasn't his at all.'

'Then whose?'

'The doctor's. Anton's.'

'You mean he raped her? And then murdered her? Wouldn't it have been easier for him to perform an abortion?'

'I don't know.'

'But . . .'

'Maybe both of those men were abusing her, and maybe Luther went too far there at the Pond,' said Konrád. 'I don't know. Fucking bastards! I don't know what those fuckers did.'

A car passed on the street. The rumble of its engine carried into the house until it moved away, then all was silent again apart from the low sounds of the old man's breathing. Sitting on the sofa in his bathrobe, he held the oxygen mask tightly to his face and inhaled the oxygen with more difficulty than ever before. It was as if each breath would be his last. He had considered calling an ambulance, but hadn't yet done so. Maybe later. He had called one many times before, and they had come and taken him to the hospital where the doctors got him breathing easier, but after sending him home, he would just start going downhill again and the same dance would begin all over.

He started coughing. His whole body shook and he thought he would suffocate. The fit finally subsided and he put the mask back on and gulped down the oxygen. He was thinking about the visit of the policeman whom he'd recognised from his past, about the girl in the Pond and what Luther had once insinuated, the rat that he was. At the time, he'd thought it was a lie, but now he felt that there must have been some truth to it.

He didn't know how much oxygen was left in the bottle. It had lasted a long time, but now he realised that the flow was losing strength. He fumbled for the phone on the table next to him and started coughing again. The fit went on for some time and that suffocating feeling came over him again. He tried to stand, but collapsed to the floor and dropped the mask.

'Luther . . .' he whispered.

Coughing non-stop, he groped for the mask but couldn't find it. He tried again and again to get some air, to no avail. He felt like he had to vomit, went on coughing and couldn't catch his breath. He groped again for the mask, but it was gone. The coughing continued to shake him and he tried to inhale but couldn't and he coughed and coughed and coughed . . .

Shortly afterwards, all was silent in the house. Nothing was heard but the sound of a car passing and moving off down the street.

59

The house no longer seemed as stately to Konrád as the first time he went there, at the request of the couple who didn't want it to get around that their granddaughter had sunk into drugs. At the time, he'd found the house handsome, with its austere surfaces, large windows and pitched copper roof, and felt that it fitted perfectly into the neighbourhood, where only the rich could afford to live. It was clear from the house's outward appearance that it belonged to people who possessed considerable wealth and knew how to enjoy it. Now, it had lost its lustre, and suddenly, Konrád found it ugly and ridiculous.

Erna had told him that the husband was an accountant, that he owned shares in a large accountancy firm in town and was known for his reliability. Many years ago, Erna had taken her tax returns two or three times to him, and he'd given her invaluable assistance without asking for a króna in return. 'He's such a lovely man,' she had said. His wife had stepped away from the political circus, and they had both retired while still in their prime. The few times that Erna had spoken about them, she'd described them as a couple who knew how to enjoy their wealth without ostentation. Konrád could tell that she had a certain amount of respect for them. He himself knew them only in passing.

Now, though, he felt he knew them better. Marta parked her car a short distance from the house and shut off the engine. She was going to resume the interview that she'd had to interrupt earlier in the day, and had asked Konrád to come with her. Marta thought his presence, as a kind of family friend, might help the woman open up, if she were really hiding something. Besides, the couple had called on him to try and sort out their problems, and few were as familiar with this matter as Konrád. In a way, he'd become their confidant. Konrád tried to explain to Marta that it had all happened against his will – to which she turned a deaf ear.

The door to the house was ajar, and after hesitating a moment, they went in. Marta called out the woman's name, but got no response. They walked slowly towards the kitchen and living room. They'd seen a dim light in the house's windows, but didn't see or hear anyone inside. Finally, they stood there awkwardly in the middle of the living room, looking at each other. It was as if the couple had run without warning out of the house. Konrád had noticed on his previous visits that two cars were usually parked in the driveway, a big SUV and a saloon. Now, neither of them was there.

They left without touching anything, except that Marta preferred to close the door properly. They were walking back to the car when a chubby man who appeared to be the couple's next-door neighbour called out to them. He had been for a jog and was stretching in front of his house, and asked them if they were looking for the old couple. They answered yes, adding that they were with the police. The man stopped stretching, came over to them and said that he'd met the old lady when he went out for his run. She'd been distraught and spoke rather quickly as she got into her car, telling him that she hadn't heard from her husband and was very worried about him. She asked the man to tell her husband, if he happened to return home while she was away, that she had gone to the hospital in Fossvogur to meet his brother.

'The poor woman,' said the man in the jogging outfit. 'I feel terribly sorry for her – for both of them, of course. All of this has been so hard on them. Understandably. For that to happen to the girl. But you just never know. Let me tell you, I couldn't have asked for better neighbours, but then you see on the news that the girl was smuggling in drugs. I would never have believed it. Never. Not from these people. In fact, I was talking about it to Tommi here in number 15 . . .'

While talking, the man had started stretching again, and was clearly going to go on doing both until Konráð interrupted him, thanked him for his help, and got into the car with Marta. Driving away, they decided to go directly to the hospital in Fossvogur to speak to Danní's grandmother. Marta said that she was seriously considering putting out an alert for the woman's husband. It wasn't normal for a man to disappear like that and leave his wife to bear all these shocks alone. Media pressure was growing. The case's main details had got out and the questions the police were being asked were more pointed, while the demand for clear answers was becoming more insistent.

'Why do you think Danní's grandfather isn't showing himself?' Marta asked after a long silence, as they drove through a drizzle into the Fossvogur neighbourhood. 'Where do you think he is? Has he run away?'

'I've been asking myself the same questions,' Konrád replied.

'Lassi said that the grandmother knew what Danní was going to post on the internet. Could it have been about him? About her grandfather? Something about him having done something to her? Something unspeakable?'

'Maybe, but he would hardly have killed her to shut her up, his own granddaughter?'

'For God's sake!' Marta exclaimed. 'Because of the secret that Lassi said the grandma knew?'

'Who knows?' Konrád sighed, before telling Marta something that had been on his mind since his visit to the man with the oxygen mask. 'I had the impression that he knew much more than he let on, and he asked me some pretty peculiar questions, too. He wanted to know if Nanna's mother sometimes took her daughter with her to the hospital where she worked.'

'And?'

'Apparently, she did, but why should he have asked about that? Why did he want to know that? Unless he knew that someone who might have harmed the kid also worked in the same hospital?'

'The doctor?'

'Anton Heilman. The father of the man who's now disappeared, whose granddaughter went to the dogs and was going to post an unspeakable secret on the internet.'

'Are you saying it's hereditary?' Marta asked after a long silence. 'Is that what you're saying?'

'What?'

'That perversion?'

60

It was late in the evening when they pulled into the hospital car park, where calm had returned after the bustle of the day. There were few people about. They went to the information desk and asked for Dr Gústaf Antonsson. The staff member on duty consulted his computer and told them that he'd left the hospital a short time ago. Marta said that she was a police detective and asked if an elderly woman had come there asking for the same man, and was told that she had come not too long before them and got the same answer, that he had left.

'Do you know where she is?' asked Konrád.

'You two are with the police?' retorted the staff member, who was wearing the uniform of a security guard and felt that Marta and Konrád didn't exactly look like officers of the law, what with Konrád resembling a tired pensioner, which he was, and Marta in her customary white blouse beneath the usual black, three-quarter-length jacket. She never put much effort into her appearance, particularly not for work.

She took out her ID and showed it to the staff member, who replied that the woman had asked where she could find Lárus Hinriksson, and that he'd given her his room number.

They thanked him for the information, went to the lift and took it in silence to the floor where Lassi was hospitalised. As they walked towards Lassi's room, Konrád asked Marta why the police hadn't posted an officer at his door. Marta said she thought that that had been the plan, but that it had probably been deemed too costly.

The door to Lassi's room was wide open, and they saw that the woman they were looking for was sitting at his bedside. When they entered, she looked up and tried to smile, but produced only a grimace. She was holding her phone, having just tried again to reach her husband.

'I have absolutely no idea where he is,' she said desperately. 'I don't understand it. He's not answering his phone and won't call me back.'

Lassi's condition appeared unchanged. He was lying there motionless, but seemed not to be in any pain. He was still connected to various devices that were unfamiliar to Konrád, and IVs attached to both of his hands administered a saline solution and drugs.

'I'm terribly worried,' the woman continued. 'This behaviour of his is very unusual. I don't understand why he's doing this.'

'Maybe we shouldn't wait any longer to put out an alert for him,' said Marta.

'No, I suppose not,' said the woman, who appeared exhausted. 'Shouldn't we just go ahead and do that? Since he seems to have vanished.'

'But how are you doing?' asked Konrád. To him, the woman seemed somewhat confused, and he was sure that she hadn't got much sleep. 'Is there anything we can do for you?'

'No, thank you,' the woman said. 'I just feel awful. I feel awful about all of this and can't sleep, and I'm so terribly worried about my husband. He's never behaved like this before. Never. I'm mainly worried that something has happened to him. That he's had an accident or . . .'

'No accidents have been reported to the police,' Marta said. 'Why do you think he isn't responding to your attempts to reach him?'

'I don't know. I so want him to be here, by my side. I'm so tired. So tired of this endless game of hide-and-seek. This endless . . . I'm so tired of this, tired and exhausted . . .'

'What do you mean by hide-and-seek?'

The woman didn't answer.

'Do you think it's because of Danní that he's hiding?'

'Because of Danní?'

'Did he do something to her?' Marta asked. 'Do you think he's trying to escape the consequences? Do you think it could be that?'

'The consequences of what?'

'We know that Danní had a secret she was prepared to reveal. Maybe a family secret that had to do with her, and that you and your husband knew about. Maybe your husband wanted to silence her.'

The woman looked at them in turn, and then down at Lassi.

'She told this young man everything. She told him who it was. How it happened. I think he was the one who encouraged her to do it, to put it all out there in public and name us and . . . there are pages on the internet where women tell what they've suffered . . .

Danní told us about them. She told us that Lassi wanted her to put the whole story on the internet . . .'

'And your husband silenced her?'

'Yes, he did,' she replied in a broken voice. 'The first time she told us about it. He silenced her. There's probably no other way to put it. We both did. I'm just as guilty. I'm just as guilty as he is. We didn't want a scandal. I had been a prominent public figure, a politician. He said that we had no choice. That we couldn't do otherwise. And then, of course . . . it was a family matter . . . no wonder the poor girl went off the rails. I told that to my husband, that we allowed it to happen. If we had only been upfront with her and helped her and tried to make amends for it and start anew. If we hadn't silenced her. Silenced the poor girl and left her alone to bear that burden, that responsibility, that shame.'

The woman was on the verge of tears.

'This is so hard,' she sighed. 'It's so hard to talk about it. I wish my husband was here. He could explain it to you. He could tell you how it all was.'

Konráð looked at Marta, as if asking for her permission to continue questioning the woman. Marta nodded discreetly.

'We need to speak to your husband,' he said. 'The police suspect him of having abused Danní, and need to question him about it. About their relationship.'

'My husband?' the woman asked in surprise.

'Danní was abused, wasn't she?' Konráð said.

A hospital bed was pushed past the door. An elderly patient was lying on it, and he turned his head and looked at them without the slightest change of expression. One of the bed's wheels creaked as it moved off down the corridor.

The woman bowed her head.

'The poor girl. She didn't tell us about it until she was twelve,' she whispered. 'She . . . she didn't like being with him at all. In our cottage in the summers or at weekends. At his place when we went abroad. She was so young when it started. At first, we thought it was just an eccentricity of hers, not to want to stay with him, because he was always so good to her, and we said that she would relax once we were gone. But it had nothing to do with eccentricities, but with that. That horror. We believed her as soon as she told us. Sometimes . . . sometimes he asked about her. If we needed him to look after her. He was like . . . an animal. I thought my husband was going to kill him . . .'

'Your husband?'

'Yes . . .'

'Who?' Konrád asked. 'Kill who?'

'Well, his brother of course. That cursed bastard . . . But then, worse, we decided to act as if nothing had happened. As if nothing had been done to Danní.'

'Gústaf?! Was he the one who abused Danní? It wasn't your husband?'

'My husband? No. Why would you think that?'

'It was his brother?'

'We should have reported him. Immediately. Had him arrested. But we didn't. We did nothing. We kept quiet. Of course, it stopped as soon as we found out about it, but he'd subjected poor Danní to terrible abuse for many years and we never reported it or did anything about it. When Danní grew older, she told us that that was no less of a crime. The denial. The silence.'

The woman took Lassi's hand in hers and began stroking it gently.

'I came here to make sure Gústaf didn't do anything to the boy,' she said. 'To make sure that nothing happened to him. I think Danní liked him. We felt she could do better. Find someone better. As if that was the important thing. Everything we did was wrong and contradictory and despicable . . .'

'Why would your brother-in-law want to do something to Lassi?' Konrád asked.

'Because Lassi knows everything.'

'Everything about what?'

'About how he treated Danní. He was just outside the door here when I came,' the woman said. 'He refused to speak to me and ordered me to go home. He wasn't himself. I think he's started drinking again. He told me the boy wouldn't say anything. He'd fixed it. I have no idea what he was talking about. He acted as if he was doing my husband and me a favour.'

'He was here?' said Konrád. 'With Lassi?'

'I asked him about Danní,' replied the woman, nodding. 'I didn't think him capable of it, but I had to ask if he was the one who stuck that needle in her arm. If he had gone to Lassi's place and was the one responsible for her overdose. He said that I was crazy. I won't remain silent about this any longer. He can't force me to . . .'

As she said this, Konrád suddenly noticed that Lassi had stopped breathing. He took the boy's wrist but found no pulse, and saw that the electrocardiograph to which he was connected, and which should have sounded an alarm, was shut off. He looked at the needle in the young man's hand that was meant for injections directly into his veins, and saw that the lid of the plastic valve at its end was open. Konrád realised that Lassi was being murdered before their eyes.

61

The girl at the guest house in Borgarfjörður had knocked twice on the man's door, trying to let him know that he should have checked out of the room some time ago. A 'Do not disturb' sign hung on the doorknob. Respecting the man's wish, she hadn't come in to do the usual housekeeping. She'd been on duty when he checked in and asked for a room with a bathtub. Each time she'd come to the room and knocked on the door, the man hadn't answered. It was as if no one was there any more. Yet his SUV was still parked in front of the guest house. So he hadn't gone anywhere. He hadn't left without paying, as sometimes happened, unless it had been on foot or he'd had someone come to pick him up. That sort of thing had doubtless happened before, though not during any of her shifts.

The room was booked for that night. The next occupants were a French couple who were travelling around Iceland by car, who had phoned to let the guest-house staff know they were behind schedule and wouldn't arrive until late evening. The girl felt as if she had shown the man the utmost courtesy until then, but now she lost her patience, took out her master key and stuck it in the lock. She called out to warn him of her entry into the room, opened the door and poked her head in.

The first thing she noticed was that no one had slept in the double bed. It was carefully made up, as if by the guest-house staff. The curtains were drawn shut, and the room was dark. Black trousers lay folded on the bedspread, black socks on the floor, and a white shirt was lying neatly over the back of a chair.

'Hello!' the girl called, to no reply.

She took the key out of the lock and entered the room. The door closed automatically, and she noticed a light in the bathroom.

'Hello! Is anyone in there?'

She was slightly hesitant about entering the bathroom, but then plucked up her courage, looked in it and was shocked to see why the man hadn't answered her.

He was lying in the bathtub, which was full to the brim with strangely rosy-coloured water that had run out onto the tiled floor and into the drain below the sink. Next to the tub was an open pocketknife. The man's head was resting on a towel on the edge of the tub, along which lay one of his arms, as well. She saw a deep gash in his wrist.

The man's face was serene, though colourless. She knew straight away that he had bled to death.

62

Konrád immediately started CPR on Lassi, and Marta rushed into the corridor and shouted for help. She ran to the glass booth where she'd seen two nurses and called to them that a patient was dying and needed emergency assistance. As she did, Konrád continued CPR, but couldn't tell if it was doing any good. Lassi lay there in his bed, not breathing and not moving.

The woman stood up and watched him impassively for a few moments before retreating to the window overlooking the car park. She stood there quietly for a moment, then turned to look down at the parking spaces.

'There he is,' she whispered.

Konrád was trying to remember the proper procedure for CPR. At one point, he'd taken a first-aid course, but had forgotten almost everything. Both hands on the chest. Press hard. Let up. Press . . .

He shouted to Marta, and she came to the door and told him that help was on the way. A team of doctors and nurses appeared in the corridor, quickly filled the room and took over. A defibrillator was hastily wheeled in and Konrád stepped away from the bed.

'He was injected with something to make his heart stop,' he said to one of the doctors. 'It was given to him deliberately.'

At the same time, the woman shouted and pointed out the window:

'There he is!'

Konrád rushed to her. She was pointing at a man in the car park who stopped and stared at them in the window for a moment before hurrying towards an SUV.

'It's him,' she said. 'There he is!'

Konrád took off immediately and shouted to Marta to follow him. The lift door was open, and they rushed into it and pressed the button for the ground floor, and the lift started slowly downward. To Konrád, it felt like it was taking ages. As soon as the door opened, they ran at full speed to the car park, where they saw the SUV drive out onto the thoroughfare and head towards Bústaðavegur Road.

They ran as fast as they could to Marta's car, but when she turned the key in the ignition, the engine wouldn't start. She had already taken out her mobile phone to call for backup, and handed it to Konrád as she focused on the ignition.

'There's a trick to it,' she said.

'We're losing him!'

'This clunker is thirteen years old! It's all I can afford on my shitty salary!'

After several attempts, the car started. Marta peeled out, grabbed her phone from Konrád and informed her colleague on the other end that they were in pursuit of an SUV driving west on Bústaðavegur.

'He might turn onto Kringlumýrarbraut Road, I don't know yet. Or head downtown. It's a black SUV; the owner is Gústaf Heilman – I mean Antonsson.'

She turned west onto Bústaðavegur, the old, ramshackle engine coughing and whining every time she tried to crank it up to full throttle. She slowed down as they crossed the bridge over Kringlumýrarbraut Road, both of them looking north and south for the SUV before they continued towards the city centre.

They passed the premises of the Valur football club, and when they reached the bridge over Hringbraut Road, they spotted an SUV similar to the one they'd seen leaving the hospital's car park, speeding westward under the bridge. Instead of continuing onto Snorrabraut Road, Marta decided to take a chance on Hringbraut and veered right, descending the narrow, curving ramp onto it. She took the turn far too quickly. The side of the car rubbed against the ramp's concrete wall with a clamour and sparks before righting itself and hurtling onto Hringbraut.

'That'll cost me,' Konrád heard her mutter to herself.

There was virtually no traffic, and they saw the SUV ahead of them run a red light. No police vehicle was in the vicinity, and Marta had begun shouting into her phone for backup. Konrád heard someone on the line tell her to calm down a bit.

'YOU calm down!' she shouted, throwing her phone furiously to the floor.

They saw the SUV turn onto Njarðargata Street, take the roundabout on the wrong side and head north along Sóleyjargata Street, where it disappeared behind the tall trees of Hljómskálagarður Park. Shortly afterwards, Marta and Konrád turned onto Sóleyjargata, but the SUV had disappeared.

As they ran a red light at the intersection with Skothúsvegur

Street, Konrád noticed rather large waves breaking against the banks of the Pond, and, looking out further, he saw the SUV in the water a short distance from the bridge.

The vehicle was upside down, almost entirely submerged, its wheels spinning fast as the engine hadn't yet stalled. The driver may have intended to turn west onto Skothúsvegur but had taken the turn too fast, lost control of the vehicle, and ended up in the Pond. Its red and yellow lights illuminated the surface of the water, giving the accident a peculiar glow.

There was no sign of the driver.

Marta braked as if for her life, put the old clunker in reverse and backed towards the intersection with Skothúsvegur. She narrowly dodged a car coming from the opposite direction and only just avoided ending up in the Pond, too.

Even before the vehicle had stopped, Konrád jumped out of it and ran to the bank, then waded without hesitation into the water towards the SUV. He heard the whine of its spinning wheels and submerged engine, which still hadn't stalled. Through the murk below the surface, Konrád could see that the SUV was filling with water. The muddy water poured in through its half-open windows. The driver's door was pinned shut by the thick mud at the bottom of the Pond, so that the driver had no way to open it. He was sitting helplessly upside down in his seat, fastened by his seat belt. He was on the verge of drowning.

Konrád stood chest-deep in the water. He took a deep breath and dived to try to open the door. He managed to open it slightly, but not enough to be able to reach the driver. He tried kicking the window with the heel of his shoe, but the water dampened the force.

The man's mouth opened wide and his nostrils flared, and

his eyes widened and then closed. His life was draining away. Marta had joined Konrád, and together they finally managed to open the door wide enough for Konrád to slip inside. He tried to free the man from his belt, but simply couldn't find the release button. When he finally did, it turned out to be stuck. Losing all hope of undoing the belt, Konrád was about to try to pull the man out from under it when the button suddenly came unstuck. Konrád grabbed the man's arm, pulled him with all his might out of the door, and hoisted his head above the water's surface.

Marta and other police officers dragged the man to shore, where they began CPR. Konrád saw two police cars parked on Skothús-vegur, and an ambulance approaching the intersection with Sóleyjargata. Marta helped Konrád out of the water and sat down with him on the bank of the Pond. Konrád was out of breath from his struggle in the water. He was soaking wet, cold, and drained of energy when a policeman came with two blankets, handed them to him and Marta and asked if they needed any further assistance.

'Will he make it?' Konrád asked, nodding towards the stretcher on which the doctor was being moved.

'They managed to revive him,' replied the policeman. 'It was really close.'

'Any news about Lassi?' Konrád asked Marta.

'I'm going to call the hospital,' she replied.

Konrád got up and walked over to the stretcher, which the para-medics were lifting into the ambulance. The man was exhausted and in shock following the accident, which nearly cost him his life. He did, however, recognise Konrád immediately, and knew that it was he who had saved him by pulling him from the vehicle.

'You didn't . . . didn't need to do that,' he whispered.

'It was a terribly close call,' Konrád replied, at the same time noticing the man's resemblance to Danní's grandfather.

'There was something . . . something in the road . . . did you see it?'

Konrád shook his head.

'And the boy . . . how is he?' asked the doctor.

'What boy?'

'At the hospital?'

In his mind's eye, Konrád saw Lassi in his hospital bed and Danní lying on the floor of Lassi's room with a needle in her arm, and he thought of the unspeakable secrets and the men who were the cause of them.

'I don't know,' he said.

'You probably know about Danní?' the man whispered.

Konrád said that he did.

'I . . . I couldn't bear the idea of it being revealed . . . I couldn't bear it . . . she was going to put it all on the internet, those websites . . . was going to tell everything, destroy me . . .'

The man stared up at Konrád as if hoping for some sign of understanding, but saw only contempt. They slid his stretcher into the ambulance and shut the doors. A moment later, the man was driven away under flashing lights.

'He survived, the kid,' Marta said as she walked past Konrád towards her car. 'Have someone drive you home when you're ready.'

Wrapped in his blanket, Konrád stood there watching the ambulance as it disappeared down the street. He looked out over the Pond, which was still illuminated by the lights of the SUV, which lay like a coral at its bottom. It reminded him of an old poem about the fallen city. He looked at the bridge and Hljómskálagarður Park, where darkness was slowly spreading amid the trees, and envisioned another event that had occurred in that same place, a death that had haunted him for days and that he knew would never be fully explained.

63

Leifur agreed to what Eygló said she had to do to honour Nanna's memory.

He had been discharged from the hospital. Lassi was recovering well and would soon be ready to testify against Randver, who was considered to be the one behind Danní's drug smuggling. Lassi grieved for his friend and said that she'd been on the verge of revealing the name of the man who had sexually abused her between the ages of seven and twelve, as well as denouncing the silence imposed on her by her grandparents after she'd told them the torments inflicted on her. The doctor, her great-uncle, had offered her both money and drugs in exchange for her silence, but told her that if she didn't keep it to herself, he would have to take drastic measures. She'd had enough of silence.

Nanna's earthly remains were buried in a new coffin, after a simple funeral service performed by a priest.

Traces of the disturbance of the girl's grave were still visible a few days later, when Konrád and Eygló returned to the cemetery with a beautiful iron cross. Eygló had bought it at a funeral home and had a small plaque attached, engraved with the girl's name and the dates of her birth and death. The cross was unostentatious, and they installed it carefully and securely at the girl's grave.

The new autopsy revealed that Nanna had been the victim of rape. She had been pregnant, and the DNA analysis proved that the father of the foetus was Anton J. Heilman. Gústaf asserted that he knew nothing about it. He said that he didn't know that his father had done the same thing to Nanna as he himself had done to Danní.

There was no way to determine how the girl had died in the Pond, although Konrád had certain ideas about the sequence of events. It was impossible to say if she had drowned accidentally or if it was the doctor's doing after he discovered the pregnancy. Nikulás had seen no reason to investigate the case further, and had apparently put no effort into doing so. Heilman had been in the perfect position to cover up the crime, by personally performing the autopsy on the girl's body. The hypothesis that he had orchestrated everything from the start and got Luther to do his dirty work was no worse than any other. Luther could have made it look as if the girl had drowned. Konrád couldn't rule out any of these theories, including that Luther had been the man whom the young poet had seen that evening on Sóleyjargata Street, so long ago.

They left the grave and the silence of the cemetery accompanied them as they drove towards the city centre and parked the car a short distance from the bridge on Skothúsvegur Street. It had grown dark and a breeze from the north rippled the surface of the Pond.

They walked onto the bridge on the side facing Hljómskála-garður Park, then stood silently for a few moments until Eygló took out the doll that Leifur had found there decades ago. They regarded it for the last time before Eygló kissed it gently on the forehead and let it fall into the water. They watched as small waves carried it out into the Pond, until it disappeared below the surface, like a memorial to the death in the water and the girl who finally rested in peace.